A Game of Romance and Ruin

A Steamy Lesbian Fantasy Romance

Girl Games
Book Two

Ruby Roe

For all the angry women out there...

Burn baby, burn.

NOTE FOR READERS

This book is intended for adult (18+) audiences. It contains explicit lesbian sex scenes, considerable profanity and some violence. For full content warnings, please see author's website: rubyroe.co.uk.

This book is written in British English.

If you would like to read the free *steamy* prequel to book 1 sign up here: rubyroe.co.uk/signup

CHAPTER 1

STIRLING

On the scale of one to *this-is-going-to-end-really-fucking-badly*, I'd say this negotiation is about three seconds from screwing me so hard I'll be limping for weeks. But then, I've never been one to back down from a deal, and I *don't* lose negotiations—except maybe to Morrigan, but that's entirely sex related.

Roman was clear: negotiate the shipping times, the boat needs to be docked by six tomorrow, and he doesn't care what it takes.

Of course, *'doesn't care what it takes'* is a sign that he cares very fucking deeply, and I had better pull it over the line in the most efficient way possible, so help me gods.

"Look, Lenny—" I start. A sharp sea breeze curls around the harbour whipping under my white shirt. A line of goosebumps freckle my arms. I'm not sure if it's the wind or the irritation. This deal means more than just Roman's poxy fucking imports.

"Don't 'look' me, missy. The port is double-booked, and

unfortunately for you, the other merchant reserved the slot first. So you're just going to have to wait."

I sniff, wipe my hand over my mouth.

There are very few depths I won't stoop to in order to pull a deal over the contractual line. Scarlett, my twin sister, might be more outwardly competitive, but I'd gut a bitch that got in the way of a negotiation. Lucky for this snivelling dock boy, I don't need to play the Roman card, because I'm pulling rule three of being a negotiator: *always* have dirt on your clients.

"Lenny, doll. There's no need to shit the bed over this." I grab him by the shoulders, spin him around and park him on a crate facing the ocean. Then I lean into his ear and whisper real low and creepy.

"Now you listen to me you son of a bitch. I know you have a nice little pregnant wifey at home. I also know you have a rather regular habit of dropping into a certain club in town, for people with particular tastes."

He swallows so loud I hear the lump go down.

"Tastes that include shoving your mangey cock in a bucket of leeches and letting them suck the erection dry. Now, I don't know about you, but I'm pretty sure my wife would take issue with that, especially if she was carrying my kid." I stand up, give him a couple tap-slaps on his cheek.

He pales as he turns to face me. "You can be a real cunt, Stirling, you know that?"

I nod, sagely. "Mmm, so can divorce. Expensive things those. About that dock slot...?"

He lowers his head, shaking. The poor bastard is translucent. I'm not sure if he's going to cry or puke. He pulls out a small notebook from his pocket and a pen.

"The slot is yours, but don't come asking for any

allowances again. This is not how I do business, and it's not how you should either. You ought to know better. I always thought you were a legacy magician, not an underworld tramp." He stands. Tall bastard, he is, straggly hair and water-stained shirt half tucked into his trousers.

"I mean tramp seems a little strong, Len. I'm just nimble with information. There's no need to *harbour* bad feelings."

He stares at me. "That's not funny."

"I mean. It was a bit. Just trying to lighten the mood. We're all pawns going about our business trying to get the best deals we can. I'll try not to be as much of a cunt next time."

I wink and walk off, the smugness already drawing across my lips.

"There won't be a next time," he hollers.

I ignore him.

It's a cute thought, but he knows as well as I do, Roman's business is booming, and that means half a dozen ships to dock and unload every week. Whether Len likes it or not, I'll be back in a couple of days and this charade will start again.

I head towards the rear of the dock and the cabin nestled in against the rusted shreds of decaying boats and scraps. I open the door, and there's a man sat on a chair with a rat on his shoulder reading a newspaper.

I stroll up to the rat, hesitate, and then reach out to stroke its head. It snaps at me. I yank my fingers away just in time to avoid it drawing blood.

"Claude, do you not think a more sanitary pet might be better?"

"No."

He doesn't even look up from the paper, just turns the

page and continues reading. I sigh internally. Why do I pick the most delightful magicians to work with?

"The next shipment is arriving at six tomorrow evening. Will you be able to—"

"Yes," he says, still not looking at me.

It's probably safer that we don't discuss what we're embezzling off these deals out loud.

"The usual payment?" Being a round of the most eye-wateringly expensive cheese for the rat, a vintage bottle of whiskey from Sangui city—which, I can't even begin to explain how difficult it is to get hold of—and my continued payment of his daily paper subscription. It's a fair price. Always amuses me how many deals I make that don't involve money. Each to their own, I suppose.

"Yes."

"Great. See you next week. I'll send payment end of the month."

He cocks his head to the corner of the cabin. There's a bag of wood wax and some new rags.

"For your project," he says.

My eyes light up, "Thanks, Claude, I needed—"

"I know."

I pick up the bag and head out. He doesn't say goodbye. But the wax and rags tell me he's fond of me.

I head out to the edge of the main harbour area and climb through a gap in the fence panels, out towards the smaller boat dock area. A hundred meters south, I draw to a halt. I scan the line of mansions set back behind the harbour and dunes. I land on a watery coloured one right behind my shed.

Home.

Not mine, obviously. I've never even stepped inside. But

it feels like home anyway. The same mansion that's kept silent guard over me while I build the boat.

I tear my gaze away and pull out my shed key, open the lock, and drop the wax and rags inside.

My fingers trail the boat hull. I finished sculpting the bow figurehead last week. I only have the wood wax left and it should be ready to sail. But no time today, so I lock up and leave. Twenty minutes later, I'm in town and pulling onto the street with Roman's biggest club—his head office. I push open Roman's club doors. DnD it's called, and while the kids of New Imperium assume DnD stands for a game with magic creatures, the adults among us know what it really means: Debauched and Depraved, which is much more my kind of game.

I enter the club's main room only to find the team sat at one of the central tables. I freeze, my heart hammering.

They don't know I work for him.

I *shouldn't* be working for him.

A couple of months ago, the Queen commissioned us to run a heist for her. We did, successfully, so she offered for us to continue working for her. Officially, we don't exist in her defence budget. Unofficially, we do everything and anything the Queen needs handling and doesn't want public knowledge.

I take a second to recalibrate. Everything is fine. The team doesn't know why I'm here. In fact, I don't know why *they're* here. But Jacob, Quinn, Scarlett, and Remy are all sat around a table.

No Morrigan.

Not that I'm bothered.

Alright, fine. I'm very bothered.

We're not speaking though. It's messy. And I don't mean lesbian drama messy, I mean a bunch of people nearly died, we probably shouldn't be together level of mess. After she came into the team, things were on track. I thought maybe we could... but no. Because then I learned she'd lied to me about who she really is: a princess.

It broke me, and we've barely spoken since.

Doesn't stop my traitorous heart aching for her.

Scarlett spots me. Of course she does, her Assassin magic mean she's always aware of everything. She frowns, a sure sign she's suspicious, but waves me over.

I head towards the table and falter. Morrigan appears carrying a tray lined with shots from the bar. Gods, she scowls at me like I burned her with the force of a hundred suns. And if it isn't the most gloriously sexy thing I've ever seen, I don't know what is.

Inappropriate, Stirling. Wildly, inappropriate.

But... That woman is ferocious when she's angry. And despite the fact she's *as* pissed at me for the deal I made two years ago, as I am at her for lying about who she was while we were together, it doesn't stop the raging urge to sweep the table clean, lay her down, and fuck her senseless.

But then I remember how I've spent the last two years. The promise I made, and my stomach bottoms out, and pins and needles trickle into my fingertips.

She can't be here, not with Roman upstairs. If he knew...

I have to get her out.

She sits down.

Fucksake.

Remy stands, opens her long arms, "Stir, babe, come sit down. We're having a goodbye party!"

"What? Who's leaving?" I say and glance at the wall-door to Roman's office, my feet twitching as much as my mind. *How do I get Morrigan out of here?*

Jacob, with his creamy curls and bike jacket waves at me.

"Wh—" I start. *Oh.*

He puffs his chest out. "Off to the Borderlands. The Queen has asked that I help continue dismantling the Border Lord's regime."

Ten years ago, the Queen and her sister had a blazing row and tore the city map in half. The problem was, the map was connected to the foundations of Imperium. Its magic quite literally tore the city in half too.

The Tearing created the Borderlands. Quinn, her father and several thousand magicians were all caught inside. Anyway, her father had beef with Scarlett so he framed our parents, who were executed for treason, and we were excommunicated. Finally, after Gods knows how many years, the Queen gave us our legacy back when we proved their innocence.

"And Malachi is incapable of doing that himself?" I ask.

Malachi is Quinn's younger brother. She decided to stay in New Imperium after their father died, and Malachi wanted to make amends for what their father did.

My eyes flick to Roman's office door and back to Quinn, who's smirking at Jacob. The pair of them have gotten close recently. Though given he's now fucking off to the Borderlands, I suspect it has more to do with the way Jacob stares at Malachi every time he visits than from their friendship.

"Malachi requested 'assistance'," Quinn says, her lips twitching as she waggles air quotes at me.

"I seeeee," I say.

Quinn and I have discussed at length whether or not Malachi turned Jacob's eye. Neither of us have any proof. I mean, hell, I thought Jacob was straight. But it seems rather convenient that he, of all of the team, happens to get the mission inside the Borderlands. Convenient indeed.

"Didn't realise the Borderlands needed a transport expert," I smirk.

The tips of Jacob's ears flush red as if he can read my thoughts.

He clears his throat. "Well, seeing as I rather rapidly picked up driving trains, and given their entire network of transport is down, the Queen thought it was a good idea."

Quinn gives me a pointed stare, a warning not to push it. So I suppress the witty snark and leave it. He'll tell us when he's ready, if that *is* what this is, of course. And hey, perhaps he is going to fix their transport. We only managed to get out of the Borderlands after an epic heist because he bought a decrepit carriage back to life.

I open my mouth to ask Morrigan for a word, not that she'll talk to me. A line of nervous sweat crawls down my spine as a woman appears with a tray to pick up empties.

She's stunning. Her hair is long and dark and blunt over her forehead. She has the kind of curves I like to trail my hands over. She gathers glasses and disappears back to the bar, my eyes following her the entire way.

Morrigan tuts at me.

I snap a glare at her. "What? You don't want me, you've made that clear." Fuck. Shouldn't have said that. Gods. Me and my mouth.

Morrigan stands. "Oh sure, that's exactly how things ended between us. *Me* leaving *you*."

I see my opportunity. I desperately don't *want* to piss her off. But winding her up might be the only way to get her to leave. So I make the killing blow that I know will end in a row.

I harden my face. "No. It ended with you lying to me for our entire relationship."

The rest of the team surreptitiously glance at each other. Probably trying to work out how to make a swift exit. *Don't worry guys I'll do it for you.*

I shove a hand on my hip. "You had three years to tell me who you were, and instead you hid this massive part of your life. I don't even know you."

"Oh my Gods. It's not like you were actually willing to listen. You haven't even heard me out since you found out, for fucks sake."

"Well go on then, Morrigan. I'm all ears."

She pulls her face, a grunted scream spilling from her lungs. "Gods you're still not listening..." she says and flings her hands in the air, expectant. As if I've missed her point entirely.

"I'm not doing this in front of the team." I head for the door pleading for her to follow. She will. I know she will. Maybe she already realises what I'm doing.

I count one breath, two, three.

The club lights flicker. Excellent, I've pissed her off enough her magic is seeping out. A beat later, she grabs my arm.

Her voice is low. "Where the hell are you going? We need to talk."

"Outside." I don't wait for her answer, I just plough out of the club.

"Excuse me. You don't dictate to me..." she says scrambling after me.

But I keep walking. She has to leave the club. Has to be away from Roman. It's not like I think he'd do anything publicly, but I'm not taking any chances either.

I pull into a side alley. There's a passageway door down

here, I know the girl who guards it. If you pay her a single tear, she'll let you through, and if you stroke the door in just the right way, it will open to anywhere you want.

"Stirling," the guard says.

"Elandra." I lower my head in deference. "I have credit still, yes?"

She nods, her hair is so long it skims the ground. "Though if you're taking a passenger that will leave you with a single tear."

That's fine, it's enough to get me back through once Morrigan is safe. She stands back, and I tickle the door's hinge.

I don't mean to do it, but the first place that comes to mind is the beach, the mansion that watches over me.

"Keep the passage open for me? I'll be back shortly."

I open the door and the afternoon sun streams through warming my skin. I pull Morrigan through and we end up in the garden of the watery coloured mansion. The one I...

The one *we* call home.

Memories of that night come flooding back, the ache, the pain. It was all here. I shove it down not wanting to remember.

Morrigan startles as she realises where we are. Her eyes are wet. "We shouldn't be doing this."

My shoulders are stiff. This might be safer than the club, but it's not exactly sensible given our history here. "It's fine."

"Why would you bring me here of all places?" she demands. I love it when she demands things of me, all uptight and serious. The force she puts into her tone makes me want to drop to my knees, worship her and lick all the seriousness out of her.

"Wasn't intentional, believe me."

"Of course it wasn't. Because of all the mansions you could bring me for an argument, you choose this one? Gods it's so irresponsible. Didn't you consider—"

"Morrigan, stop."

She huffs at me.

"Insufferable."

"So Scarlett tells me."

Morrigan stomps down the path and slips inside a glass conservatory at the bottom of the garden. I trail after her and slip inside.

I pull the door shut behind me. The circular room is bare, all glass walls and white iron structures. The only thing in here is an array of huge pillows, and Morrigan.

She's wearing a fitted sleeveless top, her cleavage peeking out. How am I supposed to take this seriously with my favourite breasts staring at me? My pussy clenches.

Her black hair is pin straight and as severe across her forehead as her mood. Her olive skin is smothered in Collection tattoos, each one a unique shape and design.

I glance down her arms, there's so many tattoos now I can no longer keep track. I used to know every single one. Every inch of her body. My tummy wrenches at the thought of how long it's been. But I choose not to be sad, instead I smile because the woman is a genius, able to suck in information like a black hole.

Our magic is sourced from mansions. In order to access it, you have to study in your chosen castle, house, or mansion. When it deems you worthy, a Collector will tattoo the mansion's magic onto your skin so the house can collect you and you can use its magic. Morrigan is trained as a Collector amongst other things. I don't know anyone else who has gotten close to being collected that many times by that many mansions and castles. I honestly think she's more powerful than her mother now, despite the palace magic her mother commands.

She tuts, livid. "It's not safe here. I don't even know who owns this place."

"It's fine. It's empty. I have a workshop close by and there's been no one in it the whole time."

"Gods, Stirling." She takes my hand in hers, it's soft, warm. It sets my stomach alight, fluttering under my ribs. I want to touch her, hold her. Take her in my arms and—

"Are you... are you still going to meet me where blue meets blue?" she asks, her eyes firmly located on the floor.

I caress her cheek, tip her chin up. "Of course. How could you ever think anything else?"

"Because it's been two years. Two long years. And it's not like we've talked properly since the team got together it was all so rushed and..."

"Morrigan. It's all I've been trying to do..." I say. "Are... are you still...?"

"Yes. Gods, of course."

The relief that washes over me is so intense my knees want to buckle, my eyes sting. She releases my hand and steps back, and a coldness spills into the space she occupied.

Her features calcify. "But I'm still furious at you."

I look at the floor and sigh. "I don't know how many times we've been through this. What choice did I have? You know why I did it."

She huffs at me. "Yes, because you never think anything through."

"Not a lot I can do about that now is there? We're already in this mess. Are we going to talk about the fact you never told me who you are?" I say, my voice quiet.

"Oh come on, Stirling. You know damn well how hard

the palace fights for its princesses to live secret lives. I *had* to stay clean, keep my head down. What did you expect me to do? Confess and break my vow of silence? What if it got out?"

"What if it got out? The fuck, Morrigan. Who the hell was I going to tell?"

"You don't get it. You never get it," she snaps.

"No, you don't get it, I loved you. I would have done anything for you."

She glares at me. The fire in her eyes burning hotter, brighter. Her eyes glisten. I want nothing more than to reach out and grab her waist and crush my lips against hers.

"Loved. Past tense," she says. It's not a question, but a statement.

I break eye contact. I didn't mean that. I don't really know what I meant. We're not together. Haven't been for two years.

But she's still Morrigan.

"You should have told me," I say. "You should've trusted me."

"Oh that's rich. You don't think perhaps you should have trusted me? We could have found a different way out. But no. Instead you chose to make that fucking deal and not just any deal, Stirling... A fucking blood bond. What the hell were you thinking? You screwed both of us."

My fingers curl into fists, my chest tight and hot. "It's not that simple. I didn't have time to think, Morrigan. He was threatening your life."

"It *is* that simple." The glass walls rattle. She needs to calm down. But the heat in her eyes is doing things to my body, my pussy.

Gods.

I wipe my face, trying to focus on her words instead of her body.

I shake my head. "Don't start this again—"

"Don't start? You give me nothing. No information. No apology noth—"

"I'm fucking *sorry*, okay? I did it to protect you. What do you want me to say?" My voice is high, loud. I'm basically screaming and that was not the point of getting her out of the club.

I step close, my resolve draining. Two years we've been apart, and still she can undo me with a look. Command my soul with a word, break me in two with a single touch. I've never loved anyone like I loved her.

I move forward.

She steps back.

Together we dance, step, step, step, until I pin her against the conservatory wall. My arms on the glass either side of her. Her chest is heaving. Her breasts rising with every inhale. Heat fizzes between us, drenching me in a hot confusion. I'm furious, but I also want to touch her. Suddenly, two years feels like a glacial age. I can't bear being apart from her anymore. I want to end this feud, I want to claw her clothes off and drink in the scent of her skin, the taste of her pussy. I slide my fingers down her cheek, caress her shoulder, dip my fingers beneath her waistband. Her eyes roll shut, her lips part, and she draws a single sharp breath.

"Stirling..." she breathes.

My name on her tongue is like lightning striking my heart. Why does she have to be so infuriating?

When she opens her eyes, her words are softer. "Protect me? Stirling, you're mad. Do you have any idea how much magic I wield? If anyone needs protecting it's you."

Her eyes are wild. Blue like mine, but where there's ice in my pupils, hers hold fire. She's a magnet.

The air compresses. My heart races, I'm not sure if it's Morrigan's magic or the searing warmth of our skin.

Maybe both.

Her plump lips part, her breath heavy. I know this look. I've seen it a hundred times before. She's livid, but she wants me as much as I want her.

"We can't," she whines answering before I've even asked. "We could ruin everything."

"We're nowhere near the club."

Her eyes flick to the mansion behind us. "We shouldn't be *here*, either. What if—"

I place a finger on her lips. " Your mouth is saying no, but your body is saying yes. I'm going to kiss you now. And then I'm going to fuck you into understanding."

CHAPTER 2

MORRIGAN

Eleven Years Ago

I think it's a sick kind of penance that a princess is bound to meet her suitor on the eve of her twenty-first birthday. A sort of fuck you to adulthood and all your duties to come.

I begged mother to forego the tradition. To wait because I wanted to keep my identity restricted to just the handful that know. The nanny, the head of staff and security.

But she said she'd make him take a blood oath, preventing him from speaking my identity until the investiture is set in motion. And that is years away yet.

I suppose a blood oath is as good a guarantee as any.

We're meeting in the city's grand library. I said it was a step too far to meet in the palace. Too risky; what if a member of household staff figured out who I was or what the meeting was? No. Better to do it somewhere open and public, somewhere I was hidden in plain sight. Which is why I suggested the public library during a collection rite. There's a collection this evening for the graduating librarians and I was asked to be their collector.

The library is in the heart of the city, not far from the palace. It's a thin, wiry castle. But its length is impressive. It sweeps as far back into the night as I can see. Miles of bookshelves line its insides like warrens and tunnels.

I enter through the main oak doors, and the library welcomes me with a rush of pressure that shivers over my body, drenching me in the smell of ancient paper, musty leather and rich ink, and all of it wrapped in the familiar smell of cinnamon and static. Of course, mother claims the palace is the most powerful building in the city, but I don't know. When you think about how much knowledge the great libraries contain, I suspect they might just clip the palace.

The receptionist nods to me. "Through to the left. They're already waiting for you."

I meander through a short corridor and into the heart of the library, its dim lighting powered by faux firelights hanging on the walls. No Magician would bring a real flame into this building unless they had a death wish. I studied here when I was just five years old. It was my fourth collection tattoo.

I should be able to Collect the three graduating librarians before my fiancé arrives for our first date. I glance down at my outfit, deciding it was a good choice after all. It's not too much, but not scruffy either. I'm wearing black cigarette trousers, a matching black corset with sheer sleeves that stop before my shoulders. If he looks close enough, he'll see the Collection tattoos on my arms, and there's no doubting the ones covering my shoulders. I want him to know he can't fuck me around. I might be young, but I wield more power than most magicians already. And so I should. One day, I'll be queen.

"Hey," a mousy woman holding glasses in her trembling hand says. She's sleight, but her arms are corded and strong, despite her nerves. I can't help but draw my eyes down her body. I lay my fingers on hers, hoping it calms her nerves.

"You're the first student?" I say.

She nods. "Larissa."

"Perfect. Don't be nervous."

She smiles at me. It brightens her whole face, an aura of calm descending on her.

"Well, Larissa, I'll just set up here then?" I ask.

She nods again, swallowing hard, only this time I'm not sure if it's nerves she's swallowing down or attraction.

I smile, trying to push the rush of heat edging up my cheeks away. I place my case on the table. "Besides, it doesn't hurt too bad, and this should be a quick Collection."

We're in a breakout section of the library, sofas and arm chairs are arranged in a neat cluster, with tables and space for lamps and box lights for those examining texts and scrolls.

"It's my first one," she says.

"Oh, even more exciting, I'm honoured. Where are we tattooing you?"

"I thought my wrist? I'd like to be able to see it."

We sit, her on the sofa, me on the armchair which I've pulled forward. I fill the tattoo gun with black ink, close my eyes and whisper incantations. I know the moment the castle hears me; the air fills with the scent of aged paper and leather. Static tingles under my skin, weaving through my arms and into my fingers until my hands ache with the desperate urge to bond a student to the castle. Wisps of pearlescent magic erupt from the library walls, and whip through the air until they hover over the tattoo gun.

"Ready?" I ask.

She blinks, swallows. "Okay."

"In blood and bonds," I say, and the pearlescent threads surge into the gun.

I tattoo Larissa first, a small book symbol on her wrist as requested. A young man comes next, and last is actually the receptionist. She's having a second bonding, taking over as head patron of the castle, and thus needed a stronger link to the castle's magic.

Larissa appears with a tall man. He fills the doorway, and I know instantly it's my fiancé. I pack up my collection gun and ink, the pearlescent castle threads evaporating.

"Don't scratch," I say, swiping Larissa's hand away from her arm.

"It itches like hell."

"I know. It will for a couple of days, it's just the castle's magic bonding to you. It will itch worse if you don't leave it alone though."

She huffs at me and then opens her hand to the man. "This is Roman. I believe he's here for you?"

"Thank you. It was lovely meeting you."

Larissa's eyes dance between us but when it's clear we're not going to talk until she's gone, she gives me a shallow bow of her head, thanks me again, and meanders off into the bowels of the library, taking the receptionist and the young man with her.

Roman bends to take my hand. He kisses my knuckles. "Your Hi—"

I wrench my hand out of his and hush him. "Are you serious? Not here."

What the hell? I thought mother had ensured he was briefed. I storm out of the library with Roman following after me.

"I apologise, that was careless of me."

Except I don't stop until I'm out of the castle. "This yours?" I say jabbing my case in the direction of a carriage.

"Yes."

I don't wait for an invitation I just climb in. He gets in after me and shuts the carriage door. It's only now that I have an opportunity to take him in. He's exquisitely handsome. His shoulders are broad, his lips are full, eyes dark like secrets and shadows. His hair is loose waves of midnight.

Objectively, I should want to jump his bones. But my mind drifts back to Larissa—her corded arms, her sweet smile.

"Forgive me, let me begin again," Roman says and takes my hand in his kissing my knuckles. I wait for the spark, the inevitable flare of heat up my neck, but it doesn't come, nor does the flutter I was expecting in my stomach.

"Lord Roman Oleg. It is a pleasure to finally meet you."

"Morrigan Lee. Please don't use my formal title in public."

He bows his head in deference, "An honest mistake, one I shan't commit again." He bangs on the back window and the carriage jolts to life.

"So we're to marry," he says. His eyes roll down my body. I can feel them crawling over my skin, and it makes me uncomfortable.

Mother was clear. This was planned from both our births. Albeit only sworn into contract once I was born as Roman is a little older than I am.

"Apparently so," I say. "Not for a decade yet though."

He shifts forward on his seat. "Indeed, most princesses have their investiture after they're thirty, is that right?"

If I had my way, I'd live my entire life in secret. It's not that I'm ungrateful for my position or the power I'll hold, it's more that I love the anonymity. I see the way the Daily Imperium rips into every decision mother makes.

Roman switches seats and slides in next to me. His body is warm, oozes a quiet confidence. He really is quite handsome.

"So tell me something about yourself, Morrigan Lee. Other than the fact you're a Collector."

"I love books, love magic, love the act of bonding castle to magician."

He laughs, his dark eyes twinkling. "Ahh, but would it not be quicker just to buy the property and own the magic than to study?"

I raise an eyebrow at him. "Perhaps. But perhaps not. After all, you can't own knowledge, only learn it."

"Who needs knowledge when you have power?"

"A fool's choice, Lord Oleg. How do you propose to control power without the knowledge of magic?"

He smiles, his jaw strong, teeth perfectly straight and perfectly white. And there, in the pit of my belly, is the first flutter of something tingly. Perhaps there's hope for us yet. I like the fire, the challenge he's bringing.

"I do believe it's you who's mistaken, Princess. You don't need knowledge to control power. Real power is all about perception. If people believe you wield power, then what is to say you don't?"

I stare out the carriage window as we move through the city, and I have to wonder if he's right. Is power really just an illusion after all?

CHAPTER 3

STIRLING

Morrigan pouts. Her expression is stiff, but her body pushes against mine. I glance out the glass conservatory wall, but we're alone; the beach is empty.

Morrigan leans closer, her resolve crumbling. This is the way it always was. Morrigan in charge, until we entered the bedroom. And I get it now, that innate queen inside her always having to think, to strategise. Practicing for the day she commands a city no doubt. But in the bedroom, she always gave herself to me wholly, knowing I'd protect her, keep her safe. It's the only thing I've ever wanted to do. And I failed.

Her tongue slides over her lips, "*'I'm going to fuck you into understanding,'* doesn't sound like a negotiation."

I tilt my head. "Who said it was a negotiation?"

I trail my finger around her waistband, and then slip my hand down. She gasps as the sudden contact, but she leans into me, tipping her pussy up so I can access her. I push my finger under her lace knickers and straight to her hole.

She's soaking wet, and all for me. A devious grin spreads over my mouth. I pull my finger out and suck her juices off.

Her mouth forms a dainty little O.

I shrug. "Your body seems to know what it wants." Gods, the absolute cheek on me.

Her eyes darken, her mouth twitches. Magic burns under my skin, a tempting pulse, begging me to use it. But I never use my magic to negotiate with Morrigan.

"For the record—" she says.

"You mean for the terms...?"

That, at least makes her expression crack.

"Fine," she sighs waving a dramatic hand at me, "For the terms *and* the record... this isn't over. I am still mad enough at you to sacrifice an entire league of magicians."

"Noted. What I heard was, make it a delicious orgasm or some poor unsuspecting fella is going to cop it for my sins."

The corners of her eyes quirk like she's trying to suppress a grin. She takes my hand, trying to win control of the situation back and places it on the button of her trousers.

I yank her forward by the button. She lifts off the conservatory as I unhook the trousers and slip the zip down in one swift motion before she rocks back onto the glass behind her.

She shakes her head at me, "So smooth, aren't you Stirling?"

I smile. It's the kind of compliment that'll fuel my ego for weeks. "I just know how to please a queen."

I slide my other hand around her neck pulling her forward. But she touches my wrist, halting me.

"This is a one-time thing," she says. "We promised we wouldn't do this… not until we fix everything."

"Agreed," I nod solemn. "Risk… danger… unresolved something… blah, blah, blah… I need you to fuck me immediately… See? I listen."

She rolls her eyes at me, "Has anyone ever told you you're insufferable?"

"Every day, baby." And then I pull her to me, crushing my lips against hers, ending the conversation.

I kiss her with the fury and ache of two long years apart.

I pull away, both of us panting already. My lips brush over hers, full of yearning and the anguish that plagues my whole body.

The realisation hits me like a carriage, almost knocking the air from my lungs. I might be kissing her, but it *is* over between us. It has been since the moment that bastard walked into my life, the moment I had to walk away to save her.

This is my fault. I broke us.

But I'd do it again if it meant saving her. If it meant I'd get to savour her lips like this. Even if this is the last time. If I never get to touch her or hold her again. It was worth it for one more kiss.

My hands trace over her exquisite curves.

Thoughts of her deception seep into my mind. She lied our entire relationship. Kept her identity secret. Was there ever really an 'us'?

Her fingers slide across my breast, my nipple hardening under her touch and my thoughts slip away. I tiptoe my fingers around the edge of her underwear and caress the flesh of her soft belly.

I let myself feel; her, us, this moment.

I push my tongue inside her mouth, and she arches off the glass into me. Her hands slide to my waist, and she pulls me against her and moans into me.

My chest swells. I'm not sure whether I want to cry with relief, laugh hysterically, or scream that she was right and we shouldn't be doing this.

Her hands tug my shirt free of my trousers, her fingers glide under the fabric and over my skin and finally, over the flesh of my breasts. My nipples are rock hard, my pussy is soaked already. Two years of longing rushing into my knickers. Gods, one touch from her and I think I might come.

I need her.

I want to feel her clench against me like she'll never let me go. I'm going to make her knees weak and her nails dig into my biceps as she struggles to hold herself up from pleasure.

I slide my finger over her warm centre and circle her clit, flicking and rubbing. She breaks our kiss and rolls her head back against the glass panting quick breaths. There's nothing more attractive than a queen experiencing pleasure. When she looks at me again, her eyes are feral. She nestles into the crook of my neck and nips at the skin. It makes me hiss, but the sensation shoots straight to my pussy.

I push into her, one finger at first. I thrust in and out until my hand is wet and I can slide a second inside, then I draw us both down the glass and onto the giant cushions. I lift her leg and hook it around my waist. I curl my fingers inside her until I make her gasp. Her eyes shut. She grips my arms for balance, her nails finally digging into the flesh of my bicep as she tightens around my hand. My excitement soaks into my knickers—it's all I can do to stop myself coming over her pleasure. Her moans grow rhythmic.

"Don't stop, Stirling."

I grip her thigh tighter, pull it higher around my waist. each movement allowing me to push deeper into her cunt. To draw more pleasure from her body. I want to drain every ounce of orgasm I can from her. It's what she deserves. What I've hungered after for two long years. I pump my hand harder, bend my fingers further inching closer to that exquisite spot.

"Look at me, Morrigan."

She doesn't. Instead she pushes her lips over mine, distracting me with a kiss. But I pull back, slow my fingers. I know why she doesn't want to look at me; the same reason I want her to: it will hurt. It will force us to confront the last two years.

I think some masochistic part of me needs the pain. Needs to see her. To hold her soul in my heart while she comes. I desperately want her to understand why I made the deal. I need her to know I never meant to hurt her.

I need to know if the life I thought we had was true. Otherwise, what were the last two years for?

"I said, look at me."

She does.

Her gaze is suffocating. The intensity of what was, what we had, it hovers between us like a spider thread, so strong and yet so fragile. It bores into me, sending a pulse of lust straight to my pussy, swelling my clit.

She grips my head, her fingers threading through my hair, "Stop teasing me and make me come."

And this time, I obey, thrusting my fingers into her, fast. Pushing her, winding her tighter and closer to the precipice. Her moans and gasps become pants. Her fingers squeeze the locks of my hair, pushing me down till my mouth devours her clit. And it is the most delicious thing I've ever tasted, sweet and wanting. I lap at her, drinking her in. Savouring every drop she gives me.

She clamps down, her hips rocking in time to my fingers. She's barely holding on, her eyes desperate to close. Her mouth opens, her hips shudder, and then she cries out, but she never stops looking.

Tears leak down her cheeks as she comes apart. When her body relaxes and I pull my hand out, I move up her body and press my lips to hers. Silent tears run down my cheeks too. I pull her in, gripping her so tight I can barely breathe. I lean my forehead against hers. I don't want to let go. I never want to let go again.

For one precious moment, we're back there. Two years ago, still in love, still pure.

But everything that's happened comes barrelling back. Neither of us are strong enough to carry it right now, and something shifts in her expression.

"Gods," she says.

But it's not *Gods that was amazing*, it's *Gods what the fuck have we done, this was complicated enough.*

"I know," I reply and lift off her. This was dangerous. A mistake.

The heat that pulled us together evaporates, and now we're left with the ugly reality that nothing is fixed and we're both still furious.

"We shouldn't—" I start.

"No," she says. But her eyes don't meet mine.

"This was..." I say but then don't know how to finish the sentence. I want to... I don't even know what I want. I want a fucking apology and I want to be mad at her and I want her to wrap me in her arms and erase the last two years.

But she doesn't do any of those things, and I don't either.

"I should go," Morrigan says. She takes a step and then hesitates. She opens her mouth as if she's going to say something. I wait, hope surging in my chest as I wonder what's going through her head. Wonder what she's not saying.

But she closes her mouth, shakes those blunt locks, and steps out of the conservatory, disappearing out of sight.

And I'm left standing there, staring after her, wondering if we'll ever be able to fix what I broke.

CHAPTER 4

STIRLING

I make my way back through the passageway door and return to the club. It's safe to say chaos has broken out.

Quinn and Jacob are on the table, a bottle in each of their hands doing the can-can, surrounded by empty shot glasses. They're screaming themselves hoarse to the music. Jacob has procured a neon green tutu that he's wearing on his head. And Remy is getting a lap dance from a woman with exquisitely large tits and... Oh Gods, Scarlett just puked in a bucket.

"What. The. Ever. Loving. Fuck?" I say picking her up.

"Stirrrrs," Scarlett slurs.

"I wasn't even gone that long, how can you be this shitfaced?"

She hiccups. Mother of Magicians I'm going to be cleaning puke up all night.

"I"—she hiccups again and points a finger at my chest

— "know what you're doing. I watch you, little sister. Was that a good id—?" she hiccups herself silent.

"Was wha—"

Scarlett wags an accusing finger at me. "You need to talk to Morrigan instead of fucking her."

I shake my head. "You're drunk, Scarlett. I'm not doing this right now."

"Then you're always going to have a broken heart." She sticks her bottom lip out like she's a four-year-old. This is ridiculous. I'm not having this conversation.

"She's the heir to the fucking throne. What do you expect me to do? It was never going to work. Even if she'd told me she was the princess, eventually she'd have to marry some godsawful prince from another city and have a thousand kids to keep the line going. It was always doomed."

Scarlett shakes her head at me, and pulls me in for a hug.

When she let's me go, her eyes are round and soft. "I love you dearly. Like a little sister, in fact."

I frown. "Scarlett, I am your little sister."

"Hicc— Exactly. You're the best negotiator I know, and you're letting a silly little thing like a past mistake stop you making the deal of your heart's desire?"

"That's not... Scar, you don't know the full st—"

She cuts me off. "My point is, you never even tried to fix it... You. Never. Tried."

I open my mouth to argue and stop. Because even though she's drunk, even though I'm pretty sure I'm about to get puked on, I have to wonder...

Is she right?

♛

An hour later, I bundle Scarlett, Quinn, Jacob, and Remy into a carriage and send them off to their respective homes.

Then I make my way back inside the club. There are two palace reps waltzing down the corridor with Roman. I duck into the reception, hiding behind the counter. It's not the first time palace reps have visited. Roman hasn't told me the details, but I'm not a fool either. I make it my job to hear rumours.

The palace, or more specifically Queen Calandra— Morrigan's mother—is worried about hostile takeovers. Especially after the King died. And to be fair, she should be worried. Roman is doing things he really shouldn't, and even though I've got plans in place to stop him, I'm just one person, and there's only so much I can do, especially when I'm not in his upper management. I don't know the ins and outs of what he's planning.

I lean onto the reception desk, shielding my face from the group as they pass.

I should confess to the team, but I don't exactly want the palace finding out.

It's not like I intended to work for both sides. It just... got complicated real quick, and I made decisions in the spur of the moment.

"It was a pleasure doing business," Roman says and shuts the front door. By the tone of his voice, the meeting was anything but pleasurable.

I hop out from the counter and Roman visibly relaxes when he sees me. "Afternoon, Stirling. I'm glad you're here as it happens. I need a minute of your time."

"Oh?"

He gestures for me to follow him. Roman's wearing a navy tailored suit. The man is so tall he has to duck under the door frame. He has the kind of build that makes me think he throws pianos at people for fun. The kind of build that I suspect most straight women would drop their knickers for.

He pushes the wall, and a door pops open, displaying a glass staircase and window-wall with a stunning view of the outside—so long as you don't mind heights. I don't, but there's something about climbing up facing nothing but sheer glass and the concrete below that never fails to make me queasy.

We reach Roman's office, which is, by all accounts, obscene. A large mahogany desk sits at one end of the room. In one corner is an enormous filing cabinet with piles of paper on top of it.

There's a bar. A fucking bar on one side of the office and several sculptures of naked men and women in delicate positions. A mahogany bookcase stretches from wall to wall, floor to ceiling behind the desk. It's so high there's a ladder attached to it that wheels from end to end allowing you to pick out a selection of leather-bound antique books.

Morrigan would cream her pants to get a look at these tomes. They're probably worth thousands. Not that she would care about the coin, she'd only be interested in the knowledge they contained.

I bristle.

Bloody Morrigan. Uptight and never able to see things from my perspective. How she thinks I could have done anything else two years ago is a mystery to me.

Roman approaches the far wall, and like the one downstairs, pushes on it. A door appears and flings open.

Well, shit. This is unexpected.

There's a naked man hanging by his feet inside the wall, his withered todger flopped towards his belly.

For a lesbian, I've had far too many encounters with

penises today—what with Len's leeched erection and now this. I open my mouth to say something, but I'm drawing a major blank, so I shut it.

Today has already been a lot.

"Am I going to have a problem with you again?" Roman says.

"Mmmhhnngs," the naked man says, his cheeks a deep shade of cherry. He huffs through his nose and then shakes his head when he realises he can't talk around the gag.

"Good." Roman, now behind the bar, waggles a bottle of whiskey at me.

"Go on then," I say my eyes skirting from him to the naked man. I've just noticed he only has pubes and body hair on his left side, there's a wax strip hanging off his butt cheek and the other half of him is... is glittery.

I need to stop looking. What kind of torture-fuckery is this?

Roman cricks his neck and bends his wrist, his fingers dancing in the direction of the naked man, whose eyes widen. His scream is muffled by the rag stuffed in his mouth. I glance his body up and down and have to suppress a retch as his balls split open and one testicle flops to the floor. Blood pisses down his torso and after an excruciating minute of shrieking he passes out.

I'm used to violence, but Gods, this is a little far even for me. Roman is clearly on one today. He waltzes over to the wall, presses the door shut, and swipes a series of finger movements across the panel. Metal grinds inside the compartment.

"Sending him to medical," he nods at the floor below and kicks the testicle towards the bar bin.

"Anyway, trouble at the docks?" There's a steeliness to

his tone, and after that little display, I'm pleased I persuaded Lenny to my way of thinking.

I shrug. "I handled the dock. I honestly don't know why you have me deal with it. It's hardly worth my skill. I'm wasted on it. I know a girl that could handle it for you instead."

Here's the thing... that's a bald face lie. What can I say? I lie a lot. But I absolutely need to continue working on the dock deals. I've been working on a plan to entrap him. About a month after I started working for him, I found out exactly what he's up to. He's importing, but it's not booze for his clubs like everyone thinks. Problem is, he's also not an idiot. He knows just how big my ego is, so protest I must, in order to keep this ruse up.

Roman smiles, his eyes glimmering under the bar spotlights. "Little Stir, you have no idea how important the dock trade is."

Oh yes, yes, I do, you maggot shit.

I shrug, "It's just booze, Roman. You could import it in a plethora of other ways. Or better you could have any old negotiator deal with it. Like I said, I know a girl. Why don't you put me to better use? Let me sink my teeth into something juicy. I'm bored."

More lies.

I'm so far from bored it hurts. However, I deserve an award for this performance. It's fucking gold.

Roman takes a swig of his whiskey. "You're critical where you are. I put you on the dock negotiations because they're vital to my business."

Vital to whatever shitstorm he's brewing up against the crown more like.

He pauses, pours a second tumbler of whiskey and then approaches the desk, placing one in front of me and keeping the other for himself. "Without the imports, nothing goes to plan."

Yes, Romaaaan, but what is the plan...? Come on, you bastard, you know you want to tell me. I edge a little magic out, just the tiniest hint of persuasion. I let it dissipate it in the air. I don't want him smelling the magic. But he cocks his head as if he knows, so I pull back. I'll try again another day.

"Because clubs need booze...?" At least I can push verbally.

Have I earned his trust enough for him to tell me what he's up to? Because that's the problem. I might know what he's importing, but I can't do shit about it until either he tells me or I can set him up. And I can't do that without a lot more information.

He smiles and takes a drink. "I hear word of change at the palace."

Not catching him today, then.

The palace reps were here, so that's not news. I also know a girl that works in the secretary office, and she said there have been rumours rumbling. That Calandra is getting twitchy. Said she thinks something huge is coming but I didn't get any more detail than that. The team haven't heard anything either. So how in fucks name did Roman hear? Unless... ahh, he's paying the officials off.

"Oh? Do I get to hear the gossip?" I say, shifting in my seat.

Roman's black eyes darken at me, a shadow full of secrets passing through his expression.

"Morrigan," he says.

I stiffen. We don't discuss Morrigan. Not after what he did two years ago. She's off limits, a silent agreement neither of us signed, but both of us agreed to.

Roman doesn't know that I'm aware she's the princess. I need to tread through this conversation carefully.

Roman sips his whiskey. "The palace is nervous. There wouldn't be officials visiting me, checking up on me to see what business I'm running or working on if they weren't."

"Good job you're paying them off then."

His eyes narrow at me. "How do you—"

"Roman, please. I'm good at my job."

He stares at me, takes a sip of his whiskey and continues. "Even without rumours, it doesn't take a genius to work out the palace is politically unstable. With the king gone, they need to establish their power base. And there's only one way to do that—with an heir..."

It takes a second to still my breathing enough to get control, and then I play the game. "What are you saying? What has any of this got to do with Morrigan?"

He tips his chin up at me, daring me to figure it out. I drag it out a little more, really driving the performance home.

I shake my head, even let a few tears well in my lids. Gods, this is a masterpiece.

"She's... She's the..."

He squints at me scrutinising my performance. Come on Stirling, bring it home.

"*No*," I shout and slam my fist on the table. I stand up, slurp down some of the whiskey and pace. "But if she's... then her mother... Oh gods." I let a couple tears fall, rearrange my face into something dark, and launch the half full glass at the wall. "Bitch."

I glance over, and Roman gives me a crisp nod.

Nailed it.

"Now you see why I agreed to save you? Why I pulled you away, and let you work for me? You were being betrayed by the one person who was supposed to love you. She's a liar. They all are in the palace. Someone needs to do something about it."

Now that is interesting. *'She's a liar'*. Such poison in his tone. See, the art of being a good negotiator is to always listen.

"How could you keep this from me for all these years?" I snarl.

He leans forward. "To protect you, Little Stir. I didn't want to see you hurt. But..." he folds his arms. "You understand what this means? What Calandra is going to do?"

The realisation of what's going to happen settles over me like a noose.

Fuck.

Bile claws at my throat, but I can't let him see the horror I'm feeling inside. As far as he's concerned, this will ensure my loyalty to him. Morrigan's own mother killed mine after all.

But I've had weeks to process this. And Morrigan isn't her mother. But I don't want this to happen.

It's too soon.

It will change everything.

I run a hand over my face, trying to wipe the realisation away. This, at least, is genuine. Suddenly, I'm sitting again, the truth shifting and like a parasite, worming under my skin. When I finally slow the racing thud in my chest, I find the words.

"Investiture? Calandra's bringing Morrigan into the public?"

Roman smiles, it's broad and white and gnarled. "Yes, and...?"

My fists ball under the table. Roman's sneering as if the

sadistic shit is enjoying torturing me. I'm too many things at once. My chest is so tight I can't breathe.

Roman leans back in his chair, his eyes narrowing at me. "Say it, Stirling."

My throat is thick. It cloys with reluctance. I don't want to say it because I refuse to believe it. What does he expect me to feel? Rage at her for lying and what her family did to mine? Regret because I did love her, and now she's...?

He laughs, a deep and gritty rumble that billows from his chest like granite and rocks.

"My Little Stir, do I detect a flicker of hesitation? Have I not given you everything?"

Fuck. I need to pull this back. I open my mouth to respond, but no words come out. Instead, I swallow the lump in my throat.

I want him to believe that nothing will get me out from under his feet. I need him to believe I am utterly devoted to him and his cause.

Roman leans forward. "What are you going to do? Fling yourself at her feet to stop the investiture? I thought you were long over this. After what I've just revealed, after discovering who she is, don't you hate her?"

"Of course I fucking do." I spit in his bin and then kick it out from under his desk. "Fuck the crown."

His gaze scans my face. "Even if you could forgive Morrigan, do you really think the crown will ever pardon you for working with their enemy? Whether you like it or not, you're stuck with me. It's time to double down."

Working for Calandra and the team was fine while the palace was ignoring Roman.

But now they're checking up, or worse, maybe they're investigating him. If my two worlds are colliding, it's not going to be good for any of us. Me especially. But I can't leave Roman. Not yet. Not until I find a way to hang the traitorous bastard.

"Don't make me doubt you. You know what happens when you make me doubt your loyalty." His gaze drops to my forearm and the scar it bears. The scar he gave me.

I grit my teeth.

"I want you to understand something, Little Stir. You work for me and only me. Morrigan going through the investiture is meaningless. You gave her up a long time ago. You and I, we're going places."

My heart turns to ice and steel in my chest. I was hoping he'd say that. Hoping he'd prove to be the malicious piece of shit I thought he was. It makes what I'm going to do significantly easier.

"It's not going to be just an investiture, is it?" I say, my voice small, intentionally weak. And even in that moment, I hate myself for it. I am not weak. I am not small. I am a fucking titan, and not even Roman will break me. I repeat it over and over in the corner of my mind. A mantra, a promise, a fucking vow.

He undoes his cufflinks and rolls his sleeves up. "No, it's not."

The backs of my eyes sting. Not for him or his vindictiveness, but for her. For Morrigan. And for what will become of her. But I won't be weak in front of him. Not when I have a pretense to uphold. I curl my fingers under the desk until magic floods my system and I harden.

I will not break.

I will not bend the knee.

Not to him.

Never to him.

He's held leverage over me for far too long. It's time for that to stop. I straighten up, pumping vicious steel into my voice, "Calandra will use the investiture to find Morrigan a husband and marry her off for political stability."

Roman raises his tumbler to me and takes a sip of rum. "Bingo, Little Stir. Cheers to the crown. The real question is, how do we use the investiture to right the wrongs done to us?"

He sips the whiskey while I seethe, hot and furious, my chest a furnace of heat.

He's going to use the investiture to attack the crown.

I cannot allow that to happen.

But I have to bide my time. Play the game, negotiate my way into position. So, I paste on a sneer and smile, "Now that's my kind of question."

CHAPTER 5

MORRIGAN

Nothing is going according to plan.

I had a plan for my life, it was a very fucking good plan. Strategic, thought out.

And Mother is ruining it.

I pull my hair up into a loose bun, my jaw grinding as I bite down the hundred things I want to scream at her.

"Would you keep your voice down, Morrigan," mother says.

"Fine," I spit through gritted teeth. The morning sun streaks through the Sanatio courtyard. The ancient plant in partial bloom this morning. Maroon blossoms float on the breeze as they peel away from their buds ready for winter. The scent of raw magic: cinnamon and static, drifts through the air. A fountain in the back trickles down creamy marble sculptures. If it weren't for the searing fury pumping through my veins, it would be a gorgeous morning.

But Mother has ruined it.

She takes my hand in hers. "This is beyond either of our

control. Neither of us would have chosen this timing. But it is what it is, and my decision is final."

"You didn't even consult me."

There's movement behind me, I sense it, magic tingling under my skin like bees, before I see it through the giant courtyard windows. It must be the team arriving. I summoned them as soon as I knew mother wanted a 'chat'. Mother's chats have never been good news.

Mother's face is sharp, tension cutting lines through her usually smooth skin. "Yes, well. What would you have me do? Delay and allow him to gain traction?"

"You're the one that set this in motion, thirty years ago."

"Don't upset me darling."

The courtyard door opens. Chatter crescendos, filling the court and then stutters into silence. I don't turn around. I know it's the team, I can sense their energy. Stirling's most of all. Gods, she's like a parasite! I can never focus when she's around. I bet her head is held high, that look of assured confidence glinting in her eyes.

"You have thirty days."

"I beg your pardon? Thirty days? How the hell do you expect me to resolve this in that time?"

"That, my darling, is your problem. Consider this a trial by fire. You want to be Queen, yes?"

My jaw flexes, and I nod.

"So fix it. I don't care how. But fix it, or I'll give the crown to Penelope."

"You wouldn't dare." This is a travesty. I'm in my thirties for gods sake, and she's making me feel like a child.

Mother's eyes narrow at me, her face dark against the morning sun. "Try me. I will not allow this crown to come to any danger, and this—*he*—is a problem that needs handling. Now, handle it like a queen, or Penelope will."

Fury shakes my body. I want to burn the entire palace to the ground. How dare she use my sister like that? Penelope is a useless bitch more preoccupied by the legacy fashions and who's fucking who than the intricacies of court politics and running a sovereign nation. Mother understands that about Penelope as much as I do.

But when I finally glance up at Mother, her face is so stern, so cold, that I know without a shadow of a doubt that she's not joking.

The threat is real.

"Over my dead body is Penelope having the crown."

Mother's face brightens. She shakes the stiffness out of her shoulders and smiles. "Just as I'd hope. Good day, Merry."

I fire a glare at her. She hasn't called me that since I was a child.

I watch her leave. She keeps the smile plastered on while giving the team a graceful wave as she exits the courtyard. And I am left standing there, tension cording my neck and my fists balled.

Stirling frowns, glances from me to mother and back again. I don't want to look at her, but I can't help it. My eyes sweep her figure. Her hair is freshly cut, neat at her shoulders, a slight kink in her locks, like she spent the morning on the docks, the ocean air swirling between the strands. Her cheeks are bronzed, too.

Her confident energy matches the curve of her eyes. So full of charm and arrogance. She catches my gaze, and there's hesitancy, but it's brief. Her expression settles into a glimmering net, as if she knows she's caught me. As if she knows she owns me, owns my heart. After yesterday and the conservatory, I don't blame her.

No one dares look at me the way she does. Most people edge away because of the power I hold. As if the current threading through my veins has a force field and they don't want to get too close.

But not Stirling.

She's never been afraid. Never looked away, never leant away from me. Never bent the knee, never succumbed to my command, my power, my authority. It does something odd to my insides. Heat pours in, but not the same fury mother ignited, something far hotter, deeper, more tingly. It drops lower, lower, until it pulses in my clit.

A memory flashes through my mind. One stupid deal ruined it all and she vanished from my life. It promptly snuffs out whatever heat was growing inside me.

And now, thanks to mother, everyone will know who I am soon. She's changed the game, changed the fucking rules.

Scarlett, Remy, and Quinn are too busy chatting to have noticed, but Stirling touches my shoulder, and it's like lightning firing through me.

"Everything okay?" she asks.

But Scarlett breaks apart from Quinn and Remy, severing their conversation. The three of them approach.

"No. Let's get out of here. I need a drink," I say to Stirling.

Stirling frowns. "It's 11am."

"And?"

She opens her mouth, but the vicious glare I give her shuts it again.

"Follow me. We have a fucking problem." I march out of the courtyard, the group sprinting after me.

I power through the palace, down the main corridor, and out into the gardens. The bushes are being trimmed by palace gardeners, probably the last real manicure they'll get before winter settles in. We skirt down the side of the palace maze and across a gravel path. It takes a few minutes, but then we approach my cottage in the east side of the royal grounds.

Mother wanted me to move into the palace after we finished the Borderlands job. But I refused. Up until that point, only four people knew my real identity. Mother, Daria—mother's head of security. Benedict—mother's chief of staff and... ugh. The last person is so abhorrent I can't even bring myself to say their name. But now the team know who I am, Mother felt I should be closer to home under crown protection.

We came to an agreement that I'd take a cottage on palace property. But that was it. I'm thirty-one, for fucks sake. And I've not lived at home in years. I'm not moving in to sit under mother's scrutiny twenty-four hours a day.

We approach my cottage, a thatched property. A real feat of architectural genius. Looks tiny from the outside but it has seven bedrooms, an office, a mini library and a huge kitchen and living room. Some Magician architect with dimensional magic designed all the cottages on royal grounds. They wanted maximum efficiency. When there are royal balls hundreds of guests descend on the palace. While the palace is enormous, there have been occasions when we needed enough rooms in cottages and houses to host a thousand magicians. So they're all enchanted to take up a tiny plot of land, but inside, they're a maze of rooms and reception areas and bathrooms.

This house is big enough that after mother decided to make the team official, slowly but surely, they'd all left more and more stuff here. At first it was an overnight bag. Then Remy commandeered a bedroom, Scarlett took another, and it went from there.

They haven't moved in exactly. But the cottage has become a mission base of sorts. When we're on jobs, it makes sense that we're together and don't have to schlep halfway across the city to have a meeting or share data. As it stands, they all have a room each and they pick and choose when they stay. Though Stirling has scarcely ever stayed, for obvious reasons.

Would've been nice if they'd asked, but apparently we're past that. I guess they're just family now.

I'm still smarting from mother. The cottage must sense my fury because the front door swings open the moment I shove the gate out of the way. Even the potted plants and flowers bend away from me as I storm up the garden path and into the kitchen.

Someone shuts the door, and I head into the kitchen. I touch my fingers and thumbs into a triangle and snap them apart. The stove flicks alight. Remy takes the kettle off, fills it to the brim, and pops it on the hob, letting it rattle away as it boils.

The cottage creaks, and the fire in the hearth on the far wall bursts to life. Bless, I love when the cottage knows what I need. I will be devastated when I have to take up residency in the palace.

"So," Scarlett says ferreting in the fridge for food. "That looked uncomfortable."

"Way to go with the subtlety," Quinn says jabbing her in the ribs.

"What? It was well awkward."

Quinn tuts and pushes Scarlett out of the way of the

fridge, grabbing sausages and mushrooms. "Get out of the way. It's not like you can cook."

"My cooking is exemplary, thank you very much."

Quinn scoffs and nudges Scarlett until she does get out the way, though it looks more like a mouse trying to move an elephant.

"Gods, you're so demanding," Scarlett says but there's no venom in her words. She gives Quinn's ass a squeeze and then ducks as Quinn throws a slap in her direction.

I smile. This at least, is normality. Seeing them like this pops the heat in my chest. I needed this. A moment of us, the team. Just being together.

I exhale as Remy pours cups of tea and coffee. Herbal tea for Quinn, though she tuts at whatever teabags I had and then rifles in one of my cupboards for additional herbs, and sprinkles a cocktail of gods know what in the mug.

Scarlett drinks straight black coffee, I have milk and sugar in mine, black tea one sugar for Remy, though she also drinks coffee the same way. And Stirling has a weak milky coffee.

It's automatic now. The last two months we've spent so much time together it's like they're an extension of me. We all know how the others move through the day, how we eat, the things we like, and the stuff that irks us.

Quinn, for example, is cussing Remy out for putting the teabags in the cupboard back to front. She pushes her out the way with a hip and proceeds to rearrange the cupboard so everything faces out in neat, precise rows.

"There," she proclaims. "Much better."

I smile to myself. I love them all. "Feels weird, without Jacob this morning. How long do you think he will be gone?" I say to no one in particular.

It's Scarlett that answers. "Not too long, I hope. He owes me a race on the track. Need to school his ass."

"Yes, because you schooled him so well last time." Stirling smirks. Scarlett scowls at her and throws an orange at her head.

Stirling laughs and catches it just before it careens into the wall.

Quinn turns the oven on and chops mushrooms and digs for beans and other items to make a cooked breakfast. Remy hands me my mug and slings an arm around my shoulder. I lean into her and rest my head on her shoulder. Stirling is curled up on a beanbag by the fire, and Scarlett is irritating Quinn by the sideboard.

"You going to tell us what that was about?" Remy asks.

I take a sip of coffee and lean onto her shoulder. "We have a new mission."

"Ooh," Quinn says, from the oven. Stirling sits up in the corner, her expression bright and curious.

"Don't look too excited. Mother has decided that I'm to come out to the public. That it's time I had my investiture and go public as the heir apparent."

Scarlett leaves Quinn cooking and pulls out a chair at the kitchen table. "How does that equate to a mission?"

I sigh, slide out from under Remy, and take a seat opposite. "The Roman rumours we talked about the other day. Mother thinks the only way to snuff them out is to strengthen the crown's powerbase. Strategically, the only way to do that is with another sovereign and an investiture."

"Right? But that still isn't a mission," Quinn says shoving sausages in the oven and turning the heat up. Stirling sits next to her sister.

"She wants Roman dealt with." I sip more coffee.

Stirling pales to a strange pasty colour I don't think I've ever seen on her usually ruddy, ocean-kissed skin.

"She's given me thirty days to 'handle it.'"

"Handle how?" Scarlett says and pulls a short blade out twirling it on her fingertip.

"Well, that's for us to figure out. Either we get rid of him, find dirt on him, or catch him red-handed making a play for the palace."

Remy whistles as she sits too. "That is..."

"A big mission," I say. "Yeah."

"What... what happens if we don't?" Stirling says and then swallows audibly.

"If we don't resolve the issue... if he's not dead, incarcerated or incapacitated, she's going to give the crown to Penelope."

Scarlett exhales and leans back in her chair.

"So we have a mission then. We're finding a way to take that motherfucker down, once and for all," Remy says.

I nod. "I've thought long and hard about it, and tactically, the best move is to catch him in whatever play he's making against the crown and then incarcerate him. If we kill him, we make him a martyr. That is only going to make the political base more unstable."

Stirling's eyes are wide. Her mouth opens and closes. Oh gods, what has she done now? The look on her that smacks of—

"I—I—I work for him," she splutters out.

No.

I'm stone-still. My breathing hitches, shallow and rapid. Quinn drops a ladle against the pan. Scarlett cringes.

How could she be so stupid?

Remy lets out a nervous laugh. "Pardon?"

"I... I'm sorry. I've worked for him for a while. It was..." she falters, glances up at me.

But I can't respond. Everything is rushing in my ears. Blood pounds in a roaring, thunderous beat. This can't be true. There's no way she could've been that stupid. She made that stupid deal, but I never thought she'd...

Gods... She has no idea what she's done. She has no idea who he is—was—to me. My throat is thick and sour.

Scarlett reaches over and clasps Stirling's hand.

It snaps Stirling out of the reverie she was in. She wipes her face. "I work for him, but not *for* him, obviously."

"What? I mean, how did this happen?" Quinn says.

"I've been trying to find a way to frame him since..." she looks up at me, shakes her head. "Doesn't matter. The point is, I never wanted to work for him. I just figured... I don't know. I guess I thought I could set him up or something. But it's been so much harder than I anticipated, and he... well, it doesn't matter now."

She glances at me, but I'm still silent. I can't say anything. I need to think. I need her to leave immediately. This changes everything. Why the hell would he want her to work for him? After he knew we were together? The sick bastard.

When no one responds, Stirling carries on. "It started while we were banished. We had nothing, and I couldn't say no. We needed the money, amongst other things. So I've been working for him ever since. But I'll stop. Okay? I'll never go back, and I'll tell you everything I know."

Quinn stirs the pan. "Stirling, you're literally working for the one man who hates the crown, who's working *against* the crown. All while also working for the literal crown. What in the name of magician-gods were you thinking?"

Stirling's standing now. "It's complicated. It's... it's not like I had a choice, I wanted to find a way to..." She catches me glaring at her and the words die on her tongue, there one minute, swallowed the next. There's so much they don't know.

"How long?" Remy says.

"Does it even matter? I'm not going back. Not now, okay? I swear." Stirling's eyes are wild, frantically skirting between the group. Scarlett's head is in her hands, Remy is kneading her temples, and Quinn is staring out the kitchen window.

The fire in the hearth erupts, roars up the chimney and then dies. Snuffed out. By me. The team snaps to look at me.

"Morrigan?" Scarlett says.

I push my chair back, the wooden legs scraping against the stone tiles.

I stand.

Slow.

Intentional.

Focused solely on Stirling.

Stirling swallows hard, her throat bobbing with the action. She shifts her footing, her eyes dropping away from mine. "Can we talk about this? Negotiate a way for me to apologise, so I can make it up to you all?" Her words tumble out like sand.

I'm not surprised. My gaze is as hot as lava right now. Bubbling and searing with the rage of a scorned women.

Scarlett twitches as if she thinks she's going to have to move quick. Defend Stirling. But she won't, not today. I just need her gone. Out of my headspace, and out of my kitchen so I can think and plan.

"Get." My word is quiet, like a whisper on a breeze, but no less potent. It hits the air like a gun.

Stirling recoils as if I shot her. Her lips twitch as if she wants to defend herself, as if she's going to spill all the secrets she's been holding. But I won't let her fuck this up anymore.

"Out," I spit and throw my hand in the direction of the kitchen door which swings open and slams against the wall.

Stirling flinches. She takes a step back.

There's a moment where our eyes lock, hers round, pleading, mine narrowed, like knives and arrows. The air swells.

And then she flees, leaving the rest of us silent in the kitchen.

CHAPTER 6

STIRLING

I leave Morrigan's cottage in a mess. My throat aches with unsaid words, but what hurts the most is my chest. It's heavy, anchored down by frustration and sadness.

I don't want to go back to Castle Grey, so I let my feet carry me to the docks. I open my shed, eyeing the ocean-coloured beach mansion with its shiplap front and huge glass windows. If I squint, I can just about make out the conservatory in the back garden.

I huff out my irritation and focus on the boat. So much for finding each other where blue meets blue. I sand wood, until my fingers are swollen and sore, and then switch to hammering a couple of extra cupboards in and knotting rigging. When my body aches, and the sun kisses the horizon, Claude finds me by the shed. That fucking rat is sat on his shoulders, the bottle of Sangui whiskey I gave him last month dangles from one hand and two glasses from the other.

He nods for me to follow him onto the sand, so I kick my shoes off drop my tools back in the shed and lock up. I meet him on the beach as the sky mottles with burnt pinks and dusky oranges.

"You look like shit," he says.

I take the bottle and uncork it and pour two glasses, and then hold it up to what's left of the dying sun. It glistens a little, and is far redder and opaque than whiskey has any right to be.

"You're sure this is whiskey?" I ask. Given this shit came from Sangui city, I'm not sure how much I want to drink it.

"Mmm, it's called Sanguis Cūpa," he says.

"Blood cask? Er... Do I want to know what's in this?"

He shakes his head.

"Right. Well, cheers."

We clink glasses and he necks an inch of drink in one go. I raise an eyebrow but follow suit, and. Holy. Mother. Of. Gods. It's like pouring the sun into my veins.

Everything brightens and glows. The sun is an orb of burning glitter. The sand between my fingers softens like candy floss, my heart thuds slow between my ribs, and everything calms. I lie back against the sand, the clouds billowing and puffing across the sky leaving a trail of rainbow mosaics.

Claude lies back with me.

"You see why I ask for it now?"

"Hell yes."

"Don't get used to it," he shrugs.

I reach out and squeeze his arm.

"You seem... sad today."

"Yeah. I fucked up." A cloud turns pink and waves at me? Or I wave at it. I think I'm hallucinating.

"What did you do?" he says.

I roll over to face the old boy, "Does it matter? I didn't fuck up today. I fucked up a long time ago, and even though I've done everything I can to fix it since, everything is still broken."

"Apologise, no?"

"Is it ever that simple?" I stick my hand out, finger pointed at the rat. Its fur has turned burgundy like the drink and stands on end. Its little head and beady eyes bob up and down, and then, in slow motion, it snaps at my finger.

"Fuck."

Claude laughs. "He can sense your dislike of him."

"He's the one who keeps trying to bite me. I'm just trying to be friends. I'm friends with everyone. Why won't he like me?"

Claude shakes his head at me, laughing. "You make good deals. No?"

"I've been known to make one or two."

"So, make a deal. Find what they want. Give it to them, that's your apology."

I narrow my eyes at him, the haze of the shot wearing off. The clouds darken as the sun vanishes and the heat in my veins lessens.

"Huh," I say. "Not just a pretty boat boy, are you?"

"I've not been pretty in three decades. What I know is friends will always love. Make apology deal. Be okay tomorrow, hmm."

Claude's right, I don't see any other way around it. It's less a negotiation that's needed and more a heartfelt apology. I don't know whether they'll accept my justification, but maybe if I just tell them what happened, I can make them see that I had everyone's best interests at heart.

I sit up. "Thanks, Claude."

He sticks a hand up but doesn't make to move off the beach. So I leave him there. The rat eyes me the whole way.

I'm about to step off the beach when Scarlett appears.

"Sister," she says, her face pinched.

"I'm pretty sure I just drank something that's about to give me a blinding headache, so unless you either have booze in that bag or you bring good news, I'm not entirely sure I'm ready to deal with you."

Scarlett folds her arms. "Roman? Really?"

"Do we need to do this now?"

"I figured you were working for him. But you never told me, and I didn't want to pry. You should have told me, Stir."

We make our way through the city, away from the harbour and toward the palace.

"And say what? How was I supposed to explain that I was working for a criminal? We were already banished. It wasn't exactly going to help our cause."

When we reach the cottage gate, the chimney coughs wisps of grey into the night. It's pitch black but there's a warm glow emanating from the windows and the smell of pizza drifts on the air. Fuck I'm starving. I didn't realise just quite how hungry I was. But working on the boat all afternoon has me ravenous.

The gate refuses to budge.

Really?

"Oh come on. I know I fucked up. Do I need to apologise to you too?"

The gate doesn't move.

I glare up at the house. "I'm sorry, okay?" I throw my hands up and the gate swings open.

Fucking cottage.

As if it can read my thoughts, the gate slaps my arse a

little too hard as I pass through. I tut but keep my mouth shut, lest it does something worse this evening.

"You need to tell them everything," Scarlett says. "Get it all out in the open, and then we can make a plan for how the hell we're going to rectify this mess.

The cottage door opens for me this time. I take a deep breath and step inside. The gentle pressure of a cottage hello washes over my skin, soaking me in the aroma of palace roses, warm cooking, and the faint trace of Morrigan's library. Scarlett follows in right behind. The team are in the living room. The fire crackles and pops, the scent of burning wood warming the house.

Morrigan sits with her legs curled under her. She's wearing pjs and a hoody and my Gods, she looks so adorable my stomach furls into a knot of butterflies. My tongue slides over my lips. I could—

"Sit down. This is your one chance to tell us everything you know," she says her tone cold.

Right yes, well that's one way to pop my lady boner. I pout but take a seat. Quinn and Remy are on the big sofa and Morrigan is in the armchair. She throws a cushion at my head, rather too hard, but I catch it before it makes contact.

Scarlett forces Remy off the sofa, picks Quinn's legs up, swings them over hers and proceeds to rub her feet.

Remy sits on the floor.

"I fucked up," I say and take a seat in front of the fire.

"I think that much is obvious, bud," Remy winks at me.

"Two years ago—"

Morrigan's eyes narrow. Figuring out that I went to work for him after our breakup. The moment it clicks, a seething poison seeps into her features. She gives me a curt shake of the head. A clear signal not to talk about that night. So I move the story on.

Remy opens a crate of beer, takes the lid off and passes it to me, along with a slice of pizza. She hands the same to everyone else.

"Keep going. What can you tell us that's useful? If the Queen wants us to take him down, and he's the most powerful magician in the ci—" Remy says.

"Third most powerful. Second to mother and I," Morrigan says.

"Right. I mean... Still. He's a powerful bastard, and all of us except you are outpowered," Remy replies averting her gaze from Morrigan.

Remy doesn't believe Morrigan's more powerful. I don't either. After what he did to us, if she had the ability to take him out, she would've done already. So would I.

Whether she likes it or not, he has a boatload of property and power behind him and that's exactly why this is going to take a team effort.

"So what is it you do for him?" Quinn asks reaching for two pieces of pizza. Scarlett lunges for the biggest piece but Quinn whips it away.

There's a scramble. Scarlett ends up victorious and takes a huge bite of the largest piece and Quinn sits back huffy.

"For the most part, I just negotiate shipping and dock deals. He imports stuff every week and I liaise with the harbour boys to make sure his boats dock."

"What stuff?" Scarlett says her eyes narrowing at me.

I shift on the cushion, the heat from the fire suddenly overwhelming. This was the bit I was dreading. The worst of the truth.

"Listen. Before anyone gets pissed at me, I had a plan,

okay? I negotiated with Claude, he's this guy I know... Never mind. The point is, I've been embezzling pieces of what he's importing. So he doesn't have anywhere near what he thinks he does an—"

"Stirling," Morrigan cuts me off. "What. Is. He. Importing?"

I glance around the room, taking in each of the team.

"He is amassing power. But he's doing it off books, importing magic from dying mansions from other realms. You remember when we recruited Remy and her team harvested the magic from the mansion that was about to be demolished? She stored all the magic in those cute boxes."

Everyone nods.

"He's using the same method but from properties in other cities and realms so it's untraceable. No chance of being caught."

"Fuck," Remy says. "That's genius."

"Remy," Quinn cuffs her up the back of the head. "Hardly the time is it?"

She shrugs. "Well it is genius. If I'd have thought of that, I could have been infinitely wealthy. There's only so many dead and dying mansions in New Imperium. You know?"

"Aren't you already like a gazillionaire?" Scarlett says.

Remy shrugs. "Yeah, but some of us like money, babe. Can always do with more."

"Anyway," I say. "Yesterday Roman told me about the investiture, right before I found you guys in the club. I suspect he's planning something for it. My gut says that's when he's going to attack."

Morrigan's a little pale, but she nods. "Mother suspects the same. That's why she gave me the investiture as the deadline. Okay. So we know he is importing power. Where's he sending it, Stirling? What's he doing with it? How is he harnessing it and how do we stop him?"

"I..." my stomach bottoms out. Two years and I'm no closer to answers. "I have no idea."

"You're joking," Morrigan says.

"I wish I was. He has a huge network of staff, layers upon layers, so we can't track each other, so that no one other than him knows what's truly going on. It's one of the reasons I've been able to embezzle magic off him--the layers of bureaucracy are insane. And I can't pay anyone off because Roman pays too well. They're loyal."

"Fuck," Morrigan says and shoves a piece of hair behind her ear.

"For what it's worth..." Remy gets up. She spreads her arms wide, and then brings her hands together, bending her two middle fingers, making the knuckles meet, and then pulling them apart to draw a rectangle in the air.

A golden whiteboard appears, hanging midair.

"...I think you're a complete numpty. This wasn't exactly your smartest idea. But we're here now. So what's say we try and figure a way out of this mess? Morrigan...? I'll scribe."

Morrigan stands too, "Help me move the sofas to the edge of the living room."

Scarlett and I shove the sofa and armchair back as far as they'll go. Quinn takes the pizza boxes back to the kitchen and returns with the last piece, taking little nibbles of it. When we're all huddled in front of the hovering board, Morrigan claps her hands.

"So what have we got?" she says.

"We know he's importing magic," Scarlett says.

Remy nods. Bends and laces a couple of fingers together

and the words: IMPORTING MAGIC appear on the whiteboard.

"Hey, this is a neat bit of magic. You'll have to teach me how to do this. It would be useful for poison formulas—there's not enough wall space in the shop." Quinn says.

"Remind me tomorrow and I'll pop in. What's next?" Remy asks.

The room falls silent. Each of us looks at the other in turn.

"That can't be it," Remy says.

"Actually, it's not," Morrigan says but her tone is grim. She raises her gaze to me, her features scrunched, apologetic.

Oh, fuck. I realise what she's thinking. And one by one, so does everyone else. Their eyes turn to me.

"But of course. We have a double agent," Remy says.

"No. Look it was all fun and games for a second. But it was hard enough keeping it secret while no one knew what I was doing. But this is serious now. We're actually trying to take him down. The chances of him catching me are infinitely higher now."

"And what do you think Calandra is going to say when she inevitably finds out?" Morrigan says.

Scarlett glares at Morrigan. "Calandra is not going to find out. Is she...Morrigan?"

Quinn places her hand on Scarlett's arm, a warning to back down.

"Well, let's hope not. Because if mother did find out Stirling was working for the very man threatening the throne, she'd want her head. No matter what she's done for the team. It's not like her record is whistle-clean," Morrigan snaps.

"I'm right here," I wave, but Morrigan just glares at me.

I sigh, "Everything was expunged when the banishment was lifted. She can't hold that against me. I'm not doing it. This is a death sentence. Even if Calandra doesn't find out, Roman will, and I'll be on the chopping block anyway."

"I really don't want to put you in danger, but we are on a timeframe here. Besides, you've managed it the last couple of months, Stir, what's another thirty days?" Morrigan says.

"Not the point. The last couple of months have been horrendous keeping everything quiet, it's a fucking miracle I haven't been caught."

Morrigan paces up and down the living room, "What's the alternative? If Roman makes a play for the throne, it's all going to come out anyway. Then what? The dungeons and a beheading? Because if we don't handle this, then it's going to be Penelope on the throne, and we all know how much she loves me. I doubt anyone connected to me will come out unscathed. So it's not just you on the chopping block, Stirling. I'd say none of us have much choice. Either we imprison Roman, or we're all fucked."

That promptly shuts me up.

Heat builds in my neck, rises over my cheeks. "Fuck." I kick the coffee table and the leg cracks, splinters and buckles beneath the weight of books which topple over the edge and onto the floor.

Morrigan pouts, "Do you feel better now? I'll have you know that's my favourite table." She places both fists together and pulls them apart. She slides her palms together and then bends her little fingers. The leg's cracks and splinters liquify and smooth. The leg slots back into place, healed as if it never happened.

"Always so reactive in the moment. This is exactly the sort of shit that got you into this mess in the first place."

My jaw tightens so much my face aches. She can't leave it alone. Always has to dig at me.

I snap. "Well at least I have emotions, and don't have to weigh up four hundred things before landing on which one I feel."

"Ladies. For fuck's sake this is not the time," Remy says and turns to the board. "Stirling. Sorry, bud, but looks like you're our double agent. So how's about we all get a grip and make sure Morrigan ends up on the throne. Yeah?"

I press my lips shut, my molars grinding my enamel to dust. I nod. I can't quite bring myself to say anything because the only things on the end of my tongue are insults and fury. My mouth is flame-hot and sour. I snatch the crust of Quinn's pizza out of her hand and shove it in my mouth, trying to get rid of the taste.

"Oh, I was enjoying that," Quinn pouts.

"I'll order another pizza," I say through my mouthful of dough crust.

But Quinn waves me off.

"If we're going to investigate, we need access to Roman," Morrigan says.

Scarlett glances at me. "Are there any big events coming up at the palace he could be invited to? Oh, Stir. Isn't there an annual party at the club? I swear you always go to it, and I always clean up the hangover you have in the morning."

"There is, but it's not due for a while," I say swallowing the crust and immediately feeling calmer.

"There's also the auction coming up," Quinn says dancing from foot to foot. "Some of the properties from the Borderlands are going into it. I bet you he's at that. Roman's always buying inner city clubs."

"Yes! Nice one, Quinn. I think I saw auction papers on his desk the other day."

"Well, we have the investiture too, but it will be too late by then," Quinn adds.

"I'll get mother to throw a masquerade ball this week. Invite everyone, even royals from other cities so it doesn't seem off that Roman's invited."

Remy furiously contorts her fingers, and all the words appear on the floating white board.

Investiture
Auction
Masquerade ball
Palace events?

"Okay, so we have a couple of major events we can use to investigate," Remy says.

"The minute mother announces the investiture tomorrow, every legacy and royal for miles will descend on the city. They'll come out of the woodwork to try and discover who Penelope and I am in advance."

My mouth goes dry. My stomach sinks. And I swear the crust I just ate makes its way back up my throat.

"Oh," I say, before I even realise the word is out. Everyone turns to me.

"Oh?" Remy says.

"She was trying to save my feelings. If the legacies come to the city it's for one reason and one reason only..." I glance at Morrigan.

Our eyes hold each other, snared together unable to say the things we want. There's a tremor in her lid, echoed in her lips. She wants to say something. I wish she would. I wish she'd tell me it will be okay, that she doesn't have to be married off. But we both know that's a lie. Like I told Scarlett, Morrigan and I, we're doomed. We always were.

I tear my gaze away before the stinging in my eyes becomes something more. "They're coming *for* Morrigan. For her hand."

"Oh," Quinn says immediately looking away.

Morrigan doesn't even try to contradict me. And I don't know if that helps or hurts even more.

When she does speak, her tone is softer. "The point is, that we can use it as an opportunity. There is nothing legacies like more than gossip. They can't help themselves. So we need to infiltrate every event that happens between now and the investiture. That means any ball, banquet, garden party, the lot."

I stand a little straighter, pull on the Stirling mask everyone expects. I jut my chin out, puff my chest just a smidge, hoping it's enough to hide the ache between my ribs. "Exactly. What Morrigan is trying to say... is that you need to be more ...Stirling."

Morrigan's lips twitch. "I cannot believe these words are leaving my mouth. But for once, Stirling is right. We need to woo and win, spy and seduce."

"Then we have a plan. Quinn, you investigate the properties coming from the Borderlands, see if there are any rumours of early sale interest. Morrigan, you convince Calandra to host a ball. Remy, you set up mission control pull any data we have on Roman, I'll work with you on that. Scar, you liaise with Calandra on the investiture. We need to know where it's being hosted, the number of guards, and schematics for the location. I'll focus on Roman."

Morrigan folds her arms and nods, satisfied with the plan. "We'll crawl through the city and talk to every single legacy if necessary. If you can't coax it out of Roman, then someone has to know what he's up to."

"You should push him," Remy says. "See if you can get closer, lure him in."

"I'll have a *think*," I say and wink at Morrigan, who promptly sticks her middle finger up at me.

CHAPTER 7

MORRIGAN

Nine Years Ago

Club music roars through my ears, the heavy base beat thumping in time with my chest. Roman closes the glass door and the thundering music mutes to a low heartbeat. I peer down. We're in Roman's favourite spot. His mezzanine office. He hasn't said it, but I reckon he thinks of it as his throne, staring down at his nightclub and all his people below.

But I'm not an idiot. What he really wants is a throne of his own. A throne in a palace next to me. Or better, without me there. I know he's only marrying me so he can get access to the palace. The council. The power.

I roll my eyes as he sets down our drinks.

"Happy birthday, Princess," he says holding out a champagne flute.

"It's not midnight yet."

"Then perhaps an early birthday celebration?" He pulls

my hand until I'm up and out of the chair and straddling his lap.

"Roman, please." I wiggle to slide off him, but his face falls. So I stay put. But the last thing I want is to fuck him in a glass box where half the city can see. And if I'm honest, it's not about the people below. It's not even about being seen. He's fucked me against the glass before. It's more that... I just don't want *him* to fuck me.

A waitress enters the box, holding a tray of nibbles. She's wearing leather bondage straps and not a lot else. Both her nipples are pierced, a chain joining them. I swallow, heat kissing my neck like a tan.

She leaves, and I glance at Roman. Fire sears through his expression. I hadn't noticed, but his grip on my thighs is bruising. His knuckles white.

Oh, shit.

"You know you'll have to fuck me eventually."

"We fuck plenty, Roman."

His eyes are white hot, sharp against the pools of black. "We've fucked three times in the last six months."

I shrug. "I'm busy."

"You and I both know that's not the truth."

He slides a hand up my arm, across my shoulder and around the back of my head, pulling me down to kiss me. His other hand wraps around my arse, tugging me close enough to his body I can feel his hard cock push against my knickers. He thrusts up so the hard end of his cock kneads my pussy.

Our lips meet, but instead of the rush of flutters my friends talk of when their boyfriends kiss them, a shudder ripples through my body. I try to suppress it, I really do. But he senses the shiver anyway.

He tuts and pushes me off him, his jaw flexing as he

kneads his forehead. I sit opposite him. The room is silent for a time, then he huffs and mutters to himself. I decide to brave a conversation I've been wanting to have for a while. It's the only way we can both make it out of this unscathed.

"How many political alliances have been made in name only over the years?"

His face darkens. "What do you mean?"

"Come on Roman, we both know this isn't working between us. What if we marry for the alliance? Would it really be so bad to conduct our affairs in private?"

His eyes flash violent. A vein in his neck throbs. The tumbler of whiskey in his hand shatters. Glass showers the carpet and the bitter reek of whiskey fills the air.

"I knew it," he spits. He's on his feet. Kicks the table of food and drinks. It splatters against the glass. Splinters of food and crockery spraying the floor. No one looks up, the music beneath us blaring too loud. His face is deep plum.

I should be afraid. Perhaps if I were a lesser magician I would. But I've witnessed enough of Roman's rages now to know where the line is. Not his line. Mine.

I will not tolerate his aggression. Then again, it's never been actively directed toward me, until tonight.

"Watch your step, Lord Oleg. It was a mere suggestion."

He pulls a hand over his face, as if trying to wash the rage away.

"I see you, you know. I watch you drool over the women in my clubs. I know what you are. What your preferences are. It's why you resist me."

"Marriages like my parents' are a much rarer beast. Most are of convenience. I'd be offering you a crown, a throne. And I'd care not who you were with so long as it was kept private and out of the media."

"Fuck you," he snarls and paces up and down the box.

"A king can't have a whore for a wife. She must show absolute loyalty."

I narrow my eyes at him. I stand now. "You forget your place, Lord Oleg. It is not you who will be king, but I who shall be queen. You are to be my consort, a king in name but not power."

His eyes burn so hot that I swear the glass box we're in trembles against the surge of power coursing through his body. He might not like my words, but it's the truth and he'd do well not to forget it.

He advances on me, a towering hurricane of darkness. Half of me wants to wait and see if he lays a finger on me. The other half knows I need to put him in his place before he really does forget.

He's ten paces away, eight, five. His hand draws up.

I cuff my fist in the air and he stops suddenly, frozen mid-step, his fingers a whisker from my neck.

"You weren't really considering laying a finger on the heir to the throne, were you?"

His mouth draws shut, the veins still pulsing in his neck.

"Now, I'm going to undo my fist and you're going to sit down and contemplate what you want. Do we have an understanding?"

He nods and I release my fist.

He spits on the floor. "Fucking lesbian."

I laugh. I can't help it.

By all rights I should be furious. I should be insulted. But when is the truth ever an insult?

So I smile, sweetly, all teeth and lips. And for the first time in a long time, I feel lighter, freer. "Yes, actually I am. And I dare say I eat pussy better than you. Shame the rumours about your exploits weren't true."

"Go fuck yourself Morrigan."

"Marriage of convenience, *Roman*. The choice is yours. You can have a crown, or you can have a wife who loves you. But you can't have both. Now sit." I swing my fist in the direction of the chair, and he slides across the carpet and down with a *thunk*. His face deepens to purple. "And think about your future."

CHAPTER 8

STIRLING

The team brainstormed late into the night, so we decided to sleep at Morrigan's. I don't normally stay; I prefer to go home to Castle Grey. I hate knowing she's so close to me and I can't have her. But it got late, and after how hard I'd worked on the boat yesterday I was too tired to schlep home.

I haven't been asleep long when I wake, after restlessly turning and kicking off the duvet. I glance at the clock. It's 2:30am.

I groan but decide to get out of bed, so I pad downstairs. There's a strangeness in the air; it's agitated like someone just left. I move through the hall, check the living room and kitchen but no one is here. So I move back towards the rear of the house. Morrigan's library door is open. I step inside but the room is empty.

My fingers caress the pages of the books. There's a Post-it note saying "Find the Sangui Grimoire". I flip some of the books over and look at their covers. Most of them are about mansion magic, and transfers of power. I wonder what weird magic rabbit hole Morrigan is studying now. There's another book titled sovereign politics and negotiation magic.

Negotiation magic? I flip the book shut, frustrated she didn't ask me for help. There's a cup of coffee, half drunk. I lift it to take it back to the kitchen, but it's still warm. I frown. Step out of the library and into the hall. She's not here and I doubt anyone else in the team would use her personal library.

The cottage door opens and if I squint, I can still make out the shape of Morrigan's curves traipsing across the gardens in the direction of the palace. I don't think, I just move. I grab my hoody out of the living room, throw on my trainers and jog after her. But not before I rub the door-frame and whisper a thank you. The cottage door closes gently behind me as the gate swings open to let me chase after her.

If I know anything about Morrigan, she won't have slept because she'll have been thinking. And after today, I suspect she's overthought herself into a rage. I don't blame her. She's going to be pissed at her mother dropping the investiture on her. And, gods, of course if she comes out as the heir in thirty days, there's no way she will be able to stay on with the team.

Everything is crashing down around her.

And then there's me. Us.

I know she's livid with me for working with Roman. Especially because working for him wasn't part of the deal. It was an afterthought, but still. It's enabled me to get this close to him. I'm sure I can use it to my advantage. I've embezzled enough magic to know he's got blind spots. I just have to find the right one, present the right offer.

Maybe if I can get Morrigan on her own, if I can convince her to listen she'll understand. Morrigan disappears into the palace through a side door. I hurry to catch up to her and shiver as I reach it, the night air whipping under my jumper. When I step over the threshold the palace hugs me in cinnamon, mint, and lilac. The pressure eases off after a second, and I close the door behind me. But I've lost Morrigan already. The enormous hallway is empty.

I touch the palace door handle and whisper, "Tell me where she is..." It's stupid, the palace has no reason to help me. But it's all I've got. Something rattles down the end of the corridor. I grin, rub the handle and thank the palace.

At first, I think she's gone to the Sanatio courtyard. Where else would you want to be, than the heart of the palace and power? But then I remember that it's where most people would go, the staffers, Magicians and any dignitaries who stay in the palace, it's essentially a tourist attraction now.

As I round a corner, I realise that she's gone somewhere else entirely. She's gone to the source of the problem.

I'm no longer sure if it's the palace leading me or if my body just knows where to go. There was once a time I didn't even have to think. I was so close to Morrigan I knew every move she'd make. That thought has me rubbing at my torso as if I can erase all the hurt.

I pull to a stop outside the throne room. The door is slightly ajar, and I know it's because she's in there.

I push it open a crack and find Morrigan sat at the foot of her parent's thrones. She cocks her head in my direction but doesn't turn to face me. Instead she sighs.

"Stirling," she breathes, her voice a whisper.

How does she know...?

"You smell like whisky, regret, and the sweetest hint of desire. How could it be anyone else?"

I open my mouth to respond. I've not even had a drink today. And what the hell does regret even smell of? Forget it. I'm not even sure I want to know.

"I woke up and realised you weren't in the cottage, so I came to see if you're okay."

I walk down the elongated throne room, passing the marble pillars, and walls sculpted with textured Sanatio plants that crawl from the floor to the ceiling. Tall soldier-plants stand beside the windows and corners in golden pots carved with intricate patterns, like they guard the palace.

She sags and gets up, finally facing me. "What do you think?"

"Do you... want to talk about it?"

"Why are you here really? You gave up the right to care a long time ago."

Irritation flares in my chest like an elastic band pulled to snapping. But now isn't the time. I don't want to fight and it's not what I came running after her for. I take a steadying breath. "We might not be together, but that doesn't stop me caring."

She purses her plump lips and I'm convinced she's going to shake her head, tell me to get out of here. But she sags and sits on the steps and nods for me to join her. She's wearing slippers, and her legs are bare. Beneath her hoody is a silk slip that finishes just below her tattooed kneecaps, and it takes everything I have to concentrate on her face and not let my eyes rake up her thighs.

"I couldn't sleep," she says as I take a seat on the step next to her.

"It's not like you to stop yourself sleeping because you're overthinking or anything..." I nudge her side.

"Oh fuck off," she says but she's smiling and it makes me laugh.

"I just... I knew this would happen. It's not like the investiture is a surprise, but I thought I had more time. The last couple of months with the team have been the most fun. Even if it meant being careful with you."

"If, by careful, you mean undressing me with a glance from across the team table, then sure."

She rolls her eyes at me but then rests her head against my shoulder. It's the first moment we've really been peaceful with each other. The first moment we haven't rowed or been on mission or had a million people around us. It's almost like before. Almost.

"The last couple of months have been the best months of my life, you know? And now, I have thirty days left and it's all over."

"It's not all over. We're not going anywhere."

She shakes her head against my shoulder. "I know. But it all changes. It won't be the same. It's already started. Jacob's gone to the Borderlands. I doubt he'll be back by the time the investiture happens."

She shifts, lifts off me, her eyes skirting up towards the thrones on the platform. Her father's passing pushed her one step closer to inhabiting the throne herself. I can't imagine the pressure. The weight of an entire city's people. The expectations. The service she will spend her life giving. She might have had a few years in secret and freedom, but she was born into a gilded prison. My arm swings around her shoulder pulling her close, my fingers absentmindedly trailing down her arm. She sighs into me, nestling closer.

"We're definitely safe aren't we? For the next month.

Calandra isn't going to suddenly put your picture in the papers, or anything ruinous?"

"No, the investiture is the moment I step out into society, so I do have a month to adjust."

"Then I guess we have to make these the best thirty days of your life."

At this, she looks at me, "What do you mean?"

"If this is it, these thirty days are all we have, then we should make the most of it. Live life to the max. Thirty days of real freedom. We're going to go to all the legacy parties as part of the mission. So what do you want to do outside of that? What do you want to do, one last time, while no one knows who you are? We could go out? We could do anything..."

"It's a lovely thought, but we don't have time to play truant. This isn't magician school. There won't be any freedom if we don't find enough evidence to capture Roman. If we fail... I lose the crown, you lose your life, and Roman steals the city. Everything will be a mess. Much as I would like to take the time to appreciate these last days.... We can't. We have to strategise, plan, think through every angle, every possibility."

I stand up. I need to put space between us.

I get what she's saying, but this is it. She'll never be able to do a damn thing after this month. Why won't she just let herself *be* for one fucking second?

I step up to the thrones. Their backs are intricately carved and gilded with Sanatio blossoms.

"You know you don't always have to be so stubborn, you can live in the moment, be present and just focus on this, on right now."

She appears beside me. "And you could... oh, I don't know. Stop shooting first and asking questions later. Have you ever considered that taking a breath and thinking things through might actually benefit you sometimes?"

"Low blow, Morrigan."

The air heats, sizzles. I'm not sure if it's because she's winding me up, or all the things I want to do to her in that silk nightgown running through my head. My bottom lip drops open.

"Gods, I am still so mad at you. I can't believe you work for him, after what he did," she says, but the words trill out in a purr and she takes a step closer.

"Liar," I say my face the picture of seriousness. She blinks slow. I tip her chin up. "I'm still furious you kept your identity secret from me."

"Liar," she breathes.

All the things I could do to her on that throne rush through my mind.

One day this throne will be hers, and she'll be Queen.

But even if we end up back together, Calandra will never allow me to be her consort. Morrigan knows that as well as I do. I'm tainted by my parent's legacy, even if they were pardoned. How could Calandra condone it? I turn away, run my fingers over the throne's arms.

A dark thought sparks. I want to fuck her on it. Mark her as mine. I want her to remember me forever. I want her to know that I owned her, that I was the one that lavished her with pleasure and made her come until she couldn't see. So that every time she sits beside her consort, she'll know it should be me next to her.

Morrigan's sucks a slow breath in, her eyes drifting between me and the throne.

She knows.

Gods, she always knows what I'm thinking.

"You're a bad girl, Stirling."

"Oh?" I say, cocking my head and raising an eyebrow at her. "I've no idea what you're talking about."

She laughs, "You forget yourself, Lady Grey. Forget how long we were together. Forget how well I know you."

I forget nothing.

Not the way her body used to arch under my touch. Not the way she used to moan my name like a prayer. Not the way magic oozes from her tattooed skin, the smell of rose and cinnamon that follows in her wake nor the faint scent of ancient books that cling to her clothes.

I forget nothing.

"Mmm. Enlighten me, Your Highness, what is it I'm going to do that makes me such a bad girl?"

"Stirling," she growls. "We can't fuck our way out of this."

"Who says I want out?"

A slow grin peels across her lips, and her eyes darken with want. The same want coursing through my body, pooling between my legs.

She wets her lips but doesn't answer.

So I take a step nearer. The room is searing. Maybe it's my skin, or maybe it's the magic rippling off her body. The closer I step, the headier I feel, as if her desire is seeping into me, leaching my ability to focus, her magic warring against mine. A cocktail of static and tingles. My eyes graze over her naked arms, slide up her legs, each intricate tattoo practically vibrating.

"Tell me you want it..." It's not a question anymore. I demand it.

I want her.

But I want her to want me more. So I won't touch her. Not when whatever this is between us is so fragile. Not when a single touch could fracture our history. Not when I still want to rewrite our ending.

"I want you to bend the knee," she says.

I look down, hiding my reluctant smile. This is unexpected. This isn't the Morrigan I knew two years ago. I hesitate, because I will not yield for anyone... except, it appears for her. I slide to the floor, realising she is the only woman who could command me to my knees. For Morrigan, I'd fall on a sword. I'd kneel until my skin tore and my legs bled, if it meant I could have her. Fuck, I'd deal my soul to the devil if I could keep her forever.

She slips into her mother's throne. Her future throne.

"You're going to bend the knee and worship me, Stirling."

I kneel at her feet and hold her gaze in mine. "Which part of you should I worship?" My words are low, seductive. I take her slender fingers in mine and place a kiss on her knuckles. Worshipping my future Queen just as I've been told.

But I know this isn't what she wants. What she wants is for me to fuck her. And I will. But if I'm bending the knee, then she'll have to work for it.

She tuts and leans forward, her fingers guiding mine to her ankle. There's an ornate filigree pattern twisted around the bone, and I wonder what magic this gives her, which house she's connected to.

She hovers there, my hand clasped to hers, her lips millimetres from mine—a dare, a temptation. I don't move. This is all a negotiation of wills. Who will break first? Who kneels and who commands? The air ebbs and flows thick with lust and power: hers, mine, ours.

My legs shake, my body quivering and desperate with lust. I'm so close to breaking. But finally, she draws her hand up her leg, pulling my fingers and the silk of her gown up, up, up.

Over her knees.

Over her thighs... until.

I suck in a sharp breath. Fuck. She's not wearing any underwear.

I can barely keep myself upright. My fingers tremble against her thigh, tracing the lines of tattoos, pulsing with the static and power peeling off her skin.

My heart races under my ribs.

I want her.

I need her.

I long to part her and slide my fingers inside her warm cunt and worship her core. I want to taste every part of her.

"Will you find me where blue meets blue?" she says.

"Always."

She leans forward, "Are you devoted to me, Stirling?"

I nod because in this moment she could ask me for anything, she could demand I cut my heart out, and I would. I'd give it to her on a plate.

She tips my chin up. "Only to me?"

"Of course."

"Then you care not for him..."

Roman? Is that what this is about?

She's jealous I work for him. But why? She knows when I left it was *for* her. She knows I'm working for him to find a way to take him down, *for* her.

"There is only you," I say.

"Do you swear it? Always? Forever? In blood and bonds?" she breathes.

"Yes," I whisper. My body thrums with need, a desperate throbbing for her to open her legs.

"And how should I serve such a devoted subject?" she asks.

My eyes flick down to her pussy.

"I see," she says. "Well, a good queen should always reward her loyal subjects."

There is nothing sexier than Morrigan embodying her power, the power she has over me. It shows me what she'll be like when she finally takes the crown. And fuck, she won't just wear the crown, she won't just be a queen. She'll be a fucking goddess. And it's in moments like these that I realise she knows it too.

Slowly, inch by inch, she shifts to the edge of the throne, and then she parts her legs wide, baring herself to me.

"So claim your reward." I lace my fingers through hers and slide my hands around her thighs leaning into her.

I kiss the apex of her pussy. A shiver washes through her body and I wonder how long it's been since I touched her like this.

The conservatory wasn't like this. That was frantic, hurried.

This is more.

I kiss her everywhere—her thighs, her clit, her opening. I take a glorious amount of time. Savouring every caress, every inch of flesh. She tastes sweet, and moreish and it drives me wild. My mind is feral, I can't restrain myself any longer. I open my mouth and draw my tongue down her pussy.

She gasps and leans back, releasing my hands and gripping the throne instead. It occurs to me that I am racking up reasons for Calandra to hang me. I'm pretty sure fucking the sovereign heir on the incumbent's throne would be frowned upon.

I wonder for a moment whether Morrigan is right.

Whether I should take a minute to think through my decisions.

But then she moans my name, and the sound melts reality away. I focus only on her, on her pleasure, her pussy.

I savour every second of right now because this could be the last time we're ever like this. Tomorrow her life shifts; a thirty-day clock will start to tick and nothing will ever be the same.

I press harder into her, lick faster. She moans, her head dropping against the back of the throne, her eyes closing. She's growing warmer, wetter. I can't hold back her orgasm much longer. But I don't want this to end. I don't want this to be goodbye.

I slide a hand up her silk shift until I find her nipple. She shudders against me as I tweak her piercing, making the nipple erect. I release her nipple and slide my hand into my own underwear, eager to ride this out with her.

I've drenched my underwear. But I don't care, I rub my clit furiously, bringing myself up to meet her pleasure. I want to come with her.

My other hand draws down her slit until I find her opening. I slide a finger inside her, curling it until she bucks into me. The way her body moves fills me with hunger. I want more, more, more.

I bend my finger until her expression ripples with pleasure and her breath fills the air with moans. She rocks and tilts her hips in time with my rhythm. Her hands find my head, her fingers curling through strands of my hair until she's grinding into my face.

She moan's my name like a whisper and a prayer. She breathes me out like a promise and then she comes undone and so do I. She shudders and jolts in the throne, her pussy soaking me with orgasm.

When it's over, I lean my head on the edge of the throne, panting.

So regal, so much power in one piece of furniture.

The throne.

The... fuck.

Something inside my chest cracks wide open. My heart aches like fire and regret. I can't breathe, my eyes sting. My ribs clamp, suffocating my mind, my ability to be rational.

"Stirling?" she whispers.

But I can't. Because I fucked her on the throne. I fucked her on the very lie she kept from me and that truth is like a blade. I'm so confused, my head swims. I want her.

I want to push her away.

"Two years, Morrigan," I say.

She tries to turn my chin to face her, but I pull away.

"Was it all a lie?"

"I don't... what is this about? What's thrown you?"

"I didn't realise it until now. But Calandra. She... You knew back then who I was, didn't you? You knew that one day you'd be invested and you'd have to find a consort. But back then, I was banished."

Her eyes widen, but she says nothing.

I shake my head, finally looking up at her. "You knew who I was, who your mother was to me, and you said nothing..." My gut hardens. Steel lining my ribs and heart.

"No. It... it wasn't like that."

"Was it all a lie? Was I just a fun fuck to keep you amused? Because you couldn't have taken us seriously. You knew damn well your mother would never let you marry someone like me."

"Stirling, that's not—"

"Gods, I'm an idiot. You were never going to find me

where blue meets blue were you? All this time, I've been working like a dog, and you've been doing what, exactly?"

Her eyes well with tears, but no words come out. She doesn't defend herself or her actions. And that hurts so much more than the identity she kept secret.

She reaches down, her fingers pulling my body round until I look at her.

Her eyes are wet. Tears streak her cheeks, the same tears cooling in rivers down mine. She's breathing hard. Her eyes are feverish, skittish. Her lips tremble as if she's trying to tell me all her silent secrets. But the only thing between us now is a thirty-day deadline and a long, protracted goodbye.

Two lovers.

Exes.

Both broken.

Both desperate.

Both on opposite sides of a crown.

I lean back. Break contact. This room is suffocating. I need to get out. I can't do this with her. I can't keep repeating this cycle with her.

"No," Morrigan says, her words breathy, the confidence the throne gave her evaporated. "Please," she begs. Tears flowing down her cheeks. "Not again. I swear to you, Stirling. I'll find it."

"No. You were right, we can't fuck our way out of this." There's too much emotional shit between us.

My fingers find my lips, stopping myself saying anything else. My heart thumps so hard between my ribs I think I'm going to be sick. I have to get out.

I shuffle back, stagger down the steps. I open my mouth to say something. Say anything.

But there's nothing left. I can't explain away the years

of hurt. I can't promise I won't make another deal. Because I'd do it again if it meant saving her.

I can't plead with her to take me back and ignore the impending investiture. I can't tell her to forget the plan. Forget Roman and Calandra. I can't even persuade her to make a spontaneous decision.

Nothing has changed. We're exactly where we were two years ago. She is a Queen, and a Queen can never leave her kingdom.

So I don't say anything.

Because it's pointless.

Instead, I turn and run. Morrigan screams, a sob cutting through my name.

I don't face her. Instead, I whisper words that will haunt me forever.

"Goodbye, Morrigan." I open the door and flee the palace, disappearing into the night, Morrigan's cries still echoing in my mind.

CHAPTER 9

MORRIGAN

THE DAILY IMPERIUM

The Daily Imperium is delighted to report that after thirty-one long years shrouded in secrecy, our sovereign heir is finally stepping into public life. Queen Calandra set the date of the Princess's investiture for thirty days' time, on the 31st of October.

The proceedings will be aired on the New Imperium screens.

We can also announce that The Daily Imperium has gained exclusive access to the palace and will be bringing you the most up-to-the-moment news and information from all the dignitaries attending the palace and events leading up to the investiture.

Prepare, New Imperium: today we celebrate the dawn of a new era and the hope that our

*new sovereign brings the promise of a more
stable future.*

The team, even with Jacob and Stirling missing, seem to fill my cottage like a teen party. Everywhere I look, there are takeaway boxes, bottles, and bodies. Remy, Quinn, and Scarlett are having half a dozen conversations, cutting over the top of each other while Remy makes everyone coffee. This is how it always goes at the start of each new mission. A flurry of late nights, plotting, and way too much food. I draw my hand along the wall, wondering if the cottage is pissed at us for dirtying it up, when usually we're so much tidier.

There's a knock at the front door.

It's Stirling. I know because it's early, and because even through the stone walls I can smell the bittersweet perfume that follows her everywhere she goes.

"Open up," I say.

In the hall, the door creaks open of its own accord.

"Thanks," I whisper to the cottage, and give the wall a little rub.

Stirling's footsteps pad softly towards the kitchen.

"Stir," Scarlett says, frowning as she enters the kitchen. "Where the f—"

Stirling shakes her head, and Scarlett swallows the rest of the sentence. I'm furious. My chest pools with heat; until our eyes meet.

Dammit.

She looks hideous, red rings around her eyes, and her skin is swollen and puffy. I should tell her. This is the moment to just come out and tell her who he was to me.

Why I was so mad at her. But she gives me this ridiculous face, and I just...

"Oh for gods' sake, how am I meant to be pissed at you when you look that pathetic?" I bark.

I hate that she has this power over me. I've never been able to stay mad at her for long.

"You're still pissed at Stirling?" Remy says, handing me a coffee with milk and sugar in it, just how I like it.

Yes, Remy, but I can't tell her that because how the hell do I explain that the man she is working for was my fiancé?

Stirling scratches at her side, then rubs her face as if sleep still clings to her. I want to shout at her for leaving mid-row last night. I want to shake her and remind her what we promised. Make her understand that just like fucking, walking away and not talking isn't going to fix this either.

"Come on, you can shower in my room." I try to snarl the words out but the bite I want to put into them doesn't quite reach my mouth.

Stirling follows after me. As she walks, she leaves a faint trail of sand.

"Did you sleep on the beach?"

She shrugs at me as we enter my bedroom and I open a cupboard to find her a clean towel. "I didn't have my Castle Grey keys and figured I probably wasn't welcome back last night, so I broke into my beach hut and slept half the night in the bowels of the boat, and the other half on the beach itself."

She scratches her ribs, I narrow my eyes at her.

"What's wrong."

"Nothing. It's fine." She snatches the towel out of my hands. "Thanks. For. Umm. This."

"It's clearly not fine," I say, snatching the towel back.

Although now it's in my hands, I have no idea why I took it.
I'm not the one about to shower.

She sighs, so overly dramatic her shoulders heave. "Can
I please have the towel?"

I go to hand it to her, and she reaches for it, but I step
back, moving it out of her grasp. "Tell me what's up with
your ribs first. You were scratching them downstairs too."

She groans, "I just want a shower. Gods, why can't you
ever leave anything alone."

"Stirling," I warn.

"Fine." She lifts her top up and over her head, revealing
her bra. I didn't see it yesterday, she was too busy fucking
me on my mother's throne. But it's lace. I catch the dark
pink of her nipples. It makes me swallow. I drag my eyes
down the curves of her body to her side.

Her ribs are red raw and smothered in welts. Her hand
drifts to the marks she scratches, but it's making it worse. I
step close, tap her hand away, and then proceed to trace the
marks on her skin. My fingers heat, desperate to touch her,
to caress her skin and...

No.

"What happened?"

"It's just a stupid sand rash. What do you want me to
say? You're right, Morrigan. If I hadn't disappeared last
night I wouldn't have had to sleep on the beach."

I press my lips together and pout, "So what did we learn
here, Stirling? Hmm? Reacting in the moment and not
thinking things through leads to what...?"

"I am exhausted, gagging for coffee, itchy as hell and
have a mouth like arse. Must you be so self-righteous this
early in the day?"

"Me? Self-righteous. Oh, that's fucking rich coming
from you. You make out like—"

"Everything alright?" Scarlett's head appears at the door.

"No," I snap. My chest rises and falls with all the words I want to lob at Stirling. How dare she. "I was just going to get Quinn. Stirling's gotten herself a nasty rash. But then, I suppose that's what you deserve for disappearing in the middle of the night."

I spin on my heel and march back to the kitchen. Who the hell does she think she is calling me self-righteous? She can't even fucking communicate. And yes, I get that I'm a hypocrite and need to tell her about Roman, but there's a time and a place. She's too stuck in whatever she's feeling and thinking. She just reacts, reacts, reacts and doesn't strategise anything. Doesn't she realise we can't all be like that? I'd have been discovered in hours, let alone the *years* I've had living free and in secret.

I swear to gods, that woman will get herself into a situation she can't talk her way out of one of these days.

I reach the kitchen and stick my head in. Quinn raises an eyebrow. "You okay?" she says.

"I..." I open my mouth ready to unleash a rant and then decide better of it. "Have you got a medical kit here? Stirling slept on the beach last night. She's got a nasty sand rash."

She slurps her tea and then hands Remy the mug. "Do I want to ask why she slept on the beach instead of here?"

"No."

"Well, okay then. I'll just grab my kit and head to your room."

Twenty minutes later, Stirling is showered and clean and sat in her underwear on the toilet. Quinn is daubing some rancid looking mixture on Stirling's ribs.

"It tickles," Stirling whines, "Fuck, its cold. Oh my gods,

is it crawling with something? Eww, eww. Get it off me, Quinn."

"What are you, five? Get a grip." Quinn cackles and slaps another dollop of cream on her ribs.

Stirling gags so hard a burp pops out, and Quinn and I collapse laughing. When we get control of ourselves, Quinn dabs the last drop onto Stirling's body.

"There," Quinn says standing up and admiring her work. "Leave it on for ten, then you should be able to peel it off. It will go crusty and just crack off, pulling the welts with it."

"Great. Thanks. I think," Stirling says her face crumpled into a grimace.

Quinn picks up her stuff and heads back to the kitchen, leaving Stirling and I alone.

She gets off the toilet and strides up to me, it only takes three paces, and then we're nose to nose. Her short, wet hair drops beads of water on the bathroom mat, her sweet honeyed breath trickles over me.

I want to slap her, shake the sense into her, maul her face with kisses. My fingers twitch, desperate to reach up, to run my finger over her lip and caress her mouth with the deepest kiss I can muster.

"I'm sorry," she says.

"Are you?" I breathe.

"With every cell in my body."

She steps closer. Pushes me against the sink. Her hand curls around a loose lock of hair, she pushes it behind my ear her fingers hovering there. My whole body vibrates when she's near and I'm never sure if it's instant irritation or my muscles holding themselves back.

"You're a drug, Stirling. Do you know that?" I say.

Stirling sucks in her bottom lip, as if she wants to disagree. She leans her forehead against mine.

"You're the drug, Morrigan. The one I have always been hopelessly addicted to. The one I'd cut my ribs open and tear my heart out for. I didn't mean to go last night. I just. It's like I think we've gotten to the bottom of it. I think we know the full truth and then more secrets spill. How am I meant to trust you?"

I wipe a hand over my face. "I wish you could understand the position I was in. I told you everything I could."

She shakes her head at me. "I know that what we had before is done... that when this is over, no matter what we said, we can't... because you'll have to be queen."

I push her off. This isn't helping anyone. "You don't know that."

"Don't I? I was angry last night, but that doesn't mean I'm wrong. The reason you didn't tell me who you were is because of Calandra. Come on. Do you really think she will ever accept me as your wife?"

I don't answer. How can I?

She looks at the floor, shaking her head. I can see this chewing her up. I want to tell her that we can still be a team, we can fix this. But I stay silent because I honestly don't know how this will end. I know that we can try. That we are trying. But I don't have the answers and if we don't fix this first, don't stop his attack on the throne, then what we are won't matter anyway.

My body, the traitor that it is, wants her despite last night. Despite the years of complication.

"Stirling, look at me. You left me with a heart full of hate. And yet, standing here in my bathroom, those ocean blue eyes looking at me... I still want you. I still want to fuck you in the shower, on the floor, in my bed, in my garden. I want to fuck you every morning, before I go to sleep at night and between every breath. Tell me you're not a drug."

She reaches up, threads her fingers through mine. I lean into her warm palm. She slides her other hand around the back of my neck. Pulls me close. I shouldn't let her. We can't keep going back and forth like this.

But she feels safe. She feels like summer nights and laughter. She feels like hunger and need and desire.

The air between us is hot. It sparks with a lust neither of us can control. With everything going on, I need to tread carefully. If we keep fucking each other it blurs the lines, makes everything riskier. What if Roman follows her? Finds us?

She inches closer, brushes her lip over mine. She sighs, her eyes rolling shut. My pussy warms with liquid desire.

No one commands me like this. No one but her.

I want to laugh because she doesn't even know how much power she has. As queen, I will wield more magic than every Magician in New Imperium. But Stirling holds my heart in her hands. She can stop me with a look, a kiss, a thought. If she commanded it, I would destroy armies for her. If she breathed it I would end lives and slaughter saints. And all for her. Every wanton desire she kissed over my skin—I would make real, if only it meant I got to keep her.

Stirling's want throbs and pulsates in the air around her. And right now, all of it is aimed at me. I can barely breathe.

I pull her onto my lips. Her hands instantly roam my body, pushing me into the shower door behind. It clatters as our bodies slam into it.

She moans into the kiss, she wants it as much as I do. Fingers skim my belt. Her nails caress the slip of flesh around my belly. It sets fire to my skin, breathes gold into my body.

"Fuck me," she says. She unhooks the shower door, pulls me inside fully clothed, and peels the now hardened goop off her ribs throwing it over the top of the shower door.

I hold a hand to her chest. "Swear to me this is the last time. One night together, and we're falling apart. We can't afford this. We can't sabotage his plans for the investiture if we're too distracted with each other."

She laughs, leans in and kisses me. "One night and I know how much of a fucking mess we are. How much both of us hurt. Hate. Hunger."

She leans back and turns the shower on. I gasp. She smiles and it brightens the whole bathroom. Lights up my chest.

Gods. I want her. I do. But this won't help.

"I've already told you we can't fuck our way out of this mess," I say as the water drenches my pyjama top.

"You think I don't know that?" She runs her hand through her hair, pulling it out of her face.

I run my hand along her jaw, cup the back of her head and pull her close. "We have to take him down. Nothing else matters."

"Everything else matters, Morrigan. Just stop being up here..." she places two fingers on my temple. "And start living here." She draws them down to the top of my breast, resting them over my heart.

She swipes her mouth over mine, but I don't feel it on my lips, I feel it in my clit, and it sends a delicious shiver up my back.

My clothes sag against my skin, heavy and sopping. Stirling must sense it because she reaches for the hem of my top and waits. Waits for me to say yes, to tell her I want this. And I do, fuck, I want it more than anything. Maybe she's right, maybe I should live more in the moment.

But she's wrong too, time is running out.

I slide my fingers over her hand.

"One last time."

She tilts her head at me. "One last time and then no more sex. We focus until after."

"Sounds like you're offering me a deal," she grins. "You know how I feel about those."

I smile as I slide the hem of my top over my head. She takes it and flings it over the shower door. Then she unclips her bra, slips it off her shoulders and flings that over. My knickers next, then hers. Until we're both standing in the shower utterly naked.

Gods, she is glorious. Her breasts are big for her small frame. She's tall like Scarlett, though unlike her, she's all torso and waistline. Her right arm is full of collection tattoos, but most of the rest of her body is bare. So naked compared to the mottled paintwork on my skin. I run a finger down Stirling's smooth skin through the rivulets of water.

"No deals, no negotiations. Just a promise," I say.

She grins deep, it covers her entire face. "Don't make promises you can't keep, Morrigan."

"Don't make deals—"

She cuts me off with her finger against my lips. "Stop talking. Get on your knees, princess."

My pussy clenches, and my eyes widen. There's a part of me that wants to chain her up for insubordination, and the other part of me wants to give myself over entirely. To do as she bids, to submit myself wholly.

And despite the fact I would never, *ever* bend the knee

to anyone, not even my mother, Stirling is something else entirely. I lower to the shower floor, obedient. And it unleashes a raw purity inside me. Stirling knows what I need. She's always anticipated what my body yearns for.

She knows I need this because this is the only way to stop me thinking. When I give myself to her, let her take control, I don't have to think anymore. In these moments, I trust her entirely and it's everything: freedom, relief and pure pleasure.

My stomach flutters, my clit already swollen. There's a strange twisting heat between my ribs, it thrums and cords down my spine, and slides into my pussy.

The shower streams down my back and over my breasts and down my legs. But the slick heat between my thighs isn't the shower, it's my own excitement.

I suck in a breath as I reach up, clasp her breasts, squeeze her nipples until she rolls her head back, dowsing her face and hair with water.

She lets out a moan, and the sound makes my nipples stiffen as if replying. I draw my hands down her body, over her hard waist and down to the bones of her hips, I yank her forward, so I can touch her without drowning.

I spin her around, push her against the cold tiles. She gasps as the cold seeps into her back. But I don't give her time to complain. I sink my mouth over her slit. Push my tongue between her wet folds and onto the hardened bead of her clit.

It's almost too much. My body responds along with hers. Stirling's fists clench by her sides.

"Gods, Morrigan."

"Shut up, and just feel, Stirrrling," I say drawing out her name. Her body tenses, as if she wants to argue, and correct me.

She needs to be quiet. If she wants to feel the moment, I'll show her exactly how in the moment I can be, I'll—

"Morrigan. Stop thinking and fuck me otherwise I will pick you up, throw you on the bed and edge you until you beg me for release."

I glare up at her and swipe my tongue hard down her slit, promptly shutting her up. I slide my fingers to her opening. She's soaking. I love that I can still make her this wet. I slip a finger inside her, curling around until I find her g-spot. My tongue laps at her clit until she's panting and rocking against my mouth.

Her pussy tightens around my finger and I know she's building. I lick faster, sucking her clit in and letting my tongue roll around her core. She moans my name and I want to soar into bliss with her.

I remember what's in my bathroom cupboard. I stop suddenly, pull out of her.

"What... the... hell? The edging was a joke," she whines at me.

"Be quiet and face the wall."

She narrows her eyes at me, but I think she secretly likes it when I'm bratty. She opens her mouth ready to put me back in my obedient place.

"Wall," I point.

For once, she does as she's told and faces the shower wall. I open the door and hurry to the cupboard, pulling out the strap we used to use. I climb into the harness and buckle it in, pouring lube over the cock. Not that she needs it.

Then I climb into the shower. "Hands on the wall."

She bends around to face me, a devilish grin in her eyes.

"Hands," I say, my tone hard, demanding.

She places her palms flat on the shower tiles and tilts

her butt towards me. It's pert and full and—fuck. I step forward and place the cock at her entrance.

"Tell me you want me," I say.

"I want you, Morrigan. I always will."

Her words are flowers wrapped in thorns. They comfort as much as they sting. But I don't want to think about why that is. Not right now.

I thrust my hips forward. She arches her back and inhales as the cock pushes inside her. I pump my hips, hard and rhythmic, until she's panting. I lean over her back, reaching around until one hand finds her breast and the other finds her clit. She takes one of her hands off the tiles and grabs her other nipple, squeezing and moaning as I thrust inside her.

My own pussy swells with heat and want. We've been in here so long the water cools, as it runs down both our bodies in ribbons. I reach up, thread my fingers through her hand, and hold it against the wall. She holds me tight.

I speed up, rubbing her clit harder and faster as I pump long, deep strokes into her pussy.

She rests the back of her head onto my shoulder. I grab her throat, pull her ear to my mouth. "Come for me."

"Don't let me go," she says.

I grip her tight. "I've got you. I always will."

Her knees go, and a shiver bucks its way through her entire body. I hold her in my arms until the quivers wracking her slow and her knees stabilise.

When she's able to hold her own weight, she turns to me, tears in her eyes. She reaches over and pulls me in to a kiss. But it's different this time, softer, warmer like autumn sun and candy floss. She kisses me like she's saying hello, like she's saying goodbye. And I don't know what I think anymore. I lock my arms around her neck and kiss her back.

Our tongues slide over each other's. And all I know is that I don't want it to stop. But it does, and when she pulls away, the water cools to freezing and I have to reach back and flick it off.

"So this is it? No more...," Stirling asks.

I open my mouth to answer, but I'm no longer sure.

"I...We have a job to do. We can't be distracted with..." I gesture at our naked bodies. "You are a distraction, Stirling. I can't focus when you're... like this. So I guess this is it. No more fucking or fighting. Just friends."

She presses her lips together and I can feel the ache in her chest. As if it's the same anchor pulling at mine. My throat closes. I can't breathe. The shower walls close in around me. Suddenly I want to be away. Out. Not near her. It feels like goodbye. And I'm not sure I was ready, even though I know it's the right thing to do. Even though I know this is the way it has to be.

"Just friends," Stirling says, giving me a single nod. "We should discuss terms."

And that makes me laugh. Of course she wants to discuss terms. "Ah yes, you're nothing if not rigorous with your deals."

She shrugs, "You know how it goes, nothing like a bit of due diligence to ruin the moment..."

She gives me a weak smile. I know what she's doing. Trying to make it hurt less, trying to take the pain out of the mess we're both in.

"No kissing or touching," I say.

"Okay and no sex?" she asks.

I nod. "Definitely no sex. No kissing, no touching. If... after this is over, and we both still... If we meet where blue meets blue, then let's talk it through then. We've done two years, we can make it another month."

"A month is a long time... Especially now we're back in each other's lives."

"And a deal is a deal."

She gazes at me, her eyes glittering like stars and something tells me that a negotiation is never just a negotiation with her. But finally she relents and shakes my hand.

The deal is done.

"I...," she starts, but the words fade and whatever she was going to say evaporates as she closes her mouth.

So that's it.

Over.

For real this time.

I push the shower door open, the cold settling into my bones, goosebumps running over my flesh. Stirling wraps a towel around herself and leaves without saying a word. I dry myself off and get dressed, but no matter how many layers of clothes and jumpers I put on, I can't seem to warm the cold ache in my chest.

This is for the best. It has to be this way. We have a plan. And the plan is always right.

Isn't it?

CHAPTER 10

STIRLING

It only takes two days for hordes of dignitaries to arrive at the palace. It's late afternoon on the day of the first ball. Of course, none of them know who Morrigan is yet, but they come knowing she's here, somewhere, in secret among the ballgowns and diamonds. It takes about three seconds for me to get irritated.

Their slimy hands all over all the female dignitaries trying to wheedle the information out, their eyes roaming over the bodies of every young woman in the palace, wondering if they're the princesses. Wondering if they can win the heart of the heir.

It makes me sick. Before I can get ready for the ball, I have some errands to run and deals to fulfil. Morrigan was in the library this morning. I noticed another pile of books, and that same piece of paper with Sangui Grimoire hand-written on it.

On the way to Roman's this morning, I delivered a bag of poisoned rats to a scorned lover's door, dropped a precious crystal off at a merchant's place, delivered another packet of I'm not even sure what—it oozed green and felt squelchy—to an alchemist, and then fed two pieces of information to two council members, *discreetly*.

After that, I had to sneak onto private property and witness an affair, capture it on a crystal ball and deliver it to the scorned wife who paid me handsomely.

I call into a magician colleague of mine's house. Quaint little thing, made of black stone and bone. Terrifying really, if I think too hard about it. She's the contact who initially helped me secure a resident contact in Sangui city so I could source the whiskey for Claude. I don't stay long, never do. She has these eyes that look through you right into your soul. Gives me the shivers if I stare too hard.

And that's how finally, exhausted and dreading the party tonight, I find myself in Roman's headquarters.

The team agreed, if I'm playing double agent, I need to act like it. Be bolshy, push him. There's no one else on the team that can play this card, so that's my role. Reel the bastard in and get him to make a deal that hangs him. Given it's Morrigan's crown and my freedom on the line, there's no one else I trust to play this role anyway.

So here I am, I'm in his office *again*, and he is behind the bar pouring drinks, *again*. I take a slow breath and remind myself I know what I'm doing. I've been playing this game for two years.

Though this time, I'm pleased to say there's no man in his closet. I'm sure there's some joke in there, but Roman is far too straight to find it funny, so I keep my mouth shut.

I'm sat on a chair in front of his desk, my legs kicked up on top, snipping the end of a cigar.

"You got some real lady balls coming in here and treating this office like your own."

I trim a second cigar, light it, and hand it to him over the bar.

"We both know I'm an asset, Roman."

He sucks on the cigar as I light my own. "Hmm, you do have a certain finesse. But it begs the question...why now?"

I tip my chin up at him. "You know why. The Queen is unsettled. You," I point my cigar at him, "have unsettled her. You're under her skin. So, if you even have an inkling of a plan, then you should use me. Forget the past. Let me use my history with Morrigan, get close to her, squeeze whatever information I can. But what do I know?"

I shrug at him, pick up the tumbler of whiskey he just poured me and make my way back to the desk. I lean back and puff on the cigar. The bitter smoke fills my lungs and numbs my heart. I hate the words coming out, they reek of lies, but I'm threading magic through my veins so hard to keep myself emotionless that there's no way he'd know I'm bluffing. Especially because Quinn brewed up this super strong moisturiser that covers any scent of cinnamon and de-electrifies the air around me, removing the static.

"And what exactly is it you think I should do?" Roman says.

I sip on the whiskey, already regretting the intense hangover I am guaranteed to have tomorrow. I clasp the tumbler, sit up straight, and pull a severe expression.

"Gain her trust. It's the only strategic move. Give her assurances," I say in my poshest voice and best impression of Calandra. "This is going to be a trying few weeks, Mr. Oleg and you are part of this city." I stand now, thrust a hand on my hip and waltz around his office like a queen. "You're my people, Roman. And my people need to stick together. This is the perfect opportunity for us to make peace and unite forces as we bring a new royal heir into the limelight."

Roman laughs. "Fuck me, Stirling you ever considered being on stage?"

"Meh. The stage is for crowd pleasers. I'm too much of a hedonist to worry about what a room full of people want."

Roman's dark eyes narrow at me. They're black like coal and dead things. They match the nightshade suit, shirt, tie, and shoes he's wearing. Like the gods damned grim reaper. And I tell you, he's killed and maimed enough magicians in my presence for me to believe it. Like his clothing, his hair is as dark as his heart.

The room shivers as he looks at me, power oozing from every pore and inch of his skin. He moves across the room, the air swelling and palpating around him. Gods, you can see the desire in the way he moves through the room. Roman is going to try to usurp the crown. I just need to figure out how. The power rippling off him... doesn't matter if I've embezzled some of his magic, he's still powerful enough.

Roman takes a seat, inhales the bitter smoke from his cigar and then blows smoke rings into the room.

"And how exactly do you think I should gain her trust?"

"Go slow. She won't believe anything out of the ordinary. So do something utterly you. Why don't you offer to host an event? There's already dignitaries descending on the city. Why not throw them a party? Take them off her hands and entertain them for a night?"

His smile deepens.

"It would have to be a very *you* party, though. None of this royal pomp. Host it in a club, maybe this one. Make it the most DnD party you've ever run. There's only so much bending you can do before it becomes unbelievable and

Calandra will see through you. But make it just believable enough and you'll lure her in."

He narrows his eyes at me. But behind the dark beads, I can see the cogs turning. The smell of agreement is sweet, warm and crystalline in the air. This is how you negotiate: give the client exactly what they want—or at least, make them think it's what they want. I'm winning. I'm bringing him around, convincing him my plan is sound.

"And what do you want, Stirling? Because as you said, you're too much of a negotiator to bring me a deal for free..."

He lets the statement hang in the air, the words thick and pulpy with subtext. What he's really asking is what is this going to cost him.

Everyone thinks a negotiator's job is to keep the peace, drag the whiners and whingers over the line. But it's not really. It's to sit and listen, to let our magic feed under the words, to seek out the truth, the wants, the desires. To find what's in a client's heart and then make sure they get it. It's the only way to get a deal done.

"What do I want?" I say staring up at the ceiling and dragging on my cigar.

"Other than an excuse to fuck your ex, and get that little pussy of yours wet." His stare is like acid, something bitter and vicious beneath his gaze.

"Don't be crass darling. But yes. I'm partial to a deal that involves getting my leg over. Aren't we all? But fuck Morrigan. Even the thought of her makes my skin crawl. I don't care if it was her or her mother. As far as I'm concerned, they're both responsible for my parents' deaths. There can be no sweeter moment than watching the horror in her eyes as I twist the blade right through her heart."

That makes him laugh so hard he kicks his head back. In

all the months I've worked for him, I don't think I've ever seen him laugh like that.

The dangerous bastard is kind of handsome when he smiles.

"My, my, you've changed."

I tap the cigar on the ashtray. "Can't do any of this without your agreement though..."

I let that hang in the air, filthy and thick with the ugly truth of what he did. There's a sweetness to know he wants this path, and yet, unless he undoes what he did two years ago, he can't follow it.

"What do you really want?" He says those dark eyes boring into me.

Morrigan.

The word flits through my mind, strong and as solid as diamond. Ironic isn't it. He thinks I want money, power. To get out from under him. And I do. I want all of those things, along with a fucking holiday and Morrigan sat on my face while several half-naked women serve us cocktails. But even I can't bullshit my own magic. Because above all of those things, what my heart really wants is her. But of course I can't tell him that.

So instead, I say what Morrigan suggested when the team was together.

"I want a promotion."

His beady eyes examine my face, his power ebbing across the table towards me. And though there's nothing touching me, I swear I can feel the faintest feather kiss of static roll across my skin. What the fuck is he doing? Checking if I'm lying?

I'm not. Or not exactly. I'm just not giving him the whole truth. Whatever he's checking on me, I thank the gods Quinn gave me the cream because he seems satisfied. So I push on.

"I'm talented, Roman. And I'm sick of being the middle-woman. I should be curating deals, negotiating bigger contracts. I should be your right-hand woman as you take over the palace and you fucking know it."

He leans forward, tapping the cigar ash on the ashtray.

"Especially if I can negotiate my way back into Morrigan's life. Then we'd have a foot in the palace doors. And that, for someone like you, is a handy person to have around."

He takes his sweet time before replying. Long enough I have to suppress the urge to twitch and run out of here.

I've blown it.

Finally, he responds. "But you're a legacy, Stirling. And given our history, how exactly do you suppose I'm supposed to trust you enough to promote you?"

He's pointing his cigar at me. A swelling bubble of panic settles in my gut. I suppress it. This is part of negotiating, part of my ability. Thank fuck I have my magic back, and I can suppress my natural instincts and reactions.

I knew this was coming. Of course he needs proof that I'm loyal. Just like he did the night I came to him for the job.

It's fine. We planned for this. Of course we did. Morrigan thought through every angle and option and possible path this could go down. '*If he does this, say that. But if he says something like blah blah blah, then go with plan C.*' On and on she drilled me, until I had every option from A to fucking Z memorised. And just like we planned, he's walking step by step along the route we lined out for him.

This is how I get into his inner circle. Maybe even close enough I can slide a knife into his carotid while the bastard sleeps.

I laugh, short, sharp, and cocky. "Please. The crown negligently executed my parents. You think a fucking pardon is enough to make up for the years of poverty and humiliation? The only penance the Queen can pay is with her fucking head. But sure. Let me prove it to you. Just like last time..." I roll up my sleeve, brandish my arm at him. "What do you want me to do?"

"You tell me..."

My fingers trace the scar along my arm, the one he gave me after a bout of insolence a few months into working for him. I have to tread carefully. A delicate balance of something believable and significant without being over the top.

"After I infiltrate the palace, after I secure Morrigan's heart, I'll feed you everything you need to take the crown."

"I never said my plan was to take the crown, *Stirling*."

My heart stops. The room is stiff. Goosebumps trickle down my neck. Shit. I fucked up. I need to think on my feet, change tact.

I focus. Inhale. Breathe.

This is just a game, a negotiation of words and wills. He's pushing me as hard as I'm pushing him. But I'm not backing down. Not this time.

"Oh sure, and I'm a virgin," I scoff.

At that, he smiles, and the atmosphere eases. "Touché. I like you, Little Stir, you got some cajones, that's for sure."

The air loosens as I draw him closer.

My stomach twists.

This is what I wanted.

Roman is agreeing to the plan. So why is every single cell screaming at me to back away?

Run. Run hard and fast and get the fuck out of his office.

I don't.

I sit perfectly still. Because this is the kind of crossroads you only get once in life. These are the moments deals are struck and broken. I know what Roman wants, the crown. I know how to give it to him, or at least make him think I'm giving it to him.

I have to follow through. This is the only way to protect Morrigan.

"After everything you've done, Stirling, after where you come from, the fact you're a legacy playing in the underground, how can you ask me to buy this?" he says.

I smile, and it's wide and toothy.

"Come on, Roman, that's exactly *why* I'm asking you. Think of it as a win-win. You get a chance to infiltrate the palace, for real. Find out everything you need before the investiture. And I get the chance to make her pay for the lies she told. For ruining my life, murdering my parents. The promotion is just the cherry on top."

He shakes his head at me. "One, what makes you think you're even capable of convincing her to let you into her life? With the investiture on the horizon, she'll suspect your motives. And two, let's say—hypothetically—I am after the crown and I get it. What then? What happens when Morrigan finds out you betrayed her? You'll lose everything."

I sniff, reach for the bottle of whiskey he brought over from the bar, and top both of our glasses up. Preparing for the toast, to sign this deal off.

"You know I can negotiate anything. Including a heart. And if I can't, I'm damn sure I can convince her pussy. And she won't find out. Because if she does, then you lose. You take the crown, and it doesn't matter what she knows. So, I guess I better make sure you win..."

He snorts and takes a deep swig of whiskey. Always

fucking whiskey. I swallow a mouthful and it burns hot on the way down.

"So, the terms...?"

"Simple. We stop pretending you're not going to attack the crown. I want a promotion in exchange for infiltrating the palace via Morrigan. And in exchange, I'll get you whatever information you need for your attack," I smile at him. Sweet lips and eyes of steel.

He leans back and raises an eyebrow and holds his whiskey glass up as if indicating I should go on.

So I do.

"I take it you're going to storm the palace on the day of the investiture? What are you going to do once we get inside the palace? Even if you secure the Sanatio tree and take the palace guards. To command the city, you still need the council and all the legacy magicians on side. How are you going to do that?"

He takes another sip of whiskey but says nothing. His eyelid flickers; it's the only tell I've ever seen on him. He doesn't know. Interesting. I decide to see how far my ego can push this.

I waft the tumbler of whiskey around. "I'm asking because I can give you the council because of who I am. You might see my history as a weakness, but you're missing the point. It's the ultimate strength. I'm your way in. There's no one else like me, Roman."

Roman stares at me long enough my skin crawls. This is it. Either he buys it, and it's game on, or I've fucked the whole thing and I'm taking both me and Morrigan down. But I hold my ground, keep my shoulders pinned back and strong. He doesn't intimidate me. I'm too good at this. At reading him, the way his fingers tap, tap, tap. He's trying to make out like he's thinking. But I can tell from the glint in his eye this is a done deal. He just needs to feel like he's in control. And if that's what he needs to pull this over the line, who am I to withhold it.

Tug, tug, Roman. Be the puppet I know you are.

His fingers continue to beat a drum against his tumbler, again and again.

"Fine. Bring me information. Significant information that helps me get into the palace. Help me take down the crown and I'll give you your promotion…"

There it is, the little stab of power he needs. It takes every ounce of my strength not to put the toxic dickhead in his place. To lord the fact I have one over on him, the fact that he thinks he took Morrigan from me, but she's already back in my life.

But I can't. This deal is too important. He needs to trust me. Trust is what will seal his fate. A moment of playing nice, of the sour lies coating my tongue like slime is worth the weight of the negotiation. I guess Morrigan is rubbing off on me after all.

I swill my tumbler, then down the whiskey in one. Fuck, it sears my throat but the warm glow in my belly soon turns to smug delight.

"Then I guess we're done. I'll get you information, and this stays our little secret. Do we have a deal?"

He reaches out, pours another shot of whiskey in my cup and then offers me his hand.

I take it, shake hard. I can't wait to bathe in the blood of this motherfucker.

"We have a deal."

And as we clink glasses, and I swallow down yet another shot of whiskey, I have to wonder whether this is the greatest deal I've ever landed, or if playing with the devil is going to get me killed.

CHAPTER 11

MORRIGAN

The gang are huddled in my cottage, all of them whining and complaining in some form about what they have to wear or how the hairdresser is yanking their hair, or how they hate their make-up. They should try growing up a princess—even without being in the public eye, this was my life at the palace. Clothes are strewn across every room, there's pots of cream and balms, razor and scissors, dyes, and powders.

After three hours, the make-up artists and stylists leave, and the team meet in the living room.

"Well, damn," Remy says looking in the long dress mirror. "I don't look too bad."

She really doesn't. Her ice white hair is slicked up and into an elegant coif. There's a lick of black eyeliner around her eyes and the ivory suit she's wearing is tailored to precision.

"Damn, girl, you could be a bride in that thing," Stirling

says plucking the thought right from my head. I try not to think about what that means, how she can read my mind.

Quinn is in an elegant royal green ball gown with crystal touches. The way Scarlett is looking at her..."Scarlett Grey!" I bark.

"What?" she jumps and feigns innocence.

"I can see you mentally undressing Quinn. Save it for after. We have to make friends with all the pompous arse-holes mother invited tonight."

Scarlett sighs, bowing dramatically at me, but agrees. She's in a matching suit. Rich dark green, so deep it almost looks black. It's tailored and tight around her muscular physique.

Stirling walks in and halts in the doorway. Remy wolf whistles, and Quinn claps. My lips part. I didn't expect to find her in a dress.

"Oh," she says, taking in our reactions. And then she straightens, pumps her lips, and tips her chin up, all glinty-eyed. She takes an almost identical mock bow to Scarlett and pretends to fan herself. "I know, right?" She grins and winks at us.

Honestly, those two are as bad as each other.

"I thought you'd wear a suit."

"I was going to. I tried this on for fun, and I thought it looked good."

"Yes. No. I mean, yes it does. But I—" I don't know how to finish that sentence.

Scarlett snorts out a laugh and promptly covers her mouth and stifles it down. "You look great, Stir," She slaps her on the back. "Your baps look banging."

Stirling rolls her eyes at Scarlett. "Do fuck off, Sister."

"No, I mean it. You look distinctly above average tonight."

"You're an arsehole. You know that?" Stirling gives Scarlett a playful shove in the shoulder.

But I can't keep my eyes off Stirling. She's wearing a fitted black silk dress. There must be boning in it because her boobs are on maximum cleavage. There's a cut-out swiping from her ribs across her stomach, showing her belly button and ending just where her body curves south. I have to focus to suppress the instant heat pooling between my legs. I'm not doing this. We're friends, that's it.

"I... umm. So, Roman? What happened when you visited?" I say and spin around to examine my face in the mirror and do anything other than look at her.

"Reeled him in hook, line and sinker, didn't I...?" She looks at me expectant. "Of course I did. You don't need to answer that."

My lips flatten, my gut churns, Gods. What did she do now? "How, exactly did you do that...?"

She raises a finger, "I had to give him something... He wasn't going to just hand me the keys to his plan. But he's given me permission to weasel my way back into your life in order to get information..." her eyes glimmer white like fire and diamonds.

Unbelievable. I throw my hands up. "That is very antithesis of what we agreed last night."

She shrugs, "I came up with a better plan."

That's it. I'm going to throttle her.

"Before you get uppity at me, this gives us the flexibility to be seen together and not panic. As long as it's not too much too soon, we'll be fine. At some point we're going to have to give him something useful. I was thinking we could start with the schematics Scarlett's getting from the palace."

I groan. "We can't just hand him a map to the bloody palace. He'll know all the entry and exit points."

"Yes, and I can't just flail around not giving him anything. Not if we want him to believe I'm on team jackass."

Brilliant. Another problem to resolve.

"Now, now," Quinn says. "We knew Stirling playing good cop, bad cop was going to create complications. We expected that."

"We did," Stirling confirms. "Besides, I made another excellent suggestion to him too."

"Oh?" Remy says.

"Throw a party. A DnD one, in honour of the investiture."

My instant reaction is to scream at her that it's a preposterous idea. The last thing I want to do is spend any time in his proximity. But I take a second to think it through, and the more I consider it, the more I realise it is actually genius...

If I can just tell her before we go, explain so that it doesn't come out at the wrong time, then... then maybe this is a good idea.

"Alright, I'll give you that one," I say.

"Obviously," Stirling says and grins at me. "Came up with it on the spot."

The skin under my eye twitches. I take a deep breath.

"What?" she says smirking. "It was a good idea. Just because I didn't spend seven hours pondering all the ins and outs and potential scenarios doesn't make it any less valid or worthy. Besides, you guys gave me the idea, asking about the annual DnD event."

"It's not the point. Oh my gods, I am so tired of having this conversation over and over. I'm not asking you to spend years strategising. Just give things a second, because, I don't know, you might actually come up with a better strategy."

"Just admit it. I was right for once. I had a good idea."

"Ugh," I half scream in frustration. "It's not about being ri—"

"And that's time, ladies. I do believe I see guests arriving," Remy says, pointing out the window and cutting our argument off.

I throw my hands up and shove past her through the door into the hall and put my shoes on. The team all follow suit.

"Right. Everyone know what they're doing?" I say before opening the cottage door.

Each of them nod in turn. We've all got certain legacy magicians we're targeting to liquor up to loose their lips. We'll convene later this evening back at the cottage to swap notes.

"Masks and names," Quinn says and hands out our ornate masks, each one matching our outfits. As she dishes them out, we reel off a list of names of legacies we're targeting.

When we're satisfied everyone knows what they're doing, we make our way through the grounds, past the rose gardens and across half a dozen gravel paths that make my ankles hurt in these heels. We scoot up the palace steps and into the building.

As soon as I slip through the door, the palace magic presses against my skin and body, a huge surging rush of a hug, like it's saying hello. I close my eyes for a moment and send a pulse of warm magic out to the palace, my own little hello.

As we make our way to the ballroom, the tension grows.

The team stiffens, as dignitaries and royals from other cities appear and join the procession.

"Just breathe," Quinn says. "They don't know who you are yet, remember." She slides her hand into mine and gives it a squeeze. She's right. For now, at least, I'm still anonymous. I can still live the life I've always been living. I can still just be me.

"Thank you," I squeeze her hand back and she gives me a smile.

"You look stunning, by the way. In case none of us have said that."

I smile. Pat my free hand down the dress. It's black and white, a fitted corset top and billowing skirt. Ironically, the dress matches Stirling's. But we're not a pair. Not today. The procession of people slows to a halt as we approach the giant oak doors, and the guards check names against their list.

Stirling nestles between Quinn and I. "Are you ready for this?" she asks.

"Not even slightly."

She throws an arm around my shoulder. Her perfume is intoxicating. Familiar hints of bergamot, sandalwood, and always a freshness underneath; today it's foresty. Gods, I want to run my fingers down the cut out in her dress, over her skin. But instead, I scowl at her.

"No touching, remember? Part of the terms." I bat her off.

"Right, yes. Those terms. Thing is, we're about to go into a banquet hall with half a dozen monarchs from half a dozen cities, the team and your mother. And let us not the forget the fact, that we need to mingle. This is a masquerade ball... So you know. That requires dancing, so I'm just saying, we might have to touch. Besides, Roman thinks I'm here to seduce you... so I guess you'll at least have to let me kiss your hand." A shit-eating grin spreads across her expression.

Unbelievable. I give her a little shake of my head, trying and failing to suppress a smirk, "You are insufferable, you know that?"

"I keep telling her that," Scarlett says from behind.

Stirling shrugs off both of us. "I'm just saying, you can't go to a ball and not dance."

"I'm going to dance with Remy. Aren't I, Remy?"

"Huh?" she says snapping around to join in. "Sorry, I was distracted by... Gods is that...?" she frowns and vanishes up the queue, heading towards an equally blonde woman.

Brilliant. Thanks for the save Remy. I glare at her back.

I turn back to the rest of them, Scarlett and Stirling are wearing identical smirks. Stirling sucks through her teeth. "Guess that leaves you dancing with me. *Such* a shame,"

Scarlett's shoulders rock. Quinn gives her a sharp nudge in the ribs, and they descend into whispered squabbles.

I sigh inwardly.

The guards check our names and let us in through the giant arched doors. The ballroom is already full. While some people are a mystery, you can work out the wealthy from the legacies, the legacies from the royals based solely on what they're wearing.

So shallow. I bet Penelope is in her element.

There are a few royals I don't recognise from other cities. A princess I vaguely remember meeting in my child-hood, her pointed ears and dark skin sumptuous under the glistening chandelier lights. Another prince from a different city, one from the north, where it snows all year around. I shudder, unable to think of anything worse. I don't see any one from Sangui City, but then it's still light out, so perhaps they'll join later. Very few vampires ever visit New Imperium, not after the war, centuries ago. But the royals make a point to keep the lines of communication open.

"So... I can hold your hand?" Stirling says, as we descend the stairs into the ballroom. My stomach flutters and furls in an unsteady rhythm.

My mouth pinches. "Stirling, we literally only said last night we wouldn't do this."

She glares at me hard, "We're not doing anything. But if and when Roman arrives, you'll have to let me at least play at wooing you. We're convincing the crowds we're dignitaries here to dance and see if we can work out who the princess is."

She says that last bit loudly.

I tut at her. "I'll hold your arm."

"Hard negotiator. That's fine. I like a girl that plays hard to get."

"I'm not playing anything. This was our agreement."

"Sure you're not," she grins.

"You really are impossible."

"I know." She leans in, her warm breath trickling down my neck. "But rumour has it the heir has a thing for taming impossible people."

I grit my teeth, her words sinking straight to my pussy.

She breaks off, heading straight for the drinks table. The space where she stood is cold and vacuous and I don't know if I want to scream in exasperation or cry in frustration. Why can't she just stick to the plan? Everything is always a joke and a game to her.

There's a scuffle at the side of the ballroom. The doors to the gardens burst open, but Daria—mother's head of security—and two guards are already blocking the way of the paparazzi, ensuring the tape and rope locking off the open doors is in place.

"Back up. Or get the hell off palace property," Daria snarls. Her words are low, cutting through the atmosphere like a sword to a throat. The paparazzi immediately draw back. Daria—while extremely effective at her job—is a narcissistic pustule of a magician and mother's second in command. She's arrogant and vicious, but I suppose the head of security needs to be to protect the crown.

I've never liked her, and she's never much liked me. But I do, at least, respect the woman. Still, my first duty as queen will be to fire her ass if she hasn't met an untimely demise in the meantime.

Mother is no fool; the paps are allowed to observe from the garden but *only* the garden. Allow them close enough to speculate and salivate over court life gossip but not so close they can listen or hear anything of value or guess who Penelope and I are. The room erupts into a cacophony of noise and chatter. Whispered gossip, gasps of breaths, shouts from the paparazzi to *just answer this question or that*.

I observe the room. I spot Penelope despite the sea of masks. She looks like a doll. Her blonde, pin-straight hair drapes down the open back of her dress. Which is fluorescent pink and short enough I'm pretty sure I can see arse cheek, Gods Pen. Hardly the demure, hidden princess mother expects. At least her pink crystal mask covers the majority of her face.

And just like that, my back itches. I turn and mother's eyes are boring into me from across the room. She snaps away, unable to stare for too long to save anyone suspecting.

The air shifts, rumbles and deepens. I glance at the door just as Roman enters. He scans the room, his eyes landing on Stirling. He gives her the slightest of acknowledgments and then scans the rest of the room. This time, his eyes land on Pen, his tongue slides over his lips and he heads in her direction. Thankfully, a man in a navy pin stripe suit intercepts him, and he's dragged into conversation.

I locate my targets and head over to engage in conversation.

"Hi," the man says, startled. His name is Gilbert. Prince Hullington the third or fourth I forget exactly.

"Er," I say, unable to find words because there's a lump of—what the fuck even is that? Bagel? Toast?—hanging from his beard.

"Sorry, I meant good evening." I stick my hand out as I reach for a glass on a butler's tray and swig it down to stop myself staring.

"Yes, quite. Good evening. The pleasure is all mine..." he holds out his hand, waiting for an introduction.

"Morrigan."

"Delightful name," he smiles.

I gag, turning it into a cough. Gods, there's bagel stuck in his teeth too.

"Well, the lady here"—he nods to the masked woman next to him—"and I, were just discussing the socioeconomic impact of migrating magicians on the culture of monarchies and changing sovereigns. What with my eventual duty as a monarch, I figure it's important to be educated on matters of the crown." He laughs, a snorting, snuffle of a thing, so loud and raucous, the piece of bagel flies off.

I lean back.

Unfortunately, not far enough, and a fleck of spittle lands on my cheek.

Bile rises in my throat.

Kill. Me. Now.

"Oh delightful," I say wiping my chin. "I'm more of a student of magic."

"I can see that." His eyes glide over my arms.

I'm not going to get anything useful from these two. They're dull as dishwater; they wouldn't associate with Roman if you paid them. It's a dead end. I make my excuses and head back to the drinks table to grab something stronger.

A strong, thick hand curls around my arm and pulls me toward the head of the room where mother stands. Fury burns in my veins.

"What the f—" I go silent as I realise who has hold of me.

My insides turn frigid. Heat licks up the back of my throat. I want to spit hexes into the air, pull electricity from the atmosphere and torture the piece of shit guiding me towards mother.

"Roman," I snarl under my breath.

"Princess. Or should I say Morrigan?"

"Get your fucking hands off me before I sever your balls."

"Now, now. Play nice. From what I remember, you seemed to enjoy my balls very much."

"Fuck you."

"Now, now, Morrigan. The papers are watching in the window. Last thing we want is a ruckus they deem gossip worthy. I think we had enough of that the first time around, don't you?"

A camera flashes through the open palace doors. Daria twitches in the doorway and steps in front of the paparazzi. But a second journalist notices Roman on my arm and ducks low to take a shot.

"You don't hold power over me anymore," I snarl. "If you think I'm afraid of you...."

"Oh, I know you're not afraid of me. You never were. That's what made it so much fun. But it's not me you should be afraid of. What's the old saying? Keep your friends close, your enemies closer?"

His eyes scan the crowd until they land on Stirling. My blood turns to ice. The air whooshes out of my lungs. Stirling, thankfully, is deep in conversation and blissfully unaware that she's being watched. He's just trying to fuck with me, shake my confidence and faith in her. I trust Stirling. I have to. We have a plan.

Scarlett, though, catches my eye. Her gaze narrows, and I know she knows something is up. Fuck. I can feel the plan slipping through my fingers. Inch by inch. The path I've woven is being knocked off course. I need to get a grip. I need to fix this.

"Smile, princess, unless you want to out yourself to the papers before the investiture. I take it you do want to keep your privacy as long as possible?"

He smiles wide, his teeth white and straight and I swear to gods it takes all my willpower not to smash them right out from his pretty face.

"Is that a threat?" I say through pursed lips.

"Do you want it to be?" He glares at me, the same old stare, the same hard, impossibly cold eyes.

Eyes I knew once.

I lean in close, pull him by the tie until his ear meets my mouth. "There will come a day when I will stand over your burning corpse, and I won't piss on you to put you out."

He inhales a hissing breath of air. "I do like it when you talk dirty to me. Have you forgotten what you took from me? What I'm owed? I fucked you once, I can do it again.

The scales have tipped in my balance." He snaps upright. "Your Majesty, so lovely to see you this evening."

"Good evening, Roman. Morrigan," Mother gestures to me a question in her eye.

"Well this is unexpected," she says. Her expression hardens, as her eyes roll to where Roman grips my hand.

"Perhaps Morrigan's changed her mind. Decided to stick to what was decreed..." Roman sneers.

I yank my arm away. He looks down at me, laughs. Piece of shit. Then he turns to mother, dismissing me.

"I was actually after a moment of your time, your Majesty." He opens his arms, raises his voice, and claps his hands.

Then he steps forward. "Your Majesty, princesses— whoever you are—" he makes a big show of scanning the crowd, his eyes hovering on me and Pen a split second longer than necessary. "Ladies, gentlemen, magicians, guards, and honourable guests from far-flung cities. As a gesture of goodwill and peace to the crown, I am throwing a party at DnD, in honour of the investiture, a week from today. Everyone is invited, and the whole evening is on me. Consider it my gift to New Imperium."

A cheer rings through the crowd, hands shoot up, whooping and hollering as some magicians cheer and others whistle.

He turns back to mother. "I think it's high time our families were united, we are, of course, all people of the city. In another lifetime, I'm sure we could have been family."

He lowers his head in deference, "Morrigan."

The rage coursing through my body is so violent, the ground beneath my feet begins to shake.

"Snap out of it," Mother says and forms a circle with her index finger and thumb, tilting her hand in my direction. A bolt of static slaps me in my solar plexus. I gasp for breath as my focus comes back to me and the ground instantly stops trembling.

"Sorry."

"I thought you were handling the situation. Or do I need to talk to Penelope?" Her eyes scan the crowd to find Pen being swung around the arms of a rather muscular prince from three cities away.

"I am handling it."

"Well, it certainly doesn't look like it, does it? Do get a grip. Time is ticking."

She leaves me standing there, my jaw flexing, and I'm no longer sure if it's Roman I want to murder or mother.

CHAPTER 12

MORRIGAN

Eight Years Ago

Watery dawn light swims through the curtains of Roman's apartment. It's my birthday. I'm twenty-four. I twirl my fingers through the dust motes dancing in the beams of light. His apartment is in one of these newfangled buildings blended with magic from other realms. It's all glass and windows built upwards on top of each other.

He snores softly, his wavy hair flopping over his eyes. As I push a lock away from his face, a memory flits through my mind. That night a year ago in the club. He was so possessive, so angry. So was I. Strange that a year on, all those wounds, all the rage has left us both. And in a way, I do love parts of him. But he shows those parts less and less. But I'm not *in* love with him and I never was. I just wish he could admit that to himself.

After that night, Mother was conflicted. As my mother she wanted me rid of him. She thought I deserved better. But as the queen, her duty is not to her daughter but the crown and so she insisted I give him another chance. For the sake of the contract. For the sake of the palace and political strife.

So I did.

Gods, I really did.

I've tried for an entire year. But this morning, I realise I just can't keep pretending anymore. I'm exhausted and it's not fair on him or me. This farcical arrangement needs to come to an end so we can both move on.

I slide out of bed, pull my underwear on, pull my top and trousers on and slip my feet into my sandals.

Roman rolls over, wipes his eyes, and before he sees me, he's picked up a square box.

Oh gods no.

My stomach sinks. Bile twists in my belly and claws at my throat.

He's already out of bed. On one knee.

Fuck.

"Thought we could make it official. The papers are already speculating. They don't have to know you're the princess."

I'm dizzy, my vision speckles. "Roman."

One whispered word and everything changes. The air cracks.

He looks up now, meeting my gaze for the first time, a glinting gem staring at me from the tiny box in his hand.

He realises I'm dressed, and there's a flicker of hesitation; it beats like a wing through his eyelids.

And feather-light, just like a wing, everything snaps, and his face is thunderous.

"No. You're not doing this to me again," he's on his feet. "I thought you were over your little phase."

I can't look at him. My throat is thick. "I tried, Roman. I really did. I tried for you, for mother, for the damned crown. But I can't do this."

He slams the ring box shut. Paces up and down, dragging his hand through his hair.

"Will you truly not accept a marriage in name only?" I whisper. But I know before he speaks this is only going one way.

"Will you truly not get over this ridiculous phase? Is this not enough for you?"

He grabs his pants and cock.

Finally, I look him dead in the eye. "It's not something to get over. It's who I am. Who I always was."

He leans his head against the wall, slaps his hands and then balls one into a fist and drives it through the plasterboard.

"Please, Roman? I don't want to argue with you. I want to find a way to make this work. It would make both our lives so much easier if you could agree. We'll produce an heir. But once the heir is conceived, we're done. You can have anyone you want. Hell, you can have five mistresses for all I care. But once the heir is born, this—" I gesture to the bed, "is done, and we keep our personal lives separate."

He pulls his fist out of the wall. His knuckles are split open, blood dripping down his fingers. I reach out, touch my index fingers together.

"Don't fucking touch me with your pathetic magic," he snarls, slapping his bleeding fist to his other palm. My index fingers fly apart.

"So what? My cock is only good enough for you when you want to get pregnant? You can go fuck yourself you dirty fucking whore. If you don't want all of me, you can't have any of me."

I take a deep breath. They're just words. They don't hurt me. I'm doing this because it's the right thing to do, for me, for him. For the crown. I can't give myself to a life of service without being true to myself.

"I'm offering you everything I can give you. If you do this, you're throwing away the contract, the crown. You're giving up everything you want. But it is your choice."

He points his bloody hand in my face.

Fire ignites in my chest, I won't allow him to intimidate me.

His expression burns like sulphur and steel. "Don't you dare tell me what I'm giving up. This is your fault. You're destroying everything. And for what? To have your pussy fucked by a plastic cock? You want a plastic dick? Fine, I'll fuck you with one, Morrigan. Will that make you happy? You filthy little cunt?"

And that's the line.

I glare at him. The air grows cold and stiff. Magic thrums in my veins, pulsing like liquid fire.

"Watch your mouth, Oleg."

A vein throbs in the centre of his forehead. Spittle flies as he barks in my face. "You won't get away with this. You don't get to walk away from me."

"So you've made your choice."

He throws the ring box against the wall. Picks up a chair and smashes it into the ground repeatedly until it splinters and snaps in half.

I leave on silent feet, padding out of the room while he continues to smash his furniture and I can't help but wonder if one day it would have been me he was trying to smash and break.

I know then, even as my gut is twisting over the conversation I'm going to have to have with mother.

But no matter how much Roman wants the crown, it will never be his.

CHAPTER 13

MORRIGAN

The ball drags, my feet ache, but I continue to meander, discussing politics and gossip. None of it useful. After a couple of hours, Remy slides in next to me.

"What have you got for me?" I say.

Remy slides her arm around my shoulder. "His associates are here."

"Oh?" I say.

"Left corner of the ballroom. Unfortunately for you, right behind Stirling," her lips twitch as if she's going to laugh. I shake my head.

"You're an asshole. I thought we were friends."

That makes her kick her head back and laugh.

"And you should stop lying to yourself. Go dance with her, for gods' sake and put yourself out of your misery. We're adults you know, we're capable of having your back and seeing this mission through while also being in love. Scarlett and Quinn managed just fine with the

Borderlands."

But I turn serious. "Remy. It's not that I don't know how I feel. But this is serious. There's so much you don't know. It's not just..." the words fade.

Her eyes soften. "There's always time for love, Morrigan. It's the only thing that matters..."

She leaves, joining Quinn and Scarlett, who are deep in conversation with some legacies on our list of targets.

I head over into the corner of the ballroom to locate the next person on my list when Stirling breaks away from a group of legacies. She spots me and her eyes flick to a cluster of magicians behind her.

She stalks over to me and slides her fingers into mine. "Dance," she commands in my ear.

"Stirling," I growl. But she throws me out wide, spins me and then pulls me back in dipping me low.

"I said dance." It's not a request. She must have heard something and needs to stay close.

"Fine, break all the rules," I spit.

"Sometimes we have to break them. Like right now." She slides her hand around my back pulls me in tight. "Earlier, I saw Roman doing a deal with someone."

"Right?" I say, curious as to where this is going.

"I know a girl, Trixie. She's a journo. But often does undercover work. Like now. She shouldn't really be in here. But I'm not going to rat her out. Not when she can help."

"What have you done?"

"Don't look at me like that."

"I'm not judging, just tell me."

"I blackmailed her. Used the fact I knew she shouldn't be in here and convinced her to charm the info out of Roman's contact."

"Stirling!"

"What? I sweetened the deal by paying her. But I gave her an enchanted coin, so the deal is trackable. It ensures she won't talk. Anyway, see that woman with the poofy back dress?"

She turns me, step, step, slide. So I can see.

"Yes," I whisper against her cheek. Her hands are warm around the curve of my back. Every pad of her finger leaves a heated mark through the fabric.

She pulls me closer, and then speaks low. "The man behind her left shoulder, eleven o'clock, works for Roman. Do you have some kind of magic to heighten our hearing?"

She turns me again, step, step, slide. Step, step, slide.

"Actually yes. But I need to, ahh. Gods, of course I have to do this." I grit my teeth, skim one hand against the very patch of skin I'm desperate to touch. My fingers skim like feathers from her belly button to her solar plexus. She stiffens against me and it sends a bolt of desire through me.

Her skin is warm, soft, and it tingles against the pads of my fingers. There's a swell of desire rising inside me. I force it down. Inhale, focus, exhale.

"Oh my, Morrigan. I didn't think we were touching each other unless absolutely necessary. Certainly not in public." She's smirking while she mimics my voice.

I shake my head at her but I'm smiling too. "This deal of ours isn't going so well, is it?"

She shrugs as I tip toe my fingers up her neck, pressing at key points before sliding my index finger along her earlobe.

"Well, we lasted twenty-four hours."

I repeat the sequence of movements over my own body. When the magic settles in my head, it's buzzy at first, the crescendo of noises a little louder than I anticipated. I can taste mint and cinnamon at the back of my throat. But there's so much floral and expensive perfume on all the guests I don't think anyone notices the use of magic.

"Ready?" Stirling says.

I nod. She leads us, dancing on swift feet, twirling and spinning me until we're fifteen feet away. Then, the music drops and the low heady beat mellows into a slow dance.

"Oh dear, how devastating, I guess I'll have to hold you real tight now. What. A. Shame."

"Speechless," I say. "It's like the universe is conspiring against me. Though if you touch my arse, I'm going to electrocute you."

She glances down at me, a devious grin in her eyes, and then she squeezes my ass. I shoot upright, my spine straight as an arrow. She's laughing so hard she can barely stay upright.

"Stirling." I slap her arse right back and that, at least, gets her attention.

She grabs my wrist, her eyes go dark, hungry. "Behave like a brat again, and I will put you over my shoulder, carry you to the throne room and fuck you until you can't stand."

"Such double standards."

"I don't make the rules," she smiles. "I just give you what I know you want."

"The plan, Stirling," I say trying to bring us back on track.

Stirling bows low, and then opens her arms to welcome me into the slow dance. I twine my fingers into hers and lean my head on her shoulder, her hand closing around my waist. My head nestles against her neck. Slotting into place like I belong. Like I was always meant to be here. For a brief moment, I wish I wasn't the heir, that once this was over, we could go back to the way it was. Just us against the world; no palace, no politics, no princesses.

But to do that, Penelope would have to become queen and I don't trust the safety of New Imperium in her hands. I glance over to her. Roman is standing with her, her hand on his arm, her head kicked back as she laughs.

Stirling shifts suddenly, turning us. She slide-steps another foot closer to the group and then settles us into a slow spin so we can hear the conversation.

There's two voices, an older gruff guy and a younger, sharper voice.

"How's farming going? You managed to negotiate the land you need outside the city?" the gruff guy asks.

"No, I need a space with import and export routes, and everywhere I've looked is too remote. Nothing is close enough to the city," the younger man replies.

"Now you know why Roman likes the docks so much. Import and export is a piece of piss from there."

This is not useful. The gruff guy might work for Roman, but he's certainly not spilling any secrets we don't already know. Stirling's fingers slip lower on my back, and everywhere they trail is like hot glitter. I'm acutely aware of exactly how much pressure she's applying. Acutely aware of the way her other thumb rubs the skin on the back of my hand where they're clasped together.

"You know that's how I ended up working for the bastard?" The gruff chap says.

"I didn't think Roman was interested in growing the export trade though," young man responds.

"When have you ever known Roman to not want to grow a part of his business? We both have the scars from his ambition."

"Don't I know it."

"Precisely. You know I lost two city centre properties to him and six in the burbs. Who the hell needs to amass that much property anyway? And he didn't even go through the official property negotiation channels." The gruff guy drops his voice, low enough that even with magic heightening my hearing, I have to strain to hear.

"About eighteen months ago, he just stopped. Went completely off books. But he continued amassing property. Calandra's a fool. I can't believe the palace just accepts his placations. Like he's spontaneously being an upstanding citizen. Did you hear him announce that party?"

The two share an ugly laugh.

"Once a tycoon, always a tycoon," the younger voice says.

"Aye, I just wish I knew what the hell he was doing with all those houses."

"Oh please, like you don't know." I can practically hear the young man roll his eyes. "Power. Roman's amassing power."

"How do you know?" The old boy says.

I spin to face them and risk a glance up.

"I don't. Not in any concrete way. But it's logical. What else do you want that many houses for? If he can't study fast enough to be Collected by all the properties, then he'll buy them up, so he gets the power by default."

"And what about the houses in the burbs, with no power?"

The young man scratches his jaw. "Who knows? But when you amass as many properties as he is, doesn't fucking matter, does it? He'll have more power than the crown soon, and then Calandra's in deep shit."

"Gods," the old boy says.

I swallow hard. Gods in-fucking-deed.

"We need to locate those properties and fast," I say.

Stirling pulls apart, her face grave. "I know a girl. I'll go find her."

CHAPTER 14

STIRLING

The carriage rocks from side to side, making it hard to stay awake. I'm shattered after the ball last night. But I need to meet the girl I know, Trixie, before regrouping with the gang at Remy's place for lunch.

The carriage pulls to a stop outside New Imperium Park, and I can already see Trixie. She's frowning up a storm, her stout little figure all folded arms and fury.

I pay the driver and ask him to wait ten minutes. I'm not walking across town, and Scarlett left this morning on her motorbike so carriage it is.

I head over to Trixie, and if it's possible, her scowl deepens.

"That bad?"

"You owe me. Pay up, Stirling."

I hand over a bag of coin. "What happened?"

"I mean... I love cock, who doesn't?"

I raise an eyebrow. "Umm, me, actually. But what has this got to do with anything?"

"Well, I love it. But last night... that was..." she shudders. "He didn't know what he was doing. Let me put it that way. And it was mortifying, but I genuinely asked if it was in."

That makes me belly laugh. "You know you're never supposed to say that."

"It was *in*, Stirling. It was *already in*. And it's not like I have a bucket-vagina. I've not even had kids, for fuck's sake." She throws her arms up. "The shit I do for you, honestly. You owe me big." Even she's laughing now.

I wipe a laughter-tear away. "I do. I won't forget what you've done."

She smiles. "So listen. He's only buying a handful of properties openly and he's doing that at auction."

"Okay, thank you. And what about the rest?"

"All off books. He's targeting desperate magicians. Those in need of a quick buck and happy to take cash buys in exchange for staying silent about who purchased the property."

"So is it going on the property transfer records?" I say.

"It must be, but I think because they're properties on the outskirts of the city without magic, he's found some loophole and slipping them through undetected."

I rub my forehead. I don't get it. How the hell is he managing to keep everything under wraps? This is going to have to be a Remy job. She's going to have her work cut out trying to trace down all the purchases.

Trixie squirrels the bag of coin into her coat and turns to leave but stops herself. "There's something else."

"Yeah?"

"I stayed most of the night. I saw you guys leave about halfway through. But once you did, Roman... Do you know if he has a girlfriend?"

"Not that I know of. I've never seen him date anyone."

"Nor me," she says a neat little line furrowing between her brows. "And I'd know. The paps like to follow him, he's good fodder for the gossip columns."

"Did you see him with a girlfriend?"

"I'm not sure, he was acting like it though. All over a woman I didn't recognise. Tall, blonde, wearing a really short dress."

"Okay, thanks. I appreciate it."

"Catch you later," she says and disappears into the park heading across to the other side.

I get in the cab and give the driver the address. He swipes his hand over his arm and Collection tattoo. A translucent city map shoots up and hovers above his forearm. He uses his fingers to zoom in and out and spin the map around.

"Alright, should be about half an hour."

I pay him the coin he asks for and we head out into the city, the watery sun warming the carriage just enough I fall asleep to the rocking motion.

I'm thrown awake by a sharp jolt as the carriage lurches forward and grinds to a halt. I wipe the sleep from my face and glance outside the carriage. "Ooh, she lives in the new quarter."

"Have a good day," the carriage driver says.

"Thanks." I hop out of the carriage and check the address again. She lives in a fancy new building. It's ugly as sin, all tall rectangles and plain squares. None of the regal beauty of old mansions, marble pillars and limestone turrets.

It's weird, these newfangled buildings. Dozens of little flats all built on top of each other. But they draw magic from the threads and connectivity between the apartments. It's the compounding of multiple units on top of each other. Skyrise, I think she called it. Apparently, they took the concept from another realm. The architects building them are at the cutting edge of magic creation and architecture. While I love new tech, they're a gaudy eyesore. Like little teeth in the maw of the New Imperium horizon.

There's a doorman at the front of the building, dressed in a dark navy uniform.

"Who are you visiting."

"Remy Reid."

"Take the lift, flat 99."

He holds the door open and as I enter, the building sends a rush of pressure over my body. This building is tingly, like static electricity and pins and needles. There's a strange plasticky smell and the hint of leather.

So cool. I suppose there's something to be said of utilising new magic as well as old. Even if I'll always be a purist when it comes to mansions.

I take the lift up to the 9th floor and the doors open into a long corridor with apartments on either side. I can tell Remy's the moment I see it.

It's decorated for one, unlike the others which are plain white. Hers is adorned with lines of tech fibres and copper-coloured cogs. It's cute. I like it.

I knock on the door expecting Remy to answer it but it's Quinn. She wrenches open the door in hot pants and a vest top, a sausage roll half eaten in her hand. She opens her arms and pulls me in, crushing pastry crumbs into my hair. Giving absolutely no shits, she drags me inside and points to the bathroom on the right.

"Toilet," she says with her mouth half full. "Bedroom. Kitchen down the end and living room and office through there. Upstairs is more rooms."

Remy's apartment is odd. Most of the rooms open into each other on this floor. I thought it was a flat, but there's glass stairs to another floor. There's so much light and glass that the place doesn't feel as claustrophobic as I expected, being sandwiched between nine other apartments on the same floor. If anything, it's kind of light and spacious. Huge great windows cover one entire wall in the open plan living room and office.

Everything is white, ivory or glass and I'm kind of nervous to touch anything in case I dirty it up.

Everywhere is clinically clean. There are a few neat sculptures and paintings on the wall, and one photo. It's a small frame with a cluster of people on it. One of the women look familiar, but I can't place her. But most of the walls, floors and counter tops are all clean and free of trinkets.

That is, until Quinn wheels me towards Remy's office area, which is about as chaotic as you can get. There's cabling and wiring piled in tight circles. There's papers and notebooks. A lattice of transparent cogs hang in the air, and next to them hovers another whiteboard rectangle like the one Remy made at Morrigan's house. There are a dozen coffee cups half full, take-out containers covering most surfaces and even scattered around the floor of her desk. Last, there's an array of little gadgets and devices in metal and plastic boxes.

"Woah, what are these?" I ask.

"Computers, phones, tablets. Magic levellers, magic feeders, testers and enhancers. All kit I've negotiated for from other cities. You'd be proud, Stir."

"I am. What are you doing with it all?"

"Reverse engineering it. I want to create an impenetrable security system and I want to blend new advanced tech with older magic systems. I think it's going to create something incredible. I'm just stuck working out how to program an interface between our runic security subsystem and the electrical mechanics of analog based computer systems."

"Right. Right." I nod. Remy always loses me when she goes off about tech. "Well I am all here for it."

Scarlett and Morrigan appear from the kitchen, bringing a plate of pasties, sausages and a tray of drinks and fruit.

"Lunch," Scarlett says.

"So what have we got?" Morrigan asks as I sit down and take a sausage. "Did you meet your contact?"

"Yes. And for everyone else, when we were at the ball, I saw a girl I know. She's a journalist. I paid her to talk to the guy I saw Roman shaking hands with."

"Oi, babe. I was sitting there," Quinn says to Scarlett.

"Well, I'm sitting here now," Scarlett glares at her.

"Don't be an arsehole, just move you—"

"Ladies," Morrigan snaps.

Quinn huffs, throws a satsuma at Scarlett's head, which smacks her on the ear. Scarlett launches at Quinn knocking her off the back of the sofa in a giant thwack. Quinn screams and cackles as Scarlett sets about tickling the ever-loving shit out of her.

I glance at Morrigan. "Should we...are we meant to stop that?"

She shrugs at me. We both turn to Remy who rolls her eyes, cracks her neck and touches her two index fingers together, whispers something under her breath that I can't hear and then her two knuckles meet. She weaves them in a circle around each other.

The screaming and laughing promptly stops, and both Scarlett and Quinn stand up. Flushed and frowning.

"What the—" Scarlett says holding up handcuffed hands. Around her wrists are translucent, copper-coloured cuffs.

"Do you mind?" Remy says. "That's a thousand-coin rug you're wrestling on. If you squash satsuma into it, I swear to the high magician I will drop you out the 10-storey window, mmkay?"

"Such a killjoy," Quinn says staggering to her feet, her wrists also cuffed.

Remy just glares at the pair of them. "Scarlett, there. Quinn, you sit over there." Both of them pout but sit on opposite sides of the room. I rub my mouth, trying to hide the smirk. The state of them both, like scolded children, is truly priceless.

I cough the laugh away and continue. "As I was saying, I paid this girl I know to go and chat up the guy I saw Roman shaking hands with. It was the kind of hand shake that smacks only of a deal. It wasn't a hello sort of shake."

"And? What did she say?" Morrigan asks peeling a satsuma.

Remy releases Scarlett and Quinn from their cuffs.

"Publicly he's just bought another club in the centre of New Imperium. But he's making off-books private purchases."

Quinn's eyes narrow, "I didn't think there were private purchases."

"Well, neither did I. But apparently he's managing to buy them, and no one fucking knows about it."

Remy grabs her office chair and sits down on it

whistling. "That's quite the feat. I thought property purchases all had to follow the same legal system. This is magic we're talking about here. He must have found some kind of loophole or..."

"Or something," I finish for her. "The ones that are off book are on the outskirts of the city. None of them have magic. And what's the public record?"

Morrigan sits bolt upright. "It's the magical property record. Everyone mistakes it for property transfers but that's not really what it's doing. It's actually recording the transfer of magic."

"I did not know that," Quinn says, leaning back in her chair.

"Most people don't. There's no need. But I was studying property transfers and it was in a little footnote."

Morrigan's whole face lights up. Her smile fills her entire face, and it makes me want to reach out and kiss her. I remember the night we met, the grimoire she was after that I'd won in a game of poker. Her face lit up the same way when I asked her what she wanted to know from it. I smile to myself. It was an underground poker club in the next city. I won, of course, poker is just another series of negotiations. But the night was especially delicious because we'd ended up playing strip poker, and, well...

Morrigan's voice chops into my memory and brings me back to the room. "So we need a list of all the property exchanges in New Imperium."

Remy sits up, "I can do that. And I might be able to do one better too. I have a couple of contacts over the magic web that might be able to help. There's a new underground magic network that a lot of deals and transfers are happening through. There might be something on there I can dig up."

"How long do you need?" Morrigan asks popping a segment of satsuma in her mouth.

"A few days?"

"We don't have a few days, Remy. It's already been more than a week since the announcement, we have less than three weeks before the investiture, and we're no further forward with finding out what he's doing or stopping him," Morrigan says.

"Alright. Give me two days and I'll get something concrete for us."

"I haven't gotten much from the Borderlands. I spoke to Mal but most of the properties coming through already have prospective buyers at the auction, none of which include Mr. Oleg, so I think we can cross that avenue off."

"Okay, noted. There's one other thing though." I'm resistant, unsure if I should actually add this. "My contact saw Roman with a woman. Tall, pin-straight blonde hair in a super short dress."

Morrigan drops the rest of the satsuma on the floor. Her eyes bugging wide.

"Penelope?" she breathes.

"I don't have confirmation, but it certainly seemed that way. What the hells do you think she was up to?"

Her expression darkens into something born of steel and vengeance and it makes me shift on the sofa. I should not find that level of rage attractive, but fuck it looks like she'd burn the world to the ground right now, and I'd follow her anywhere picking up the ashes.

"I can confirm it. I saw her with him briefly. You know she didn't even come and say hello to me when she got back to the palace. It was only at the ball that night that we finally spoke."

"I could always give her a nasty bout of dysentery to keep her out of the parties," Quinn grins.

Morrigan snort laughs. "Much as that would be deeply pleasurable to witness, should mother ever find out, despite the fact you work for her, I think there would be some severe consequences. No. I'll have a word with my little sister."

"Let's meet in two days. By then, Scarlett you'll have gotten the schematics," I say.

"Meeting Daria tomorrow," Scarlett nods.

"Perfect. That means I can take Roman the palace plans, or at least partial plans. Remy, you'll have a report for us on the sales?"

She nods.

"And in the meantime, I'll try not to commit sororicide," Morrigan says.

CHAPTER 15

MORRIGAN

"What the hell do you think you're doing associating with Roman Oleg?" I spit at my sister over evening meal.

She sticks her little piggy nose up at me. "What's it got to do with you? Isn't he *your* problem?"

"Yes, precisely. I'm here trying to find a way to ensure he doesn't usurp the crown while you're off galavanting around trying to swing your giraffe legs over his cock. What the fuck? You know who he is... what are you thinking?"

"Oh Morrigan, darling, you're aware of how bitter you sound? It's not a good look for you."

My fists ball, and the lights in the dining hall flicker. Penelope's make-up caked face turns on me. Her exterior beauty is unparalleled. She is, by all conventional standards, stunning. Heart shaped face, piercing blue eyes, and smooth skin that looks like it was carved by marble loving gods. Legs for days, and thin limbs--even her hair is perfectly smooth and straight and static free.

Unfortunately, that is where the beauty ends. Inside, she's a nasty, petty, malicious bitch out for whatever she can gain for herself. And worse, there's no brains behind her actions. She doesn't think like a Queen. She thinks about herself and that's it. The prospect of the crown being handed to her is not only terrifying for me, but for New Imperium too. She used to watch some of the magician council meetings in the early days, and she'd come up with the most ludicrous suggestions.

And of course, all of them benefitted her.

Which is why I'm not swallowing the innocent bullshit act she's trying to give me.

"Don't avoid the question, *Pennn*."

She narrows her eyes at me. Her top lip curls. I wish mother were here to see who she really is. But of course, mother is never here when Pen is being a cunt. Only when she's got her perfect princess smile on.

"Fine." She picks up her napkin, wipes the corners of her mouth, then drops it on the table. "I'm done with dinner anyway. Yes, I approached Roman at the ball. It was a delightful conversation, if you must know. He's quite the man."

She winks at me. And I have to swallow down a lump of chicken to save myself from gagging.

"And what is that supposed to mean?"

"It means I'm going to see him again."

I find myself standing, my shoulders heaving where I'm breathing heavy.

"No."

"Excuse me?"

"I *said* no."

She sniffs, wiggles her shoulders at me, all affronted. "And who are you to tell me no?"

"I'm your sister, your future queen. And you know exactly who he was to me. You know exactly what his temper is like. You will listen to me, and you will leave this alone. It's not your fight, Penelope. You don't know what you're getting yourself into."

"You don't know shit. All you know is who he was, not who he is now." Her mouth is pinched, her nose upturned.

She's not got a clue, and there's only so much I can tell her. I don't trust her.

"Well?" she sneers.

Somewhere deep inside I'm screaming. "Penelope, he was my first, for gods' sake. Think this through. How could you want to go there?"

But the stiffness in her jaw, the set of her shoulders is so tight, so rigid I know she's already made up her mind. Anything I say will only convince her to keep going. Unless I tell her the truth and that's the one thing I can't do.

I lower my eyes, I can't bear to look at her. "You know what, do what you need to."

She gives me a smug smile. "I thought as much. Gods, *Morrigan*, I am so tired of your self-righteous entitled bullshit. I don't know whether you realise this, but you're not always right. You might have gotten the bulk of the brains in this family. But you don't know everything, and I am sick of your attitude. Your incessant need to control everything and everyone. So, I'm going to prove to you and to mother you're not the right choice for heir."

"I beg your pardon." One of the lights hanging on the wall sears bright and then the glass bursts.

She shakes her head at me. "You're pathetic. You had the chance to have the most powerful husband in the city.

You have all this power inked onto your body and it's completely wasted. You can't even control it."

"How dare you!" Heat rises and seeps between my ribs, clogging my throat until I have to physically bite my tongue to stop myself screaming spells at her.

She stands, pops her chair back into the table. "When you inevitably fail to bring Roman down, I will be right here to take your crown and your precious city and you'll know once and for all, that I am the better sister."

"Bitch."

She smiles, it's small and tight and filled with a perverse spite. It makes her face ugly as sin—I hope it stays like that.

She places her hand on the door handle. "Unless, of course, I get there first and find a way to stop him attacking us before you have the chance. Toodles." She waves and then she's gone.

Fuck, fuck, fuck. I thought I'd planned for everything. But Penelope is a variable I hadn't accounted for. She has the power to get close to him in a way I never will. And she won't move slowly, she'll seduce him and coerce him into doing whatever the hell she wants.

I need to think and I need a new plan. And quickly.

I shove my dinner away, no longer hungry and head to the cottage, grab my coat, change shoes and pick up a notebook to make a new plan.

♛

Three hours of strategising later, I find myself by the harbour. I don't really know why my feet took me here, but for a while, I sit on the wooden pier and watch the fish. I dangle my hand over, trailing it through the water, and just think. It's a few moments of serenity with the cool breeze on my skin.

When my butt hurts from sitting, I get up and stroll. There's a hole in one of the fences cutting the beach off. I glance around but there's no one to stop me so I squeeze through. I strip my shoes and socks off and let the sand trickle between my toes. It's soft and warm, though not as scorching as it is in the height of summer.

I want to close my eyes and let the dying afternoon heat beat down on my skin and soak up what's left of the day. So I meander for a while, directionless. The beach is empty save for someone working on a wooden boat. They're stripped down to short shorts and a vest top, a pile of clothing next to them.

It's a woman.

Her arms and legs are tanned from hours in the sun waxing the wood I assume. The muscles in her arms are corded and toned, and gods, I feel wrong for ogling her. Not that Stirling and I are together. We can't be. But still. There are so many unsaid things.

The woman looks up. Deep blue eyes locking on mine.

Stirling.

Of course it's Stirling, a tiny bubble of hysterical laughter fizzes up. I manage to stifle it as Stirling's face breaks out into a smile and she waves me over.

"Hey," she says, beaming. And I swear to gods her face lights up like the glistening sun on the ocean and I just want to fall into her arms.

"Hey yourself. What are you doing?" I scan the boat she was... what? Waxing? Varnishing?

She shrugs. "It's my... hobby I suppose."

I glance at the sand around her, there's hammers and nails and strange clamps and odd bits of tools. The boat is almost complete and it's beautiful. At the front... is front even the right word? Bow? Helm? I make a mental note to study boat magic this winter. At the front of the boat is a beautiful carved woman, a mascot I assume. She's...

"Oh..." the word pops out in a squeak.

Stirling's face flushes red. She flings her top over the sculpture sealing it away from view.

But I saw.

I saw enough to know who it was. Who she modelled it off.

The air is thick. I had no idea she could do any of this, let alone carve wood like that. I wonder how long it took her, how long she's been etching and chipping and sculpting. Does she even realise who she carved? By the searing pink covering her cheeks and tracking down her neck, and the fact she covered it, she must do.

She holds my gaze, daring me to call her out, to ask her why my face is carved into her boat. But I don't. It seems like this project is just for her. She must have been building this boat for months, years maybe. All this time. Her hands shaping a piece of me.

I can't think about this anymore. I peer inside the hull and there's a glass bottom. I assume, so she can see the fish.

"I can't believe you built all of this," I say.

"Not just a pretty face, am I?" She grins, folds her arms her chin tipped high. Unbelievable, can't even be modest over a compliment.

"Why don't you just buy a boat?"

"Where's the fun in that?"

"I had no idea you liked sailing."

"It's not for sailing. Truth be told, I'm not even sure I like boats. But I love swimming and love the fish even more. There's something peaceful about them. If it weren't for the fact we own Castle Grey, I'd love to live on the oceanfront."

Stirling cocks her head at the row of mansions, her eyes trailing the property we broke into the other day. There's something forlorn about her expression, the way her eyes turn down.

She snaps out of it and turns to me. "What are you doing here, anyway? Haven't you got something to do on the Roman case?"

"I needed to take a walk to clear my head."

"What's wrong?"

I slump down on the sand. "She's awful, Stirling. She doesn't think I'm worthy of the throne."

My eyes sting. I rub at them but the more I rub the worse the sting gets. Stirling presses her lips together, drops the wax and cloth into the boat and grabs my hand, hauling me up off the sand.

"Come here."

She pulls me into a hug and it is so warm, and so safe that I let out a little choked sob. "She said horrible things. And what's worse is I couldn't even get a comeback out. Because if I'd opened my mouth, I'd have done something awful. Like slit her throat. My magic was so consuming, I burst one of the lights in the dining hall."

The words come out in a rush. Stirling stays quiet and rubs my back. I nestle into the crook of her neck, the curve of her body against mine a comfort.

"She more or less said she was gunning for the throne."

Stirling releases me, picks up her tools, and drops them into a rickety shed. She leaves the boat where it is, it's far too heavy to drag anywhere. She rifles around the shed for a while, cussing and clanging. Then, finally, she brings out a wrapped parcel.

She slides her hand in mine and tugs me away from the beach. "I know it doesn't feel like it, but we've got time to sort Penelope out. Come on, I'm going to show you something."

Her pace is quick as she pulls me off the beach, up and over a sand dune and into a copse of trees with gnarled branches like witches fingers.

"Erm... Am I about to get murdered? Because if I'm about to get murdered, I should probably tell you a few things."

Stirling laughs up ahead, but doesn't elaborate any more. I *should* tell her a few things, maybe I should confess everything.

No. I can't.

"Stay here a second," she says and vanishes for what feels like forever. When she returns she's no longer carrying the parcel.

She stops and looks up. The sky is burning like wildfire across a dessert. Ochres and oranges crumble into clouds the colour of maple syrup.

"Shit. We got to hurry up." She drags me faster now, pulling and yanking me up the path as the incline grows and my calves burn.

"This better be worth it, I'm sweating and I think my legs are going to fall off."

"It is, I promise."

A few excruciating minutes of sweat forming on my brow, my thighs screaming, twigs snapping, and me almost slipping on several rocks, we break out into a clearing and I gasp.

"Holy shit. It *is* beautiful," I breathe.

"Told you it was worth it."

We're high up, the ocean a field of blue beneath us. At

our feet is a steep drop and gushing waterfall. The water below is crystal clear, glistening white crystal even as the sun sets over the rushing water. Craggy rocks stick out behind over the lip of the fall.

I sit, just drop right there into crossed legs, leaves crunching beneath me. And admire the horizon. We're high enough that the city's lights twinkle to life as the evening revellers make their way into town for a night of debauchery. If I strain, I can just about make out the peaks of mountains outside the city limits. Beyond them and to the south and west of New Imperium are the other cities, not that you can see them, even at this height.

"It's breathtaking," I say. "Thank you for bringing me here."

"Do you trust me?"

I narrow my eyes at her. "Why?"

"I want to show you how to let everything go."

"What if I like holding on to everything, controlling everything? What if I need to?"

"You're the most powerful magician I know. You don't need to hold on. Maybe that's the issue. Because you *can* control everything, you do."

"Are you trying to start a fight? Because that's exactly the so—"

She places a finger over my lips. "No. I'm sorry. I should think before I speak. Just... Do you trust me?"

"No."

She raises an eyebrow at me and waits...

"Fine. Yes."

"Take a deep breath."

"What?"

She grabs my hand and pulls me full pelt, running at the waterfall edge.

"Stirling! What the *fu*—"

But before I have time to yank her back, she's leaping off the edge and tugging me over with her.

The scream that rips from my lips is enough to shatter glass and burst veins. At first, it's sheer terror. Pins and needles blossom in my chest and then I'm just falling, falling, falling, and everything is free, and the only thing that's safe is the strong hand holding mine, squeezing, telling me she'll never let go. It's like the whole world is suspended in this moment, free and floating, held up by molten clouds and a grin I could drown in.

And then we're plummeting into water, and it's ice cold and the shock almost makes me open my mouth. But Stirling is still gripping me and she's kicking and pulling me up, up, up and then I'm bursting through the surface and—

"Are... Y-you... Insane?" I say through ragged breaths.

But Stirling is cackling and splashes me with her hands. "I thought your eyes were going to bug out. What was it like?"

I want to scream at her. Lie. Tell her it was horrendous and if she ever does anything like that again I'll personally turn her into a cockroach. But I can't because it was... it was...

"Magical."

She nods, a knowing look in her eye. "Is it really so bad just be spontaneous?"

I press my lips shut. I'm not going to answer that. "Being spontaneous was..."

"Brilliant? Amazing? Something you're definitely going to do again?" She's wearing a grin I'd like to slap off, except I can't because it lights her whole face. The way her lips plump and curve when she knows she's won. Insufferable. One smile and she unravels all my self-control.

I swipe my arm across the water, splashing her. "Unexpected."

She shrugs in the water. "You know what? I'll take unexpected. I can work with that."

We swim to the edge of the water and that's when I notice the parcel there.

"You mean we could have avoided the hill and just come for a swim this whole time?"

She laughs and hands me the parcel.

"I got you something. It's... well, let's call it a *friendly* gesture. Me trying to stick to the rules. Open it."

I unwrap the paper. It's dark maroon, like the colour of drying blood. When I open the package I nearly drop it.

"Holy fuck, where the hell did you get it?"

She lays her hand on it. "Don't get too excited. It's not the original. But I know a girl, and she managed to uhh, borrow, shall we say, the original Sangui Grimoire. So it's an unauthenticated copy. But it was the best I could come up with and I'm hoping th—"

I put the book down and crush my lips to hers.

I break all the rules I set. And I don't care one bit.

Her fingers find my shoulders, my hands find her waist, and I pull her in. And then she's kissing me back just as deep. I push her lips open, slide my tongue inside, skimming and caressing hers like our mouths are pirouetting.

She pulls back. "I didn't source the book for this... I was trying to be friends... We said we wouldn't."

"Oh my gods, would you shut up and fuck me already."

She opens her mouth to argue.

"Come on Stirrrrrling, live in the moment. Roll with it," I say in my best impression of her.

She shakes her head at me, a smile curling the corners of her eyes.

Her hand slides around my neck, and she pulls me in for another kiss, gentler this time. She guides me through the water until my back is against a rock. There's a stone close to my foot. I hover on it and hook my other leg around her waist.

She stares at me a moment longer, her eyes flickering across my expression as if testing, trying to work out whether I'll regret this.

I won't. Gods, I really won't. For once, I figure we can worry about the consequences later. She lifts her hand out of the water, lets her fingers kiss my shoulders. She follows the droplets running down my arms all the way to my fingers, picks my hand up and places her lips against each knuckle.

There's something tight behind her gaze. She pushes a loose lock behind my ear and leans into my forehead.

"I really was trying to be friends. I want to be better for you. I want to stick to the job," she says and peppers a trail of kisses down my cheek and along my jawline. "Even though we're meant to convince Roman I'm back in the palace's good books, there's only so far we can push this. If we get caught, if he thinks what we're doing, what I feel, is real and not fake for his cause... he could..."

Everywhere she touches, electricity tiptoes in its wake. It surges through my body as if she is the spark and I am the flame. She ignites me, heat pooling in my core. I burn for her.

"I know," I pant. "We shouldn't... it's dangerous."

I kiss Stirling, my fingers kneading into her back, pulling her closer, tighter, the air magnetic and charged around us.

Stirling moans into my neck. "What are you doing?" she says, her teeth nipping my shoulder. It sends a shiver down my spine and straight to my pussy. My power claws at the edges of my skin, it wants to be released, Stirling makes my body, my magic wild.

"I lose control around you. I can't help it."

Her hands find the bottom of my top and tugs it up and over my head. "So we're agreed?" Stirling says grabbing my throat and pulling me to her mouth. She nips and kisses and sends glistening tingles all over my body, and I'm no longer sure what's her and what's me losing grip on my power.

"Agreed?" I breathe, swinging her around and pushing her against the rock.

"We're not doing this...?" she says an eyebrow raised at me.

"No, we're absolutely not doing this," I say smirking.

"Right. Right," she nods. "Got it... Morrigan?"

"Yeah?"

"What happens if I need to fuck you? Cause I really feel like you should be touching me... Like right now."

I slap my hands together, pull them apart and touch the tips of my middle and index fingers together.

Stirling gasps as her top slides off her body and over her head. I continue the series of movements, stripping her of her clothing without touching her.

"Oh dear. You seem to have lost some of your clothes," I say.

She slow-shakes her head at me. "You're a bad girl, princess."

"I was always a bad girl."

I touch my index and middle fingers together and then draw power deep from inside me, I snap them apart and her bra pings open. Her breasts fall free, her nipples instantly hard against the cooling evening air.

I throw a hand up, click my fingers, and a blanket of glistening static orbs fill the clearing. They sparkle against the frothing waterfall, and give us just enough light I can see how hard her nipples are. I swallow, desire throbbing deep in my pussy. I draw my hand down through the air, her knickers slowly slide down her long legs and off her feet. I flick my hand away and they ping up and out of the water and onto the rock.

"Oh dear, it appears you're now naked."

"A crying shame," Stirling says. "Whatever are we to do?"

"I have bad news for you..." I bat my eyelids at her. I can't wipe the smile off my face.

"Oh?" she purrs.

"I'm afraid we're going to have to break the terms of our agreement."

She tuts. "That is a shame. I believe there's a break clause. It's point seven of I don't give a fuck, get over here and touch my clit before I die of need."

I laugh, "Gods I missed you. I missed us. I missed—"

Stirling lunges at me, pulls me in and presses her lips to mine. "Stop talking."

I wrap my arms around her neck and kiss her. I kiss her like we were never apart. I kiss her like she's air and I need to breathe.

We're a mess of hands and lips and mouths and tongues. And everywhere her fingers trail send sparks of need straight to my core. I slide my hand down her waist, into the water and over her slit. Despite the water, I can tell how wet she is. The smooth slick of her folds makes my whole body shiver with wanton need.

I rub circles around her clit, her fingers dig into the flesh of my back hard enough it touches the edge of pain. But that only makes me rub faster. She pants in my ear.

"Fuck. Fuck," she breathes, and I know she's climbing higher.

I draw a finger down her core and circle her opening. She growls into my neck, desperate for me to be inside her. But she doesn't get to come that quickly. Not tonight.

I enter her, pull back, push in a little further, slide all the way out.

"You fucking tease," she moans.

"Always."

And then I thrust into her hard. She throws her head back and grabs the rock for stability. And then her hands are all over me, gripping and yanking at my remaining underwear until she pushes it aside and finds my wet heat. She slips a finger inside me, then two. And then we're both thrusting and panting.

"Stirling," I say.

Her name makes goosebumps rise over her skin. She pulls out of me, hops up onto the rock and opens her legs for me.

She holds out a hand, "I don't care what happened between us, it doesn't matter what's going to happen. You will always be my queen."

I lace my fingers through hers.

"I'm going to make you come now," I say.

"Oh gods, please," and then she drags me through the water to her pussy. She cuffs a hand through my drenched hair and wraps it around her fist, holding me to her cunt.

I moan, relinquishing control of myself to her, allowing her to guide me, to own me as she rocks and rubs her pussy over my mouth.

I reach out, sliding one hand to her core. I enter her and

drop my other hand through the water to play with my own aching clit.

Her pussy clenches around my fingers and I know she's close. She moans, cries my name, begs me.

"Morrigan. Morrigan, gods. Harder."

My name in her mouth, so feverish, so hungry, is enough to tip me over the edge. I pump my fingers inside her deeper, faster. She crushes herself to my face, and then she tips over with me, and we're both floating together, our bodies connected, a shower of tingling pleasure roving from her body to mine.

She releases my hair and hops back into the water. Kissing me soft this time, so gentle and tender, her warm lips caressing mine.

"There you are," she says.

"Here I am." In this moment I really am present. That right now, I am breathing her in. Breathing us in. And I just wish that this could last forever.

But as she breaks away and the cool night air fills the space her body was in, I know it won't last. I know that when the investiture arrives, when Roman is dealt with, whatever we had, whatever we were will end when she finds out the truth I've kept from her.

CHAPTER 16

STIRLING

Days pass. The team gather, investigate, disburse, the frustration growing between us as we struggle to find the evidence we need to capture Roman.

It took a day longer than Morrigan wanted, but Remy found a selection of properties Roman has purchased.

Which is why, long after midnight, Morrigan and I are on one edge of the city limits. Quinn and Scarlett are on the other side of the city and Remy is leading us from her apartment.

Stars spotlight the inky sky. The air is cold and still, the chill of winter nights to come pressing at the remaining warmth. It's so quiet that every movement I make, every footstep crunches against gravel and twigs. All of them like gunshots ripping through the night.

I look Morrigan up and down, my jaw flexing because I'm not sure if I want to keep staring at her with her clothes on or tear them off with my teeth. Tonight, she's wearing a black skintight catsuit. Her body all tits and tempting curves begging to be pinched and squeezed and adored.

"Stop looking at me like you're about to maul me," she says.

"What if that's exactly what I'm about to do?"

"Do I get an orgasm out of it?"

I laugh and pop the earpiece Remy gave me into my ear. Static crackles as it connects. It's an odd feeling, and it makes me shudder as her voice plays through.

"Yo?" Remy says in my ear.

Morrigan grimaces as the earpiece settles in her ear too.

"We're in position," Quinn's voice comes over loud and clear.

"Scarlett?" Remy says.

"Hearing you loud and clear," she replies.

"Morrigan?" Remy asks.

"I got you too."

"Superb. We're all set. You've got the property maps?" Remy says.

"Yes, we're just outside the first property's perimeter," I say.

"Us too," Scarlett says in my ear.

"Right. On three, enter the land. Approach with extreme caution. I knocked out the perimeter security remotely. After hacking some of the local security nets, I can't see anything beyond what I've already taken out, but stay cautious. Get in, search, observe, and get the hell out again. Got it?"

"Got it," the four of us say in unison.

Yesterday, Remy managed to hack into the property database—a crime worthy of the noose I might add. But she did it, clever bitch, and she managed to download all of the property transactions over the last six months.

We spent the night poring over the documents, trying to triangulate any purchases that seemed off. We narrowed it down to a collection of deals that were concluded faster than the rest, thanks to Trixie's tips. We found sales that were all coin buys rather than through the banks.

The strange thing is, there were no names on the records. So although we've found the properties, the negotiation details have been scrubbed. Something that's also illegal. We decided the next course of action was to get out to the properties and look for evidence.

So here we are out in the burbs, practically the sticks. There's not another house for ages. Surrounded by fields and wooded areas, we're miles from a shop or anything remotely looking like the New Imperium I know and love.

"Scarlett, I've disconnected the perimeter security for your property too. You're both good to go in three, two..." her voice quiets.

I step onto the property grounds first.

We tiptoe through the gardens, keeping to the edge and tucking ourselves close into the hedges to keep the shadows cloaking us.

I'm pretty sure there's no one here, but I don't want to take the risk. Not with Morrigan here. We reach the patio. I motion for her to stay against the hedge, and I make my way to the house wall. It's a small property, in a state of awful neglect. The windows are filthy, there's trash spilling out from the bin in the corner. Broken bits of pottery and herb jars, an abandoned cauldron. The place looks like someone could no longer afford the upkeep of the house, so they left one random afternoon and never came back.

I peer through the dirt-smeared window. The house is definitely empty. It has that dead energy, a stillness you only find in spaces no magician has trodden for months.

I hail Morrigan over and she sprints across the grass.

"It's abandoned," I whisper.

"Roger that, ours too," Quinn says through the earpiece.

"I have a feeling they all will be," Remy says. "I'm scanning the rental networks and I'm not seeing any of the properties on the rent register."

"What the hell is he doing then?" Morrigan asks.

"Do you think this is where he's storing all the power he's importing?" Quinn asks.

I shrug, and then remember she can't see me. "Could be, I guess. There's only one way to find out."

I walk around the front of the house, no longer worried about being caught. The door is locked of course. I pull out two thin pieces of metal and jam them into the lock, twisting and nudging until it clicks and the door swings open.

"You're a lock pick now?" Morrigan says. "You know I could have just unlocked it using these..."

She waggles her fingers at me and then points at one of her Collection tattoos on her knuckle.

"Where's the fun in that?"

"All about the fun, you."

"Of course." I give her a look that tells her exactly what type of fun I'm thinking about right now and she waves me off as if she isn't thinking exactly the same filthy thoughts.

I step over the threshold and into the property.

Morrigan stays put while I investigate and clear the house. There's definitely no one here. The house is empty. There's the faintest hint of mint and lilac on the air, and if I strain I can just about smell a trace of static and cinnamon.

"There's something here," I say. "I can smell magic, or almost smell it. It's odd. It's in the air, but I can't feel the static on my skin. It's here but not."

"Er. We have a problem," Scarlett's voice rings out in my ear.

"What's wrong?" Remy says. And then the audio goes quiet. I hesitate, wondering if I should head back and find out what's wrong. I decide Scarlett can take care of herself. I make my way further into the house poking my head into every room but there's nothing out of the ordinary. Most of the rooms are empty. There's not even any cupboards or storage units. Just empty room after empty room and a film of dust and grime that covers every surface.

I go to leave but notice a strange lattice of lines. A small design emblazoned on the wall at head height by the entrance to each room. It moves as if alive. It's not a symbol I've seen before, but I make a mental note of its shape and design. When I squint, the moving lines almost look like a snake. I leave the room and open the solitary cupboard on the landing, but just like every other room, it's completely empty save for the dust motes and the crinkled corpses of dead spiders.

"This is so weird," I say. But no one responds. "Hello? Guys?" I tap my ear, but nothing comes through, not even a crackling static.

It's almost like there's a field blocking it. But I can't see anything. What, oh what, have you done here Roman? I head downstairs and into the kitchen.

Morrigan's face is pale, her foot right on the edge of the door about to step inside.

"What the hell, Stirling."

"What?" I say confused. "What's wrong?"

"Didn't you hear the audio?"

"No, it cut out the closer I got to the heart of the house."

"Fucksake. I nearly came running in after you."

"What's wrong?"

"Scarlett and Quinn can't get in. There's some kind of forcefield stopping them. They're literally bouncing off the open space as if there's still a door there."

She pokes the air, her head tilted, face crumpled as if she's wincing.

"So why the hell can I get in and no one else can?" I say.

"I have no idea," Morrigan answers.

"New plan, check a couple of the other properties tonight while you're out, we have to know if this is isolated to just the properties you're at, or if this is something else," Remy says over the earpieces.

"Good idea. We're making our way back towards the road. Ping us coordinates," Scarlett says.

"Will do," Remy answers.

Morrigan is already edging away from the door.

"I think the magic is here," I say. "There's a lattice-like symbol on the outside of the rooms. Given I could also smell magic, I think the lattice is protecting the power he's importing."

"We need proof, and to figure out what he's going to do with the magic," Remy says. "Get to the other properties and see if you can dig up anything else tonight."

We check three other properties each. It's the same situation in each one of them. Scarlett, Quinn, and Morrigan can't enter. I'm the only one that can.

Around four in the morning we regroup back at Morrigan's cottage. We're all too exhausted to go over the data and findings so the team take their bedrooms and collapse for the night.

I make my way to my room but as I open the door, Morrigan's hand finds mine and she pulls me into her room.

"Stay with me?"

"You sure?" I ask.

"I have a feeling the cottage won't let any prying eyes see us and I just need..."

She opens the duvet, climbs in and pats the space.

I scoot in next to her. "I'm pretty sure he's paying off palace guards. What if he's told some of them who you are? What if they're watching?"

"He wouldn't. He wouldn't jeopardise his plan like that." She smiles into my chest. "When did our roles change? When did you become the one to think everything through?"

"I guess you rubbed off on me."

She looks up at me, "Will you hold me just for tonight?"

I wrap my arms around her, pulling her back to my chest. She nestles in against me, our bodies finally warming up after being in the cold too long. She wraps her legs around mine, locks my arms tight around her and it takes everything I have to suppress the rising ache. Knowing that even though I have her now, once the investiture is over, she'll leave me this time. Maybe not because she wants to, but because she has to find a consort worthy of a crown.

And that will never be me. Not with my history. Not with an overturned banishment to my name and a legacy that, while it's been restored, is arguably in tatters. Not when I've worked for Roman and betrayed the crown. How can I explain to Calandra it was all for Morrigan?

No, I just have to accept that these last couple of weeks are the last moments we will have together.

If letting her go is best for her, I'll do it. But I'll treasure every single second before then. I nuzzle into her neck and fall asleep to the slow rhythm of her breathing.

CHAPTER 17

MORRIGAN

Five Years Ago

I loathe poker. It's just another game where everyone feels the need to waggle their dicks around, rather than focusing on the game.

I enter the nondescript building. All plain walls and faded whitewash. The club has magic though. As I step over the threshold it curls through my palms. It tingles like the quick fingers of childhood tricks and thievery. There's a hint of cigarette smoke and whiskey too. Best to keep my wits about me then.

I'm led through a warren of dark corridors. Every twist and turn the light grows dimmer until I'm led to a plain door.

The magician gestures for me to enter and closes the door behind me. The room is dim. Muffled talking fills the air and the heavy scent of booze and smoke lingers under the ceiling like a rain cloud. There are at least half a dozen tables, though only three are occupied, a dealer passing cards at each.

I spot the grimoire at the fullest table. Four magicians; three men and one woman with her back to me. The woman has the grimoire. She leans back, kicks her legs up at the table and puffs on a cigarette.

"Come on Brutus, time to play big. Stop giving me such pussy-whipped bets," she says.

I smile inwardly. So she's that type of player.

I make my way toward the table, and the woman pulls the grimoire closer to her. Brutus, the chap in front of her has an enormous scar cutting through his lip, it's feathered like he was kissed by magic. I wonder what he did to piss off a mansion for it to attack him like that.

The dealer nods to me as I take a seat.

"It's a fifty-coin buy in," he says.

I slide him a bag and he pushes a stack of chips toward me.

"If you have other items you wish use as collateral, Jerimus in the corner is the antiquities dealer. He will set your item value."

I shake my head. I came for the grimoire the woman is guarding. Though I notice there's also a huge silver coin far bigger than normal currency, a vial, and a pouch in the middle of the table.

"Raise," Brutus says and slides three more chips into the middle of the table.

The woman removes her long legs from the table and leans forward, her tongue skittering over her lips.

I take her in properly now.

She's absolutely stunning.

Her hair is shoulder-short. It's cut into points as sharp as her ocean-blue eyes. When she smiles, her eyes glitter and my body responds. My breathing hitches, my knickers stick to me. Gods. Who is this woman? I glance down her body. She's wearing a vest top, and her arms are covered in Collection tattoo scars. She's had magic stripped? Interesting.

"Now that's the kind of play I like to see, Brutus ol' chap. Finally found your balls have we?" She winks at me.

I want to roll my eyes at her. Smash her ample ego into pieces. But I just can't seem to bring myself to do anything other than swallow down the lust pooling in my pussy. I push my hair behind my ear, force myself to look away.

"Go fuck yourself, Stirling." He slugs a huge mouthful of blue liquid and glances at the other players.

Both have dark hair and pale skin. They don't look like magicians. I wonder where they're from, but I'm distracted as they fling their chips into the centre of the table.

"Showdown," the dealer says.

One by one, the players reveal their cards. Stirling last.

"Fuck," Brutus growls, as Stirling reveals a full house. Stirling? I know the name, but I can't think why or where I've heard it.

She grins, those eyes sparkling like lightning and storms. She has the kind of look that will be the death of me. She's wearing a thumb ring and holds herself with the charm and ease of an arrogant lesbian. Exactly the kind of woman I like.

I'm in so much trouble.

Stirling reaches to the centre of the table and pulls all the chips, the vial, the bag and coin to her side of the table.

The two players with dark hair huff and leave the table.

"Care to go again, Brutus?" Stirling says and lights up a cigarette drawing a deep pull.

His top lip raises into a snarl.

"I'll take that as a no. Thanks for doing business." She lays her cigarette on an ashtray and pockets the silver coin. I almost miss it, but her shoulders sag. So that's what she was here for. She slings the dealer a handful of coins and reaches for the grimoire, but I slide my hand over hers, stopping the movement.

"Not so fast," I say. "There's still players at the table."

Her eyes fall to where my fingers graze her knuckles and then back up. She captures me in her stare. She smells like bergamot, sandalwood, and a hint of fresh pine or maybe it's mint. My head is woozy; she's the kind of intoxication I could get addicted to. The dealer gets up from the table and busies himself behind the bar.

"You know," she flutters her lashes at me, "if you wanted my attention, all you had to do was ask."

I yank my fingers away. Lean back, let the cold ice queen I keep locked away for occasions just like this ooze out.

"Who says I want *your* attention. I'm here for the game," I say. The room is unnaturally quiet. I glance around. The room is clear. All three tables now empty, save for Stirling, me and the dealer.

The dealer clears his throat from behind the bar. "Shift is over. If you're playing, you're on your own. Lock-in is in five."

"Too bad...?" Stirling says gesturing for my name.

"Morrigan. The name's Morrigan." I tense. I can't let her leave with that grimoire. I've spent a year tracking that grimoire down. I'm not letting her leave with it.

"Morrigan," Stirling says rolling my name around her

mouth as if tasting it. "Cute name for a cute woman." Her eyes sweep my body like she's stripping me one piece of cloth at a time.

So she *is* into women.

I'm going to win this night and the grimoire. The tattoo scars on her arm are mostly a massacre of skin, but one of them is a shape I recognise. She's a negotiator, I'd bet money on it. Let's have a little fun, shall we?

"You're not as good as you think you are, sweetheart..." I say, leaning back in my chair.

"Oh?" Stirling says, raising an eyebrow at me.

"You have a tell."

She recoils in her seat. "Psht please. I'm the best negotiator in New Imperium. I was born without tells." But her expression twitches, like I've hit a nerve. I've got her attention.

"Care to wager that confidence?" I lean, tip my cleavage forward so she gets an eyeful. I lift her cigarette from the ashtray and suck the last draw out and stub it in the tray. Her bottom lip drops open as if she can't believe I'd take her cigarette.

I pull the whiskey bottle from the centre of the table and a spare tumbler and pour myself a shot.

"What are the stakes?" Stirling says.

"Runic poker, three games, winner takes all," I purr the words. I could slip magic through my voice, force her hand. But she's a negotiator, or was. Which means she'll be more resistant than a normal magician to coercion. No. I need to play this cool. Tempt her.

She shuffles the cards. "High stakes, indeed. What's say we raise them a little higher? Lose a round, lose a piece of clothing." She grins as the dealer leaves the bar with a set of keys jangling from his waistband.

"Last chance..." he waggles the keys at us.

"Stirling...?" I ask.

"Morrigan..." she says, her voice low, heady with lust.

There's a pregnant pause where both of us stare at each other, and the intensity makes the hair on my arms stand, my pussy clench. Gods, tonight could be dangerous.

I turn to the dealer. "We'll deal with the lock-in."

CHAPTER 18

MORRIGAN

The next morning, we use a portal orb to call Jacob over breakfast. Remy, Quinn, Stirling and I are all clustered in the kitchen, sleep still crusting our eyes.

"WE MISS YOU," Quinn squeals into the hovering image.

Jacob gives us a toothy grin, "I miss you too. Where's that wife of yours?" he says and runs a hand through his creamy coloured hair.

"Lazy ass is in bed still."

Scarlett appears and slings an arm over Quinn's shoulder to cup her boob, which she promptly squeezes. "Oi. Rude."

Quinn laughs and slaps Scarlett's ass as she goes to the kettle and fills it up at the sink.

"Glad to see nothing has changed in my absence," he smiles into the portal orb.

"These things are so cool," I say to Remy picking up another orb on the table.

"Do I want to know how you created them?" Stirling says.

"I suspect Morrigan would find it interesting but you'd probably take a nap if I went off." Remy smiles.

"For what it's worth, I do want to know. I think they're incredible." I poke the translucent mirage of Jacob's face. "Does that hurt?"

"Does what hurt?" he asks as my finger distorts his image.

Remy laughs. "It's not actually him, Morrigan. It's just a projection. I connected the two orbs through a lattice network of—"

"You're right, we definitely don't care, we just love the fact you made it, you veritable genius," Stirling says and sits down next to Quinn.

"I care," I say and squeeze Remy's shoulder. "Tell me later, we can nerd out while these dimwits fight about pizza."

Scarlett hands out everyone's coffee. Tea for Quinn who tuts and gets up to raid my herb cupboard and sprinkle a concoction into the mug. She fusses with the cupboard, lining everything up until it's straight and face out and then plonks herself down again. When everyone has their cups, we crowd around the projection.

"So how are... things?" Quinn can't quite bring her eyes to meet Jacob's and I have to suppress a smirk. Why Jacob can't tell us that he's got a thing for Malachi I do not know. But I'm pretty sure we've all clocked it.

Malachi appears in the background and settles next to Jacob so he can see us too.

"Quinny," he says waving. His voice is above a whisper now, it's still quiet, but it's definitely tonal. There's a husking rasp under his words because he spent so long voiceless that the chords don't quite work the way they should. But it's amazing to hear him make sounds nonetheless.

"Hey. How's the program going?" she says.

"Really well now I've got help." Mal turns to look at Jacob and there's a longing in the curve of his eyes so acute I actually have to glance away. I can't bear the hunger. It reminds me of the way Stirling looks at me, the way I look at her.

"Most of the soldiers have been reallocated new roles. Some have gone to the Queen's guard, some elected to go back into training. I think we've secured places for at least two dozen at the assassin's guild."

Jacob interrupts. "There's a big group that have stayed and taken on construction work with the architects the queen kindly gifted to us. So we have been working on a program of building works too."

"The last big project is to sort the militia. We've had an armistice--anyone who wants to hand themselves in will be taken through the program and assigned a new job and given an opportunity to start again. But there's a stronghold still in the Never Wood that needs handling."

"Sounds like you've done incredible work already," Scarlett says taking a sip and wincing at the scalding coffee.

"We make a great team," Jacob smiles at Malachi so sweetly my teeth hurt.

Stirling glances at Quinn, a knowing look shared between them. I'm excited for Jacob to discover this part of himself.

"So anyway, what's new with you guys?" Jacob says a slight tinge to his cheeks.

"Oh, you know, the usual. An impossible mission, with an insane deadline, two of our lives at risk and a dry spell hard enough I'm considering relocating to a city where there are single women," Remy says.

The rest of us turn to face her.

"You alright there, Rem?" Quinn says.

"Fine. Just got blue ball-vagina. And you lot all soppy and in love is sickening." She waves us off. "I'm going to dive in the shower and get ready. When you're done, tap the base of the orb. It will shut the projection off."

She leaves and Jacob raises his eyebrows. "That bad?"

I sigh. "It's not great. Mother put a tight deadline on this mission. She wants me to find evidence sufficient to imprison Roman for treason."

"And you're making progress?" Malachi says leaning in close to Jacob so he can see all our faces.

"We know he's buying properties, but they're all off books. We broke in last night but they're all empty," I say.

"I contest the empty. You didn't go in. There was definitely magic in there. I swear he's storing it in the houses. We just need to crack the lattice or whatever it is that's covering it up so we can steal the magic back."

"Hold up, what? Why didn't you go in?" Malachi asks.

"That's the weirdest part, only Stirling could enter," Quinn says sipping her tea.

I stay quiet. Listen. Observe, strategise.

"Every building I went in had the faint stench of magic in the air. But I couldn't see it. Couldn't find it. It's like it was hidden. And then there was some kind of magic field affecting the comms," Stirling says.

I suck in a sharp breath. The first time I ever met Roman we debated what power was. He said, '*I do believe it's you who's mistaken, Princess. You don't need knowledge to control power. Real power, is all about perception. If people believe you wield power, then what is to say you don't'.*

"You okay?" Stirling says knocking me out of my thoughts.

"If you think about it, it makes so much sense. He's hiding the power he's importing in plain sight. That's why he's using the properties in the burbs. No one would ever think to look there because they're *not* magical. Everyone knows if you want magic, you go to the heart of the city. It's all about perception. It's kind of clever," I say.

"I really want to hate that man, but he keeps making such exceptional moves," Remy says.

Stirling fires Remy a dirty stare. "So he's using a lattice field to hide it?"

I nod.

"But that doesn't explain why you were the only one that could enter," Jacob says to Stirling.

"That's the next mystery to solve. None of us have a clue," Quinn says.

"Alongside figuring out what he's going to do with the magic," Stirling adds.

"Well what do the property contracts say?" Malachi asks.

"That's the strangest bit. Remy pulled as many as she could from the public records, but they're all missing names," Scarlett answers.

Jacob laughs, "Well you could always break and enter Roman's office."

Malachi nudges him and laughs. But Stirling isn't laughing. Her face has gone blank, her eyes distant, far off.

"Well good catching up, but we've got to go. Catch you later," Jacob says and the orb goes blank their faces vanishing.

"Stirling? You alright?" Scarlett gives her sister a soft shake.

"He has a filing cabinet in his office. It's enormous. What if he's keeping paper records instead? Because there has to be a record, right? He can't transfer a property unless there's some record of it. The only way that doesn't happen is—"

"Is if the property is dying and the magic is taken," Remy says reappearing. Her slender figure is dressed in shorts and a sports bra, a towel ruffing her hair dry.

"Right," Stirling says.

"But we know the clever bastard is importing magic from other cities. I still wish I'd come up with that," Remy adds and puts two pieces of toast in the toaster.

I've been studying property transfers and we're missing the point. "He's using non-magical houses to store imported magic. The only time magic reverts to the owner is if the house is magic in the first place."

Everyone turns to me, as if they only just remembered I was in the room. I stand up, leave the room and go to my library picking up a book on property transfer magic.

I drop it on the table to an open page. "Read the line. There's nowhere that says the transfer of magic or legal ownership has to be public record. What the law says is that the exchange of coin needs to be recorded to prevent embezzling. The irony is that no magician ever considered the fact someone might be embezzling magic. Son of a bitch." I slam the book shut.

Stirling stands. "We need to get into his office. We have to check that cabinet and check the coin transfer records. If we could break the lattice and get the records, it would be enough proof to put him away."

Quinn sits up. "Well, Roman is hosting a party in honour of the palace, isn't he? It's in a couple of days."

"And it's in his club," Scarlett adds, her eyes soft, lust making her lids heavy.

"Ladies," Stirling snaps. "Stop thinking with your libidos. If we're going to the party it's to orchestrate a break in, not fuck in the sex rooms."

"But we could do both..." Quinn says.

"You know, after we break in or whatever..." Scarlett grins.

The pair of them are insatiable, have been since they finally decided to get over whatever nonsense they had going on and just get together.

"Remy. How do you feel about hacking the most secure nightclub in the city?" Stirling says.

"Well I'm the only one here not getting laid, so it's not like I've actually got anything better to do is it?"

"Hold up, let's just think this through. Stirling, what if we get caught? What if *you* get caught? We need you in place close to him for as long as possible. You need to unearth his plan for the investiture. I don't know if putting you in this position is a good idea. Maybe we just go back to the properties and try and remove the field," I say.

Scarlett reaches for my shoulder and rubs it. "I think it's a pretty solid plan, Morrigan. I know it's risky, but we need unequivocal proof that he's breaking the law and in control of that much power and in all likelihood it's going to be in his office. That club is a fort if you're not there with an invite. Stirling is our inside man. She can handle this," Scarlett says.

"Agreed," Quinn says.

My heart pounds inside my ribs. We should've found the magic in the houses. We're getting too close to him.

"The club will be crawling with press. What if they catch us? What if I'm outed before we have a chance to secure evidence?" I say.

"This is our chance to get the evidence," Stirling pushes. She reaches for my hand. "Besides what if he has physical attack plans too? We might be gathering evidence of his crimes, but we still don't know what he's planning for the investiture."

"I..." I start.

"What's the problem? It's not like you to doubt. We're doing what you planned, we're thinking before we act. We're planning this out. It's going to work." Stirling squeezes my hand.

"But the plan is to break into a secure office in the most popular nightclub in the entire city on the busiest club night in a decade. With every royal from ten cities, every legacy and magician on the site. And we're what? Just hoping we won't get caught?"

"Exactly," Stirling beams.

CHAPTER 19

STIRLING

I knew he was coming before the dawn sun rose over the ocean. I sensed him in the air like a bristling wind and the static of lightning desperate to land.

Roman was pissed, and I got it. I hadn't given him anything useful, yet. But then, that was the point, wasn't it? Keep him at arm's length, give him what I find as late as possible so Morrigan and the rest of the team have enough time to build a case of evidence that he can't escape.

As the sun crested the horizon, the ocean glittered like stars and diamonds. Watery warmth caressed my skin, making the job of attaching rigging considerably easier. Once I'd finished waterproofing, the harbour guys helped me move the boat and it's now docked with all the other ships.

I paused, knowing I'm about to be interrupted. *Focus, run over the plan, Stirling*. The thought of me enacting a plan makes me laugh. Perhaps Morrigan is influencing me after

all. Though I'm loath to tell her there's something benefi-
cial to all the strategising.

This morning is critical. If I know Roman the way I
think I do, he'll react with aggression. And then I'll play him
just like Morrigan wanted and hand him what I've dug up.

My fingers ache from yanking the ropes. I rub my
hands, kneading my thumb into my palm.

A way in the distance, a school of dolphins rise and leap
out of the water, playing and splashing, waiting for the
fishermen to bring in the morning haul so they can steal the
escaping fish.

Claude spent the better part of an hour helping. I was
surprised to see him pre-dawn, but he said he couldn't
sleep. He's struggled to sleep ever since his wife passed.
Claude makes a swift exit the moment Roman's footsteps
slam into the wooden dock. His feet assault the planks so
hard I'm not quite sure how he hasn't put his foot through
one. As he draws nearer, his steps soften and cease as he
steps onto the boat.

"Little Stir."

"Good morning, Roman." I hand him the end of a piece
of rope, and he steadies himself, placing his feet wide. I tug
the knot until it's tight.

"Thanks," I say as I take it off him. "Hands hurt after an
hour of this."

He presses his lips shut and admires the boat.

"It's yours?"

I nod. The distraction working to ease the stiffness in
his shoulders. Sure, he's pissed at me, but at least I can take
the poison out of his sting. Besides he'll be smiling shortly.

"Here, help me lift this, it weighs a fucking ton."

Together we lift the rudder over the stern and slot it
into place.

"You built this?" he said.

"Building. It's almost finished. This has been my project for the last couple of years."

I pick a rag up off the deck and drop it casually over the bow, hiding Morrigan's sculpture.

"Well, I didn't come to help you build. I came because you're supposed to be earning yourself a promotion, and yet you've given me nothing."

I sigh, open a flask of coffee. I rifle in one of the boat's cupboards and pull a second cup out.

"It's not hot anymore, but it's drinkable."

I hand him the mug and take a sip of my own coffee.

"Stop prevaricating, I've got shit to do today," he says, and there under the breeze is the first change in tension, his eyes narrow--the air tightens and I know this is his hard limit. My fingers trace the scarred line along my arm. The bastard bites, I know that better than anyone.

I pull out a file from one of the cupboards on the boat.

"Palace schematics. This should help you lay out your plan of attack. It has every entrance and exit, every hidden wall route, and a few extras."

He snatches it and flicks through the pages. "Is this it? I sent you off days ago and this is all you bring me? Hardly worthy of a promotion."

I figured he would say that, no matter how much I gave him to begin with. Which is exactly why I only gave him the schematics.

"Daria," I say and gaze out to the ocean as I take a sip of lukewarm coffee.

"Daria?"

I nod. "I met her the other day at the palace. She's Calandra's head of security. If you want access to Calandra, or the palace, it's Daria you need to take out."

Roman snorts, "You think that is sufficient?

I sigh audibly, make a show like his irritation has put me out.

"I think handing you a key to enter the palace, at whatever time of day or night, is more than nothing. But perhaps it's not enough to satisfy your hunger."

"You want the promotion. Would you give it to you based off that scrap of information?"

I smile, the morning sun now rising in the sky, showering us in a kaleidoscope of watery orange and pale pinks.

"You didn't ask me to conduct a break-in, you didn't ask me to kill anyone or commit any crimes for the promotion. You asked me to bring you information. Daria's name is information, *Roman*. So are the schematics. Always specify the verbiage. You should know better."

He lunges fast, his hand around my throat. My face instantly heats from the pressure and lack of oxygen.

I steel myself. Force my mind to calm and not react to the bruising pressure of his fingers.

But then, I don't need to react. I'm holding a three-inch knife to his gut. One flick of my wrist and he'll christen my boat with blood. I can't say that though because his vicelike grip is crushing my airway.

I press the knife into his abs just enough he hisses. His eyes draw down my body to the knife in my hand. He lets me go.

"You hurt me once. I won't be fooled again." My fingers automatically skim the mottled skin on my arm where he'd 'taught me a lesson'. Roman's lips draw into a fetid sneer.

"Or would you rather have a meek, submissive right-hand woman? Hmm?" I slide the blade back into the secret pocket in my waistband.

He tilts his head, examining me. I know he's impressed.

Of course he is. This was all part of my play.

A negotiation of wills.

I wanted to rile him up. Irritate him enough I took him right to the line. That's where a person's will is the most vulnerable. That's where I can manipulate the easiest. Everyone thinks Scarlett is the deadlier twin. They're wrong. I am. She might be able to break a body, but I can break a mind.

"You're right. You wouldn't be in this position if you were weak." He walks up and down the boat, running a hand along the gunwale. "But I'm not happy."

"What if I get you the guards' schedule too? I'll have Daria followed, steal the guard roster for the investiture."

He nods. "Better. Not perfect."

I narrow my eyes at his back, trying to form a plan and think it through before I react, just like Morrigan would want.

But I realise I can't. I'm missing something, and the only way to get it is to dig deep and react to whatever he gives me.

"What is it you want, Roman? What is really going on? You want the palace, but where's the plan? The finesse? You're not a man lacking in vision. Tell me, so I can help you."

He rounds on me, leans against the hull. "I had a way into the palace once upon a time."

He did? "What do—"

"It doesn't matter. That path is long dead. The point is, I'm owed, and I want what's rightfully mine."

"And what is yours?"

"The crown, Stirling. Either they give me a crown, or I take it by force. I wasn't born to serve, I was born to lead."

I don't understand what he's saying. How can he be

owed anything? The ocean waters are still but I'm off balance.

Who the hell is he? It's like he's given me a single thread in a golden quilt. Somewhere the stitches all meet and there lies the truth of who he is, what he's doing. But this is more than he's ever given me, and I don't want to lose it.

This is where Morrigan's plans fall down. Because how could she predict this? How could this be the plan B or C? This is not something any of us knew. So I capitalise. I think fast, an idea forming to hook him in.

"Then take it."

He laughs. "And how, precisely, do you propose I do that?"

I think fast. Trixie said she saw Roman with Pen. If Roman is busy with Pen, and Pen is busy with Roman, she won't be going for the throne. And Roman will be distracted enough we could frame him, set him up. This is a solid idea.

I stand tall. "How does anyone get a crown without a birthright? Marriage."

This makes him roar. He kicks his head back, a deep rumble echoing out like cannons.

I fold my arms. "You met Penelope the other night. She's ambitious, hungry. She hates Morrigan. I'd be willing to bet she'd take your hand in marriage just to spite her. Imagine that. Penelope the princess unites the underworld with the crown. She'd shit all over Morrigan's investiture."

My magic hums under my skin. It turns my words to liquid silk, so they tie loops and knots around Roman, snaring him in a net he can't escape. It is inevitable. I will win this, I will protect Morrigan, I will find a way to imprison him. It's the least he deserves after everything he's done. And what a play by me, if I do say so myself. The perfect suggestion. He thinks I hate Morrigan for the lies, for the fact her mother destroyed my family. So making an outlandish suggestion like this is the perfect cover.

"It's the political play of the century," I add, tempting him.

There's a dark glint in Roman's eye. It grows like the rising moon at midnight, a silver-promise full of potential.

My magic deepens and throbs, oozing into the space between us, surrounding us like meshes and blankets, like a siren song neither of us can hear.

"Marry a princess... just like that?" he says.

"Well, hardly like that. But a little birdie told me you already made an impression on Penelope at the ball. I'm sure you can turn the Roman charm on and draw her in."

He straightens up. "Well, well, Stirling. It appears you're a master strategist after all."

I want to laugh. Oh how Morrigan would spit and froth at Roman's words. She thinks I can't be strategic because I think on my feet. But this is the game play to end all game plays.

"Fine. The promotion stays on the cards. For now. But do better Stirling. I want the crown and you're going to give it to me."

He steps off the boat and back into the harbour and I sag against the hull.

It's only then I turn his words over again. *'I want what was promised to me, what I'm owed.'*

What the hell was he promised?

The night of the DnD party, we all get ready together at Morrigan's cottage. There's a carriage due to pick us up at 7:30pm but currently, there's a frightfully rhythmic thumping coming from Scarlett's room and I'm pretty sure I saw Quinn sneak in there twenty minutes ago.

"They're fucking again, aren't they?" Remy says leaning against my doorway.

"Dayum girl, I don't think you're going to have any issues getting laid tonight. You look fine."

She's wearing a white jumpsuit the same colour as her hair. It nips in and gives her usually pencil-straight figure the appearance of a waist. Her boobs are strapped into an uplift bra and she holds the jacket over her shoulder, looking the picture of a badass ice queen.

"Thanks Stir. I'm not really that desperate. But you guys are rampant at the moment."

"No one turned your eye recently?"

She shrugs, "I love my job. I love the industry and magic. I've not met the girl who makes me want to put her above it all."

"You will. And not to be a total cliché but it will be when you least expect it."

She smiles, tips her head in a nod at me, and leaves. I glance in the mirror. She's right, I do look good. I'm in a black and grey checked suit. It's tight fitting and I'm wearing a lace corset style top underneath.

If my jacket moves too much one way or the other, you can definitely see some nip. I better keep the jacket done up. I button it and slip the brogue shoes on, smear a sweep of liner over my lids, and grab the hair spray and spritz a few more squirts over my hair. It's straightened and set sharp at my jawline, a little lower at the front than the back. I take a look and admire myself. We're good to go.

I make my way downstairs into the living room and stop dead.

"Fuck. Me," the words splutter out before I even have a

chance to stop them. Morrigan stands between the sofas looking like a goddess. She's in a black dress that's slit on both sides. Lace threads criss-cross over her hips. The top of the dress is strapless, and corseted tight. Tight enough her breasts bulge out the top.

Remy sidles up behind me and pushes my chin up to close my mouth. "Catching flies there, bud."

I blink, shake myself out of it and stutter out. "Wow."

Morrigan flushes. Her hair is in a smooth chignon updo, and she pushes a loose strand behind her ear. "Thank you. You look incredible yourself."

Remy coughs. "Oh you look amazing too, Rem. Really fashionable. Jumpsuit lights up your eyes. Blah blah." She smirks at us.

But I just roll my eyes. She knows I think she looks good.

Scarlett and Quinn finally appear and they also look incredible. Scarlett's wearing a fitted suit like me. Hers is dark green though, matching Quinn's body con dress. And while they look smart in their outfits, they're clearly tousled. I raise an eyebrow at Scarlett.

She shrugs at me. "What? Look at her. She was asking for it, dressed like that."

"And you couldn't wait until later?"

"Would you?"

She has a point, so I concede. If I could tear Morrigan out of that dress I would. To be fair, I'd happily bend her over and fuck into bliss while still wearing it. I adjust my underwear and force myself to think about the list of deals I need to finalise for clients. Anything so long as I get the image of me smashing Morrigan's delicious ass all night long out of my head.

"Right. Ready ladies? Our carriage awaits," Morrigan says.

We file out of the living room, Morrigan bringing up the rear.

"You look stunning," I whisper.

She smiles, her eyes glimmering under the smokey eyeshadow. She leans into my ear. "I'm not wearing any underwear."

I straighten. She saunters off out the front door.

Out.

Rageous.

That does it for my willpower. She doesn't get to tease me like that without getting fucked into a sopping mess.

CHAPTER 20

MORRIGAN

The carriage ride doesn't take long. We pull to a stop outside DnD in what feels like a blink. When we step out, we're greeted by a mob of paparazzi, flashes of white and a chorus of questions, name-calling, and shouts of this way, look here, and answer a question or two.

I step on to the red carpet, followed by the rest of the team, and I'm immediately swamped by dignitaries and royals all jostling to get inside the club.

There are two bouncers on the doors, impossibly large magicians with hands as big as my face. I wonder what magic they harbour, because their bodies seem to expand and contract as they greet guests and the dignitaries pass into the building. I make a mental note to research appearance magic. Then I scold myself for not studying it prior to this mission. It would have been significantly easier to just appear to be Roman and pass through the venue undetected.

The bouncers ask for our names and scan a list. When they're satisfied, we pass through. The building is in fine form, sending a rush of sensation like fingers sliding up my thighs and under the lace at my hips. The air smells deep and heady like sex and cigarette smoke. For a moment, it's ten years ago, and I'm here with Roman. My skin flushes with goosebumps. Not because of him, but because I still haven't told Stirling.

I'm handed a black goodie bag as soon as I step over the threshold and the memories vanish. I glance inside, and there are toys. Adult ones. There's even a strapless strap-on. I pull it out and examine it--an egg shape on one end for insertion and anchoring, and a full vibrating cock for the recipient. How delicious.

The staff member distributing the bag grins at me. "When the egg is inside, it makes the cock sit in a naturally erect position. It's genius, really."

"Ooh, you got one too," Stirling says.

I flinch. I stand a little straighter, my pussy wet at the thought of Stirling using this on me. Now is not the time, but Stirling must have the same thought because her eyes darken, an intense hunger cloaking her expression.

"We have a mission," I say.

"Yes, and a girl has needs. Perhaps I could focus better if they were attended to. Besides..." she leans in close, close enough her warm breath trickles down my neck as she whispers into my ear. "I'm not the one who left the house without underwear on."

She runs her fingers up the flesh of my thigh, the split in the dress giving her all the access she needs. Her fingers inch under the split, stroking up, up, up until she's millimetres from my swollen pussy.

I gasp and grab her wrist. "Focus...! And if you're a good

girl, I'll reward you later." My voice is a purr and a growl, a promise and a warning. I push past her grinning expression and gasp as I round the corner into the main club area.

"What the—" I say.

"He had the architects come in and rework the building structure especially for the party," Stirling says drawing close to me. Her hand settles so close to mine I can feel the heat from her fingers. I want to lace mine into hers, I want to pull her around and press my lips to hers and never let go. I want to fist my hand through her hair and pull her down to my cunt.

But I can't until later. Tonight is too critical. I need to stay alert, not be preoccupied with the need slicking my thighs. If we're successful, then we'll celebrate in style.

Tonight, when the crowd is at its peak and everyone is distracted, we'll break into his office, get into his filing cabinets, and get the hell out. We need to know why Stirling is able to access his properties and the rest of us weren't. What's his play? What is Roman hiding that could screw us over? There are too many variables, and we need to cut them off at the neck.

Remy sidles up to Stirling and I. She slips earpieces into our hands and continues walking into the heart of the remodelled club.

"Woah," Scarlett says as she pulls up behind me and itches her ear, a feint. Standing so close I see the earpiece slip into her ear canal. "It looks totally different to the other day."

Quinn appears, her mouth dropping in surprise.

"Architects worked fast," Stirling says.

I observe the newly modelled club. We're in a circular room. The main area is a sunken pit, the perimeter of which is a sweeping set of stairs descending around and into the pit. Dotted in the lower area are dozens of round tables with poles on them. Each one with at least one dancer. The walls are shiny black, and every few feet is a door. They're backlit, cycling from black to grey to opaque white. The shadow of bodies fucking behind them shiver across the perspex and then vanish as the lights drop to black. Each door is marked with a symbol of figures indicating the kind of kink you'll find behind it.

In the centre of the pit is a circular bar. It's heaving, but I need a drink, so we head for a table. Stirling, Scarlett, and Remy go to the bar, Quinn and I secure seats around a pole with a triad of dancers. Two women and a man.

As we sit, the women strip their knickers off and continue to dance, naked save the tassels hanging off their nipples. The man dancing with them has a raging boner and honestly, I'm not surprised. I'm having a hard time focusing on the team and the plan. It's almost like there's something in the air.

The women dance together, their fingers locked as they pirouette around the pole. One climbs up the pole and then with the grace of a ballerina, splits her legs, baring her bald pussy to us. Quinn's cheeks flush.

The woman slides down the pole until her pussy is the height of the other woman's head—who happily leans in and swipes her tongue down the dancer's flesh. They lock eyes and the woman on the pole mouths the words, "Fuck me."

The other woman obliges, lapping and sucking at her pussy. The dancer arches her back, pulls the man's underwear out of the way, and takes his cock in her mouth, sucking him deep enough she gags.

On the tables are little saucers of mushrooms, a hazy

purple smoke shimmering up from them. There are also decanters of a similarly shimmering liquid.

I glance at Remy who returns carrying three drinks between her hands.

"Drugs?" she asks.

I lean forward, take the tiniest of sniffs and immediately recoil. "Fuck," I say as the room warms and glows and my body loosens. Want, like glistening gold and melted desire, courses through my body. Fucking idiot. What the hell was I thinking smelling the smoke?

"Sex magic," Remy says.

"More like 'gives you a raging girl-boner magic' and you don't even need to eat them, they're so potent you'll get high off the fumes."

I grip the sides of the table, my clit throbbing so hard I think I'm going to pass out. I bite down a moan as my pussy clenches at the thought of sex. This is not good. Stirling barrels over, carrying the rest of our drinks, Scarlett follows suit with a tray of shots in her arms.

"We do have a job to do," Remy says laughing and picking up a glass anyway.

"Ooh, pretty," Stirling says and leans over the saucer of mushrooms.

"N–" I start, but it's too late.

"Woah," she says standing straight her eyeballs blown wide.

"Gods," Remy says. "Are we all just getting shitfaced now?"

"I suspect that was Roman's aim. Besides, there's hardly anyone here yet, We've got time to sober up." Quinn promptly leans over the saucer to inhale the smoke too.

"Quinn," Scarlett snaps. But Quinn grabs Scarlett's jacket and pulls her down so she breathes in the scent too.

"A little fun won't hurt. It's early, hey, Morrigan?"

Doesn't matter what I say, Scarlett's pupils are so wide, she's whacked off her ta-tas.

Gods. My legs shake under the table, and I swear to gods if I don't sit on Stirling's face in about three seconds someone is going to get sacrificed.

Remy rubs her hands together, "Looks like it's going to be a team effort tonight." She leans over the saucer and sniffs the shimmery smoke. She whistles, her eyes now as wide as Stirling's.

"We've got a long night ahead. I suppose there's no harm in taking a moment to enjoy it. One hour, we all regroup. Agreed?" Remy says, her eyes landing on a door in the far corner that indicates orgies.

My jaw stiffens. Logic tells me we should just stay here, bide our time till the club is full. But I have a need over-riding everything right now. And the more I stare at Stirling, the stronger the need grows. Stirling gazes at me with the heat of a sun, as if she can't make up her mind whether she wants to eat me or fuck me.

Everyone nods agreement.

Remy leaves first darting straight to the orgy door and vanishing inside. Quinn stands and pulls out a set of hand-cuffs from the goodie bag she was given, straps it to Scarlett's wrist and hauls her off towards one of the rooms.

And then there's only Stirling and I.

"Is this a good idea?" Stirling says.

"It is if you make Roman think you're luring me in." I'm already standing. I glance at my hand, still holding the strapless strap-on. "Make sure he sees, do that wink thing you do to make him think you've got me under your thumb."

She scans the room and I know the moment she's

locked eyes with him. I busy myself with the goodie bag toys hunting for anything else.

"Done," Stirling says.

"Good. Now, are you coming?"

"Not yet, but you will be." She grins at me.

I pull her by the hand, leaving the table and marching towards the door with two women on it. I suspect the only way any of us will focus is to rid ourselves of this insatiable drug-induced lust through an orgasm or two.

I open the door, wrap my hand around Stirling's neck and pull her in, pressing my lips to hers. The door closes automatically behind us.

When I pull myself off her and gasp for air, I notice a woman bound in shibari ropes. Her arms tied behind her, ropes crisscrossing her breasts and torso. She hangs from the ceiling. Her legs are spread wide and two women kneel beneath her, one licking her pussy and the other lapping at her arsehole. Her head is tilted back but she can scarcely moan for the ball gag wedged into her mouth. She twitches and grunts as waves of orgasm rip through her and she sprays the women beneath her in come.

The room has ample furniture, beds, chairs, chains, boxes and an array of leather straps and devices to bind and gag those willing.

"There," I say. Nestled in the back of the room are small booths designed for privacy. It's not that I mind fucking in public. I've gotten off more than once being watched. But this close to the investiture, I don't want my face remembered for the expression when I come. It's hardly befitting a queen, is it?

I pull Stirling towards the booths.

"Shame, I'd have rather enjoyed binding you up so I could have my way with you."

"I didn't say you couldn't." I grin at her.

She raises an eyebrow.

"Later."

I step inside the booth. It's tiny. There's only the bed and some straps on the wall. The room is dark, mood lit with red lighting. The ceiling is painted black and sprinkled with little lights that twinkle like stars, and I wonder how long it will be before I'm seeing stars too. I close the door and push Stirling against it.

My body flares, sending flames of heat through my body. Stirling pushes that loose lock of hair behind my ear.

She slides her hands through the slits in my dress, grabs my thighs, picks me up and throws me on the bed.

Gods, it makes sparks of pleasure shoot through me when she owns me like this. Such a juxtaposition to what I should want: submissive, pliant lovers. I can't stand lovers who treat me with deference. Stirling's never done that, unless I've asked, of course. Every time I give myself to her, she marks me, owns me, and makes me hers.

She climbs on top of me, leaving a trail of kisses across my dress, teasing me by peppering my skin and pulling back.

She yanks my dress down until my breasts spill out and takes one in her mouth, sucking and nipping at the bar piercing. I moan into her, arching my back as a shock of electricity ploughs into my body. She breaks away, leans up, and takes my chin between her fingers.

"You are everything," she says.

The way she looks at me freezes time. Her eyes trace the outlines of every tattoo as if my body is a work of art. She doesn't rush, just showers me in kisses as if Roman, the investiture, the mission, none of it exists in this moment. It makes me wonder if she is the real magic.

How is it one woman can command my soul the way she does? It's as if she were made only for me and I for her.

I breathe in the scent of her skin. She smells like oceans and wood. Like a thousand years of worship and the sweet perfume my heart craves.

It's right here, laid beneath her, with her ocean-coloured eyes holding me like precious gems in her gaze, that I realise I will never stop loving her. No matter how mad I am, no matter how much she enrages me, she stole my heart five years ago and I'm never getting it back.

As much as the drugs are driving up my lust, they're driving up my emotions too. Everything I feel for her compounds. My chest aches like there's a blade between my ribs, my heart throbs like it's caught in a snare. I want to laugh and cry. I want to pull her close and push her away. I want Imperium to bend the knee and for us to reign free. The room brightens and pulses. The beat of red light pumps through my veins like fuel.

"You're thinking too hard," she says and wipes a stray tear making its way towards my ear. But I know by the way she's looking at me, that her mind has met me in the same place. The bittersweet confusion of want and hurt.

"Then make me stop," I breathe.

She kisses me so deep, so pure, our tongues caress each other like long lost lovers. When she breaks away, there's a furrow in her brow.

"What's wrong?"

"I'm afraid of what happens at the end of this. I'm afraid your mother will never allow me to stay by your side and I don't think I can lose you again."

My whole body wrenches like she's gutting me. This is the first time she's said the thing we both fear out loud. I'm terrified too. There are a thousand reasons we can't be together: her tattered legacy, her banishment, my need to produce an heir, the secrets I still haven't spilled. Like Roman— I stop the thought. I don't want him invading my mind right now.

Stirling brushes a thumb across my cheek, bringing me out of my thoughts and back to her.

I clasp my hand to hers. "I don't want to lose you either. But for the first time in my life, I don't have a plan." The words pour out of my mouth, I know it's the drugs talking. I keep secrets like this stowed away. These aren't words for sharing, and yet they're tumbling out of my mouth like sand.

She huffs out a laugh, "You picked a hell of a time to stop planning."

"Stirling...?"

"Yeah?"

"Stop talking. Just be... with me. Right now. Let's not worry about what comes next. Let's not worry about the future. Let's just be together right now."

She smile-shakes her head at me, as if she can't believe the words leaving my mouth, and honestly neither can I.

I reach for the strap-on and hand it to her.

She unbuttons her trousers and slips them off along with her underwear and corset top. Then she pushes the egg inside her, making the cock bounce up into position.

"Oooh... it's kind of impressive, whoever desi—" she shuts her mouth as I hit the vibrate button on the remote and waves of pleasure course through her.

Her cheeks grow pink, the drug-induce lust firing up the closer she gets to fucking me. She pulls my dress flap aside, displaying my pussy.

Then she pounces, grabbing my thighs, pulling me down the bed until my arse is on the edge. She kneels between my legs and draws her tongue down my slick cunt. My eyes shut against the warmth of her wet tongue separating my folds. It sends tingles from my clit to my spine.

I gasp.

I moan.

My fingers scrunch the silk bedding.

Stirling thrusts her tongue inside me, eliciting a deep, carnal moan.

"Stop teasing me and fuck me, Stirling." I grab tufts of her hair and pull her up until her lips are over my clit. I rock my hips against her mouth, my whole body quivering as her tongue teases my apex, slow then fast, hard then soft. I soak her with my excitement, but it only makes her lap faster. Her fingers dig into the flesh of my thighs hard enough to bruise, and it only makes me drench her more.

My legs quiver against her cheeks, my core dissolving into pleasure as waves of starlight course through me.

When I'm dripping wet, and desperate to tip over the edge, Stirling stops and stands, the cock still erect. I reach for the remote, ramp up the vibrations inside Stirling. She buckles as she adjusts to the new sensation. I wiggle up the bed, making room for her.

She laces one of her hands through mine and guides the cock to my entrance.

She looks up at me, catching my eyes, waiting for permission. I nod, and she pushes inside me, slow at first, then a little quicker. Until she's thrusting so deep that I gasp from the fullness.

She reaches for the remote, a devilish grin spreading across her lips and she hits all of the buttons.

The cock buzzes to life inside me and I roll back, unable to speak. She slides her hand around my head, I lock my legs around her back and then she drives into me, pumping in long hard strokes. The vibrations flood through both of us. The ripples of pleasure-threads we feel simultaneously bind us, connect us, and ground us in this moment.

She kisses me like the universe exists in my lips, like I'm made of gold and secrets, and I suppose in a way, I am. Deeper and deeper she kisses, her hips pumping the cock inside me. I suck her bottom lip between my teeth, it makes her thrust a little faster, her moans a little louder.

The vibrations must be on a timer because they speed up, causing both of us to moan. The room spins, our bodies drown in each other, in ecstasy. She cups my face, draws her lips down my jaw as a swell of emotion rushes from my clit to my core.

I want her.

Only her.

Forever.

"Stirling," I pant her name as she smothers me in kisses. "Make me come," I moan.

She snaps to attention, pulls the cock out and flips me onto my front. She drags me up and back so I'm on all fours and thrusts the cock back inside me hard and fast. My pussy clenches around the shaft, tensing and quivering as the vibrations drill into me. Stirling pumps faster, her hands dragging nails down my back. She draws me up by the throat, holds me tight against her breasts. Her fingers hold my neck with just enough pressure to know she owns me. That I am hers, now and always.

I lean away, resist enough she tightens her grip. It winds me higher, sends bolts of pleasure to my pussy. As if she can read my body like a book, she reaches a hand around to my clit and rubs in time to her thrusts, pushing me higher and tighter, until I close my eyes, panting, and moaning and she makes both of us come undone.

We collapse on the bed, our bodies still joined by the cock. She slides in and out once, twice more until we're both quivering in pieces, both seeing stars in the ceiling and behind our eyes. I flick the remote off before I destroy myself completely tonight.

But finally, finally, the orgasm has drained the drug out of my system. The room lightens, the desire lifts, and the two of us are left holding each other in the knowledge that we're irrevocably in love. That our bodies confessed what our mouths could not.

And that is utterly terrifying.

CHAPTER 21

STIRLING

And this is why they tell you drugs are bad. When Morrigan and I emerge from the sex room, something has shifted between us. We're not just Stirling and Morrigan anymore. We're not squabbling, we're not broken lovers. We're something more, something bigger, something tighter. We're connected in a way that terrifies and excites me, and I don't understand how we can make it through this.

It doesn't matter what we want, her mother will see to it that she's married to the perfect consort. And that thought makes me want to fall apart and burn the palace to the ground in equal measure. I will not let her go without a fight. Not after everything.

But there isn't time to figure that out tonight. An hour has past, and we need to meet the rest of the team back at the table. We're the last to arrive, but not the only ones with red cheeks and wrinkled clothing.

"No more drugs," Remy says, and wipes her forehead.

With wide, startled eyes, everyone nods in agreement.

"Everyone got their earpieces reattached?"

We all nod, and Quinn places hers back in lightning fast. The club is absolutely heaving now. There are bodies everywhere, all of them as mashed off their tits as we were an hour ago.

"We need to use the fact they're not all fucking the drugs out of their system as cover. While the floor is still busy, we can sneak out back undetected," I whisper. I don't need to speak loud anymore, not with the earpieces in, everyone can hear my voice inside their heads.

"Remy, you ready?" Morrigan says.

"I'll leave now. I left a carriage two streets away with my tech gear set up in it. You're all wearing the orb-broaches which will give me a view of what you can see. Good luck, and don't fuck it up."

She squeezes my shoulder and Morrigan's hand and then she's pushing her way out of the club.

A few minutes later, her voice crackles in my ear.

"Testing. Testing. This is Remy. Can you hear me?"

"Loud and clear," Scarlett says.

"Everyone check in," Remy says.

"Here," Quinn, Morrigan and I say.

"Great. I've opened up the viewing screen, so ready when you are."

I give Scarlett a hard stare, "You two are the lookouts. Make sure no one follows us. I still need to find the door to his office because the architects have moved everything."

We make our way through the crush of bodies, sweat pours off the dignitaries, hips and asses gyrate into each other in a rhythmic beat that matches the music's bass.

"I've run a scan, and the schematics for the building match the original. So you're not seeing the real layout. I can't help you find the original office door but it will be in there," Remy says.

"Split up. You start that end of the room," I say to Morrigan.

Scarlett and Quinn take up strategic positions, Quinn dancing on the edge, her body moving in time with the crowd, but her eyes focused on the guards, the wall and us. Scarlett stays a few feet away. She's sourced a drink and looks as though she's taking a short dance break.

I place my back against the circular room wall and my hands flat. I inch my way around the room feeling for any crack in the smooth surface. But I come up short.

I meet Morrigan in the middle. "Nothing?"

"Me neither," she says.

I glance at Roman, who has sauntered onto the main stage. He raises his hands to quieten the music and audience.

When the crowd is settled and silent, he opens his arms.

"Welcome honoured guests. It's a pleasure to have you here this evening. I won't take up much of your evening. But what I will say is that there will be an exciting announcement later this evening. Do make sure you hang around to find out what it is."

There's a cheer and then Roman nods at the DJ who makes the music flare to life again.

"Announcement?" Morrigan looks at me.

I shrug. "No idea."

There's a crackle in my ear that makes my inner ear itch. Then Remy's voice comes through, "Ladies, we have a prob—."

There's static, a muffled scream, more static, banging and the splitting of wood. My eyes bug wide.

"Scarlett? Go. Remy's in trouble."

Scarlett sprints off the dance floor, her hand slipping to her waistband. Quinn glances between us and Scarlett but decides to stay. She can handle herself in a fight, but she's no trained assassin.

Morrigan and I jump back into action. The office door isn't in the main room, so we decide to check the reception corridor.

"Follow me," I say. And one by one, Quinn, Morrigan and I proceed keeping our movements as spaced apart as possible without losing sight of each other.

I slip out the exit and freeze. There's a guard.

"Quinn. Morrigan. Assistance."

As soon as she appears, Morrigan's fingers bend into a circular shape, a shimmer and haze snaps, and the sound of the club instantly mutes. She's created some kind of mirage.

The guard frowns and kicks off the wall.

"I got this," Quinn says.

She stumbles forward and then slips, her arms flinging up. The guard lurches forward to stop her falling. There's a flash of movement, a waft of shimmery powder and the guard drops to the floor.

"Oh bravo, Quinn," I say and lean a hand against the wall. It jars and I almost fall through it. "Ha. It was in the same place all along, just the opposite side of the wall. Right, put him in the cupboard," I say and indicate the wall a little further down. Then I slip inside, Morrigan right behind me.

Quinn shuts the wall door and I assume leans against it to prevent anyone else from entering. The moment the door closes, the noise and thumping beat of the club room vanishes completely. Even with Morrigan's mirage lowering the music, the shock of the silence makes my ears rush with static.

Scarlett's voice cuts through the earpiece. "I got Remy. She's been beaten bad. Two of the guards followed her out. I'm going to take her back to Quinn's shop. Quinn, can you meet us here after you're done? I'll patch her up best I can till then."

My arms flush with goosebumps, a sickness coiling in my gut.

"She'll be okay. We have to keep going. This is the only chance we'll get. No one is paying any attention."

She brushes a palm over my cheek, her eyes soft, expression warm.

"Okay," I say.

We tiptoe up the glass steps, keeping our backs pressed against the wall in the shadows to prevent anyone looking up outside and seeing us. Tiptoeing makes the climb agonising, every step slow and arduous, but eventually, we reach the top of the building. I hold her back, press a finger to my lips as we reach his office door.

I slide the door open and scan the room to make sure it's empty. My heart thuds in my chest, so loud I swear Morrigan can hear it. The room smells of stale whiskey and cigars. My nose wrinkles but his office appears to be empty. When I'm confident it is, I grab her hand and pull her inside.

"Right, you check behind the paintings, see if there are any safes. And I'll go through the filing cabinet."

She makes her way around the room running her hands behind the ornate frames. I pad to the filing cabinet and pull open the top drawer. I rifle around but it's all staffing records and HR files.

Useless.

I shut the drawer and try the next one. This is even more useless, full of the shipping records and dock deals I've been negotiating for him. I let out a frustrated huff.

There's a clatter.

It's coming from the the staircase. I freeze. Morrigan glances at me her eyes wide. A shiver runs down my back. *Shit.*

I move faster, push the drawer shut, and open the final one.

Bingo.

"I'll check, Roman," a female voice hollers from the corridor.

Morrigan hisses and then pulls up straight. Her face crumples into a frown. She mouths the next sentence at me. "It's Penelope."

Morrigan pads her way to me on her toes trying to make as little noise as possible. I pull files out, sorting through the ancient records until I find the most recent ones. And there are the addresses of the houses we visited. I angle the orb at the papers hoping that whatever happened to Remy, the orbs are still recording.

"Bastard," I spit as I read record after record. But I don't have time to discuss it or talk about it because the office swings open.

Penelope steps inside, her eyebrow rising. "Oh, this is truly delightful."

"Pen—" Morrigan starts.

But Penelope cuts her off. "I wonder what Roman would do if he knew you were in here."

"Now hold on," Morrigan starts.

"Oh do bore off Morrigan, don't lecture me. I'm not going to tell him. But only because I'm feeling generous this evening."

"Oh how benevolent of you."

"Your sarcasm isn't appreciated, I could always call him in." She takes a deep breath "RO—"

Morrigan slaps a hand over Penelope's mouth, a violent stare shivering across her eyes.

"Don't you dare."

Penelope shrugs. "You owe me," she mumbles against Morrigan's hand. She shucks her off and steps over to his desk grabbing the cigar box.

"Well, have fun, sister. Do stay around for the announcement later. I think you'll appreciate it." She sneers, a dark glint in her eyes. She approaches the door, her fingers sliding around the handle when she turns back to us. "I would hurry up if I were you. Roman wants to use his office for...reasons." She grins and Morrigan turns a deep shade of purple, fury etching lines in her face.

"Oh, and maybe don't use this door. He's at the bottom of the stairs, it might be a hard one to explain."

She opens the door and vanishes into the stairwell.

"Bitch," Morrigan spits. "I told her to stay away from him."

Somewhere deep inside me her words ignite a flare of panic. I thought it was a good idea, I figured encouraging him to pay attention to Penelope would get him off our backs.

But Morrigan seems... livid. She's practically vibrating, her eyes dark, expression violent over Penelope's insinuation.

I know Roman is our enemy, but her reaction is... a lot. She doesn't even like Penelope. Why does she care?

There's no time to ponder, I hold up another contract to the orb on my jacket, shove the papers back in the filing cabinet and stand up, just as Penelope's voice echos behind the door again.

"Oh Roman, Roman. You could always take me here." Her voice is excessively loud. She's warning us.

"Shit," I hiss. I grab Morrigan's hand and stagger to Roman's bar. My heart races, palpating and tingling all the way into my fingers. We're going to get caught and then all of this is over.

"How the hell are we going to get out?" Morrigan breathes.

I scan his office desperately trying to find a way out of this, when my eyes trace the bar and the bin next to it.

"Testicle."

"What?" She says.

"Doesn't matter. There's a lift. We can use the lift."

I rush over and press my fingers against the wall until I find the sliver of a crack and I shove all my weight against it to get it to pop open.

"How the hell are we going to fit in that?" Morrigan spits.

The office door shudders and thuds as if bodies are pressing against it. The thudding becomes rhythmic. Morrigan's eyes bug wide. She shifts as if she's going to charge at the door.

"There's no time. Just get in. You're going to have to make it move but it's a shaft that will take us to the basement. I just hope the room it lands in is empty."

I slide in and pull her towards me. She squeezes herself inside, her body pressed against mine so tight that her breasts compress my chest, her lips millimetres from mine. If this were any other moment, any other day it would descend into a bout of intense fucking.

"Quick," I say.

As the office door swings open, I yank the lift shut. Morrigan's magic fills the tiny space with the scent of cinnamon and mint and the floor judders as the lift shaft grinds into action and we descend. I just pray that Roman is distracted enough he doesn't hear the mechanisms grinding as we descend into the basement.

Even as we spill into the darkened medical facility beneath the club and make our way through the belly of the building back up to the dance floor, I know there's something deeply wrong. Morrigan is silent the entire way. The shadows never leave Morrigan, they seem to deepen and spread to her whole body.

My stomach rolls, and a chill passes through me as I have two awful realisations.

First, Roman is trying to frame me: my name was on every single building contract. And second, Morrigan is keeping something from me.

CHAPTER 22

MORRIGAN

Five years Ago

Stirling leans over the table and grabs the bottle of whiskey. "You should know, I fucking hate whiskey. But *it* hates me more. I'm a terrible drunk and a liability when I've been drinking whiskey. Sure you still want to play...?"

"Sounds like exactly the kind of fun I want to get into." My gaze falls to the grimoire.

Her eyes twitch. "You want the old book?"

"It's called a grimoire. And yes, as it happens, it's what I came for. But I see I'm too late."

Her fingers dance over the surface of the tome. "Perhaps not. I'm always willing to negotiate. Besides, you've already agreed to three rounds of runic poker."

"Then, game on. I'll deal first round."

We play and Stirling bets big. She throws cards and coin around like toys. Every round we play, she changes her tactic so I can't predict what she's going to do. I swear she uses magic to suppress her tells after I called her out on them.

"You're fucking with me, aren't you?" I say, throwing down a pair and shoving my chips across the table.

"You pout like a princess when you're losing."

I laugh to myself. Pout like a princess? She has no idea. I swirl my tumbler of whiskey.

"Top," she says.

I take a glug of whiskey, finishing the tumbler off. I'm already stripped of my shoes, jacket, earrings, and watch. My actual clothes are the only legitimate items I can lose.

Thankfully, I win the next round with a flush, though part of me thinks she lost intentionally.

Doesn't matter, I demand her trousers.

"Straight for the big guns, hey? Anyone would think you're trying to get into my knickers," she smirks.

"Interesting, and to think I thought you were flirting with me..." That hangs in the air as I slide a set of cards across the table to her.

She places two fingers on top of her cards, before sliding the corners up to check what she got. Her eyes draw up my topless body until she reaches my gaze.

"What if I am?"

My lips twitch. But I don't respond. I know women like her. Arrogance oozing out of every pore. She probably thinks she can have me, have anyone she likes.

The thought annoys me, especially because, if I'm not very much mistaken, she could have me. And I actually *do* want her to be flirting with me. I'm annoyed at myself. I'm better than letting a pretty lady turn my eye.

I'm here for a reason. I have work to do. And still, there's something about the way she kicks those long legs up on the table, leans back in her chair like she owns the bar, already owns me. My mind drifts, wondering what it would be like to have her slender fingers trail down my skin.

She's wearing a perfume that's intoxicating, hints of bergamot and forest. I want to lean forward and inhale her, encourage her to tiptoe those fingers across the table and slot them into mine.

When she realises I'm not going to answer her question, she draws back.

"All in," she says.

Sunrise peeks through the window, a blush of orange and watery light spilling into the clubroom.

I glance down at my dwindling chips. Her eyes are steely. I can't work out if she's bluffing. I stare at her, the fire and iron in her expression. In this moment, she's a predator and she's hunting me. Too bad for her, I'm not prey and I won't be caught.

"Fine, I'll see you. All in." I shove the rest of my chips into the centre.

Her grin deepens.

"Raise."

"Raise? How can you raise? We both went all in."

She pushes the grimoire into the centre of the table. "This is what you came for, isn't it?"

I nod. "But I've nothing left to offer."

"Oh there's always something more to offer... if you want the deal bad enough."

"Okay...What would you have me offer?"

She leans back, kicks her legs up onto the table like she owns the place. "A single kiss."

A tiny laugh squeaks out. Small and nervous. "You want to kiss me?"

She doesn't respond, just nudges the grimoire further into the centre of the table.

I scan her face, but she's giving nothing away. I can't leave without that damn grimoire.

"Alright fine. I doubt you've won anyway, I've got my best hand yet."

She grins, shakes her head at me. "You should know, I never make a deal I can't win…"

She flips her cards over, and my chest tightens.

Shit. Shit. Shit.

The royal runes. She's won with the best hand you can get. I've lost the grimoire.

"I'll take that kiss now." She flicks her legs off the table, pulls my chair towards her. We're so close I'm breathing her air as she's breathing mine. The room around us softens and blurs until the only thing left in my focus is her. My breathing hitches, rushes in my ears. Up close, I see just how deep those blue eyes really are, as if they hold more than just pigment, as if she's a well of secrets and stories. Stories I want to hear.

Suddenly I don't just want to kiss her. I want to keep her.

"I'm going to kiss you now," she breathes, but I can't find my words, they're lost in her eyes and the stuttering of my heart.

When her lips brush mine, they're soft and warm. Her kiss is so sweet and so tender I stop breathing. More, I stop thinking altogether. And that is the strangest, most wonderful thing. Nothing else exists, all my whirring and wondering ceases as her mouth moves over mine. As she pulls me in and her fingers caress my jaw, I sink into her kiss. My whole body is alive with sensations. No one has ever kissed me like this.

When she breaks the kiss off, she stares at me, her expression trembling as much as my body. Her fingers skim her lips, her brow scrunching.

Then her gaze returns to me, deeper, more intense than anyone has ever dared to look at me. I swallow hard, and I know without doubt, I am in a world of trouble.

CHAPTER 23

MORRIGAN

We enter the club's main room and I head straight to the bar. I shove my way to the front, sending a stream of static shocks into the queuing magicians. They need to get out of the way. I need a drink and I need it now.

I get to the front and as the barmaid places a shot down for the customer beside me, I lift it and neck the whole thing.

"Er—" the magician says but the look I give him shuts him up. I'm not in the mood.

"More," I snap. The barmaid frowns at me but lines three more shots up and then thinks better of it and just hands me the bottle.

I give her a nod of thanks and make my way back to the table we agreed to meet at.

"What happened?" Stirling says as Quinn appears and takes a seat.

"I had my handful convincing two guards to stay put. Hell, I've never been so charming. They were old acquaintances of Scarlett's from the assassin's guild. Thankfully, I'd met them once before. You'd have been proud, Stirling. But I couldn't do anything to stop Roman. It's his club. How do I explain to him that I, a random stranger, don't want him to go up to his office?"

Stirling opens her mouth to protest but shuts it again. "Penelope intervened. I think she saw you leave and made assumptions."

I stiffen at Penelope's name and take another swig from the bottle I procured.

"What is going on?" Stirling says glaring at me.

"Nothing."

"Sure looks like it too," she snaps.

"Penelope is ruining everything, destroying years of careful planning."

"Penelope?" Quinn says.

I nod, swig, and explain. "The other day, we got into an argument. She basically thinks I'm not worthy of the crown. But it was more than that. She said she was intentionally going after Roman because she didn't think I had it in me to take him down."

Stirling pales and slumps down hard in the chair. She wipes a hand over her face. Her eyes flit to mine and I know she's trying to work it out.

Tell her. Just fucking tell her.

But I imagine the hurt in her expression. I imagine all the ways she'll tell me she hates me, and I can't do it. I don't want to lose her. Not again. So I hide it away and decide I'll wait for a better time. There *is* still time.

I need to get out of here, to think.

Quinn must sense it because she narrows her gaze at

me and glances between me and Stirling. "What's—" she starts but the music cuts out, and Roman appears on stage.

"Morrigan," Stirling says. "I think I need to tell you something." She grabs my arm, a tremor running through her hand. Stirling is never nervous. My stomach sinks.

"What have you done?" I say swallowing hard.

"Gods, I thought it would be helpful. I thought it would get him off our back."

"Stirling," I hiss.

"You told me to be strategic."

My teeth grind together. Roman appears back on stage to a round of applause.

"I swear to gods I thought it through before I suggested it," she says, her voice is practically a whine.

I knead my temple. Somewhere deep down I've already pieced it together. Penelope meeting him at the ball.

Stirling having to give Roman dirt. If she couldn't do that what else would she do?

"Suggested what?" I say, trying to slow my breathing and keep my voice low.

Roman raises his hands for silence. "Ladies and gentlemen... It gives me great pleasure to make a special announcement this evening."

"What. Did. You. Do?" I say between gritted teeth.

Her eyes dart from me to the stage.

Roman claps his hands together. "I'm afraid to say history is repeating itself, and New Imperium's most eligible bachelor is single no more."

There's a gasp that ricochets through the entire clubroom.

I close my eyes, shake my head. "Stirling, tell me you didn't."

"I—I—I thought you'd be impressed at my strategic

thinking. I had to give him something. He's been on my arse wanting more and more from me. I don't understand why you're so pissed. This is a great play. It gets him off our backs and they'll both be distracted w—"

Penelope makes her way on stage, and the blood drains from my face, my toes and fingers turn to ice. I round on Stirling.

"Of all the stupid, preposterous shit you've done. Of all the idiotic crap I've had to clean up. This surpasses them all. How could you?" I'm whisper-shouting now. My whole body shaking with rage.

Roman clears his throat. "It is with great pleasure that I announce my engagement to Penelope Lee."

My stomach sinks through the floor. Bile claws at my throat, I'm going to be sick. I see static, and I'm not sure if I'm going to pass out or throw up. I point a finger at Stirling's chest. It sparks, embers of flames threatening to explode from my fingertip.

"You never think anything through, Stirling. You... He's..." the words are right there... but what good will it do now?

"I—" she starts.

But I don't want to hear it.

I can't.

I shove my seat back and march out of the club leaving Stirling mouthing the air.

CHAPTER 24

STIRLING

THE DAILY IMPERIUM
The Daily Imperium is pleased to announce the
investiture of the heir apparent in one
week's time. The investiture will be held at
the palace commencing at 11am sharp. The
masquerade celebration ball is ticket-only.
However, the event will be aired on the New
Imperium city screens.

I spend the night in Castle Grey. It's been a long time since I spent the night at home, but the way Morrigan reacted in the club made it clear she was furious with me. She left the club in a frightful storm without another word. I tried to run after her, to get her to stop, but as she rounded the street corner, she vanished.

Quinn found me and asked what happened, but I didn't know how to explain. I wasn't sure I could because I still don't really know why she's so pissed. I thought diverting Roman's attention to Penelope was genius.

I followed Quinn back to her shop. We tended to Remy's injuries. Thankfully, they were mostly surface damage. A couple of bruised ribs, a bruised eye socket and split lip. Most of which Quinn was able to treat that evening.

We took Remy back to Castle Grey and the four of us slept there. But it's gone two A.M. and there's so much running through my head I've barely slept. I try again, but spend the next two hours fitful and unable to get comfortable. When four A.M. rolls around, I finally get up. I slide thick slipper-boots on and throw a jumper over my pyjamas. I pace the corridors trying to piece everything together. I walk and walk until the shadows evaporate and the corridors are showered in light.

Roman isn't who he says he is. Or maybe he is, but there's something more to it. He has a vendetta against the crown that goes deeper than just wanting the power. I always thought he wanted the throne for the sake of the throne. But his words turn through my mind over and over.

'I want what was promised to me, what I'm owed.'

On the boat he said he's owed a crown but what the hell does that mean? Whatever happened, this is why he's going after the crown, after Calandra and Morrigan.

And what about Morrigan? Her reaction to Penelope and Roman getting engaged was severe to say the least. She was livid. I don't think I've ever seen her so cross.

And then there's my name on the house contracts for all the properties Roman's been buying. Page after page of properties belonging on paper, to me. Why does he want to frame me when all I've done—as far as he knows—is be loyal?

If it weren't for the fact I'm trying to take him down, the

bastard would've hurt my feelings. If I'm honest, he may still have.

I glance in a large mirror. I look like shit. No surprise, given my eyes ache with exhaustion, and my head feels swollen from all the thoughts and threads. It's light outside, and there's no point going back to bed so I make my way to the dining hall. The only thing saving me today will be an obscene amount of coffee.

I enter the hall to find Quinn and Scarlett laughing over breakfast. Quinn kisses Scarlett playfully, the pair of them whispering and giggling. I think I preferred the squabbling to this sickening display.

"Morning lovebirds," I say and sit down, filling my plate full of eggs, beans, sausages, hash browns, mushrooms, tomato and toast.

"Hungry much?" Quinn says.

"I didn't sleep well."

She eyes me and then pours a cup of coffee. "Here, it's extra strong."

"Thank you. How's Remy?"

"She's fine. Still sleeping. I took her some toast an hour ago but she decided to nap off the last of the healing. Give her another hour, and she'll be back to normal. I'm the best medic in town for a reason, you know," Quinn smiles at me.

"Are we going to talk about what the hell happened last night?" Scarlett says leaning forward and pushing her knife and fork together.

I shake my head, "I have no idea. The pieces are there... actually... I have something to tell you.... Last night's engagement was my idea. I had to give Roman more than just the schematics in my last meeting with him. But he said something so strange that it was the only thing I could

think of. I thought it was a great idea. I guess Morrigan
didn't."

"What did he say?" Scarlett says.

I shovel a few mouthfuls of food in, chew, swallow and
feel a little better. "He said *'I want what was promised to me,
what I'm owed.'*"

Quinn frowns. "That is weird. Have you checked the
birth and death records?"

"The what?"

Even Scarlett turns to stare at Quinn.

"When I was living in the Borderlands, I used to spend a
lot of time in the old palace library. They're huge, but they
also have a lot of historical records. One section is all the
births and deaths. Of course, any records since the Tearing
will be kept in the new palace. But Roman's old enough
that his records would be in the old palace."

I sit stunned. "That is actually a brilliant idea."

"I've been known to have them occasionally," she grins.

"If only I knew a girl who could get easy access to the
old palace..."

My words hang in the air, I wait a moment for them to
sink in.

Quinn pulls a hand over her face. "Oh gods, I'm the girl,
aren't I...this is the thanks I get for coming up with a great
idea."

"Please? Come on, Scarlett can go with you... you can
show her the palace and all your old haunts."

"Oh how generous of you," Quinn laughs.

"It will leave the team decidedly understaffed," Scarlett
says.

"I know. But I have a feeling we're being kept in the
dark. There's something else going on here. How are we

supposed to fix it or take Roman down if we don't have all the information?"

Scarlett and Quinn glance at each other.

"It's fine, I'll go. Scarlett, you stay and help. But you owe me, Stir." Quinn says.

"It's a deal..."

CHAPTER 25

STIRLING

There are only four days left until the investiture. It's been three days since the DnD party and I still haven't spoken to Morrigan properly. I've tried. But she was too cross to speak to me.

I've not slept properly. Not been able to focus. All I can think about is fixing things with her. I've done the bare minimum for Roman, though I feel like he's close to telling me what the plan is for the investiture.

This evening is the annual New Imperium auction. Roman's told me he'll be there. So I have to try to sort things with her before the team meets before the auction.

Plus, time is running out, we have a loose plan for the investiture, based on the easiest attack points in the palace. Scarlett and Daria have spent the last couple of days plotting out potential ambush scenarios, but without confirmation from Roman, and without dismantling the power he's hoarded, we're still sitting ducks.

I head to Morrigan's cottage to confront her and to

apologise for suggesting Roman marry Pen. Her cottage must recognise me because as I approach, the gate swings open of its own accord.

The lunchtime sun is warm on my skin and face, I close my eyes to it and let the rays radiate over my body. I take a deep breath and head to the front door. But the door handle swipes out of my reach and waggles in the direction of the back garden. I go to grab it again and it sweeps out of my reach, the handle waggling more insistently in the direction of the back garden.

"Okay, Gods. I get it." I step away and the handle sags, releasing a rush of sound that sounds disturbingly close to an exasperated sigh.

I want to tell it off for being patronising but decide better of it. It's in a helpful mood at least. I make my way across the grass of the front garden and onto the paving slabs towards the back of the cottage.

Attached to the back of the house is an ornate wooden deck. Intricately carved arches separate the decking from the garden. They're draped in blossoms and vines that twist their way up and over the wood and arches. Swollen blossoms and pastel leaves coat the arches despite the fact summer is over and most of the plants are shedding.

It's stunning. There's a water feature in the centre of the garden flowing and glistening against the sun.

Morrigan is sat on an enormous u-shaped sofa, her feet curled beneath her, glasses on, a mug of steaming coffee in her hands beside an enormous pile of books. She's wearing a tiny string vest, her arms exposed displaying her mosaic of intricate Collection tattoos. I stare at her in awe of the power she holds and commands. The people of New Imperium should be on their knees, grateful for the studious queen they will have one day.

She looks up over her glasses, letting the book she was scribbling in rest on her lap. There's a moment of silence where we just hold each other in our gaze.

"Hey," she says. Her tone is cold, reserved, it slices through me like a blade.

"Hey," I say.

She presses her lips together and I wonder if she's about to shut down. To refuse to engage with me, and my stomach rolls at the thought of not fixing things. But then her shoulders sag and I thank the gods that as reluctant as she might be, she's still willing to talk.

"I was so mad. But I guess we need to talk."

"Yeah. We should."

"I ordered tapas for lunch, I'm pretty sure they've delivered enough for two. Let me go get it."

She pads barefoot into the cottage and comes back pushing a mini trolley laden with little plates and bowls of food. Potatoes smothered in tomatoes, garlicky vegetables, chorizo, mini mushrooms, and an array of other foods that make my mouth water.

"Damn, the chefs are on fire today," I say.

She smiles and pulls out a bottle of wine from under the trolley. I nod and she opens the bottle pouring us both a glass. I help place the dozens of bowls and plates on the coffee table and sit next to her picking a selection of bits I want to eat.

"I'm sorry. I really, truly thought it was a good idea. Roman wants a crown, and I figured it would keep both him and Penelope off our backs."

Morrigan's lips draw into a thin line, like she's trying to hold something back. Her eyes narrow and relax so quickly I almost miss it. But then her shoulders slump and she says, "I'm sorry I got cross. It's not like me to overreact like that. It's just, she's my sister and he's..."

"Roman."

She nods.

"If it helps, that wasn't my plan. I didn't go to him intending to make that suggestion. I gave him Daria's name. But that wasn't enough for him, so I had to give him something else. And he said the strangest thing about wanting what he was owed. He felt like he was owed the crown. So I suggested he marry Penelope to get it."

She shakes her head, her features tremble, but when she looks up at me, she's the picture of calm. Her face is completely blank and my magic is tingling under my skin, and there's the faintest hint of mint and cinnamon in the air. Is she hiding her emotions?

"Do you know what he was talking about? Are you aware of the crown owing him a debt at all?"

The silence stretches between us, heavy and thick. Morrigan's eyes scan my face. Flickering as if she's debating something. I open my mouth ready to demand she just say it when she finally answers.

"No. I don't."

And I swear, there's a crackle in her voice, something buried underneath the words, but the smell of magic has vanished and there's no static in the air, so she must be telling the truth.

And yet, there *is* something wrong. I've known Morrigan a long time.

"What aren't you telling me?" I say.

"Nothing."

"Morrigan."

"Stirling."

"I'm serious. I can't keep doing this with you."

She shuffles closer, bringing her hand up to my cheek. Behind her, the sun descends behind the garden bushes, wrapping itself in the horizon and throwing a spray of blood orange and burnt yellows over the sky.

"I'm sorry I overreacted at the club. But I realised something that night."

I frown. "What do you mean?"

"About us. Having you this close to me again, I realised I can't let you go. After... I want to find a way to keep us."

I lean down, touch my forehead to hers, "I truly hope we can."

I pull her into my side, wrapping my arm around her and then pick up a piece of chorizo. "This reminds me of the night after we met," I say smiling as I take a bite.

"Oh my gods," she says, laughing. "That poker house."

"The day after we got tapas, the food wasn't half bad. I don't think I've had tapas since then."

"The whiskey was delicious in the poker club too. Shame about the players." She nudges me in the ribs.

I smile at her, the warmth we normally share returning to us finally. "I could barely focus on the game, I was so enamoured with you."

A wash of memories filters through my mind. The black skin-tight jeans she was wearing. Her arms weren't as covered in tattoos then, but she was still the most collected magician I'd ever met. That was what drew me to her. So young and yet, so much power.

I grin, "I rather enjoyed the game of strip poker."

"Of course you would, you negotiated my knickers off me."

"I'll drink to that," I raise my glass of wine and she clinks hers to mine shaking her head at me.

"Do you remember the city in the jungle?" she says, her

eyes distant, staring at the horizon as the sun drifts closer to it.

"That was wild. Never, ever doing a deal involving those jungle jumping spiders again. Didn't you manage to pick up a tattoo there?"

She points at a tattoo near her ankle.

"Though I still think the scariest trip we ever took was to—"

She grimaces, "—Yeah, don't remind me. I'd rather not do that again, they're a vicious species."

"You know that's why I built the boat?" I say the words spilling out. I drink more wine, pick at the food, each morsel as delicious as the last.

"What do you mean?"

I grab her foot, knead my fingers and thumbs into the sole. "I guess I thought that one day we could visit other cities and realms. Those trips we took, we were so free, just exploring and never knowing what would happen or what magic we would stumble upon next. Don't you think that sounds exciting?"

She smiles, but it doesn't reach her eyes, instead they well up. She wipes her face. "It does, and I wish that for you."

And that's when I realise it's a dream we can never share. All this time, I had a dream that could never come to pass. If only she'd told me who she was, I'd never have dreamt the impossible. In a week's time, her life will change forever and she will never have the freedom I do. Never have the privilege of being able to take off and just leave or adventure.

"I'm sorry," I say. But I don't really know what I'm apologising for. This isn't either of our faults. But the fun of our memories fades and we're left in the stagnant present. It's cold and hard and neither of us want to face it.

She takes my hand from her foot and threads her fingers through mine. I rub my thumb over the back of her hand.

"Don't be sorry. It is what it is. I might not have chosen this life. But I will choose to embrace it. You could choose it with me..." she says.

I look up at her, my expression resigned. I know what she said earlier, about wanting to keep us. But I also know Calandra.

I realise our relationship is a cancer. It's dying a slow, protracted death that we can both see coming but are helpless to stop.

So instead, we live in denial.

She runs her fingers across my décolletage and over my collarbone. Little flashes of static ripple off her fingers hitting my skin in a shower of sparks, it sends bolts of pleasure into my body.

She cups my jaw, guides my mouth to hers, placing a gentle kiss on my lips. She tastes like cinnamon smoke and happy memories. My chest aches with yearning for her as she moves her lips over mine, the soft kiss deepening, sweetening. I sigh into her, the familiarity of this, of us. I crave her.

I crave the feeling of home.

Her fingers slip to my neck, pulling me in tight. And then her hands are all over me, my chest, my arse, my waist. She pulls and tugs at me, the need overwhelming.

"Morrigan," I breathe. "If you keep touching me like that I'm going to strip you naked and fuck you on the couch."

She sucks in a breath between her teeth, her eyes heavy

with lust. I swallow hard. She loves it when I tell her what to do. No one orders a queen around.

"You're mine, Morrigan. Now and after the investiture. I don't give a fuck what happens, I'm not letting you go."

I lean into the denial because it tastes sweet and safe.

She closes her eyes and kisses me deep and hard. Her lips bruising against mine as she moans into me. Her hands grab at my body. She slips her fingers under my top and pulls it over my head. She places kiss after kiss on my shoulders, neck, the swelling flesh of my breasts. She unclips my bra in one swift movement, freeing my breasts and taking them in her hands.

Her mouth is all over me, licking and kissing and nipping at my hardening nipples. She moans as she takes each breast into her mouth, a sound filled with the same yearning I feel in between my ribs. A want that is hungry, ceaseless, that claws at my soul and settles in my bones.

When my fingers reach her shorts she clasps her hands to stop me. She glances up, a question in her eyes.

"What's wrong?" I ask.

Her eyes round into a devilish grin. "I learned a new form of magic." And as soon as the words are out, the hum and fizz of static buzzes in my chest.

"Oh?" I say, already liking the sound of it.

"It's a sex magic. It will allow us to share our orgasms."

I raise an eyebrow, "Sounds kinky, I'm in."

She laughs, picks up a needle from a bowl on the coffee table and pricks her index finger, then she gestures for me to do the same. She presses the bead of blood on both our fingers together. She mumbles some words I can't hear and then a bolt of heat flows from my finger into my chest and straight to my clit and I'm instantly wet. I want to roll my head back and luxuriate in the need throbbing between my legs.

"Fuck," I say. "Is that—? What is that?"

"That, Lady Grey, is me," she grins. "And how much I want you right now."

I sit up straight. Done messing around. "Take your clothes off," I demand.

A slow smile spreads across her lips. "I do love it wh—"

"Now, Morrigan," I say silencing her. A flicker of rage flashes through her expression and then evaporates as she gives herself over to me and the pleasure of submission.

She slips her top and shorts off, I help her out of her underwear, and she tugs my knickers off, until we're both naked on the sofa. The sun vanishes and a chill whips through the air. Morrigan's flings a hand out, and a free-standing chimney flares to life. A string of lights woven between the wooden arbor above us flash to life.

"Lie on your back," I say.

Morrigan dutifully obeys. I shuffle forward, placing my knees either side of her face. "Now be a good princess and lick my pussy."

Her eyes flash like fire. She grabs my thighs and pulls me down onto her mouth. I suck in a breath as she drags her tongue down my pussy. Her tongue twirls around my hardening clit and waves of pleasure radiate into my thighs. The burn of holding myself up furrows into my muscles mixing with the pleasure of having her tease my clit.

Morrigan releases me, a moan rushing past her lips. "Fuck," she says. "I can feel it, I can feel you."

"I want to play too." I shift back. Carefully, I flip over, manoeuvring so that my stomach lies flat on hers. I shuffle until my pussy meets her mouth and then I lower myself to her soaking cunt. "You're so wet, and I haven't even touched you."

"Yes, well, I could feel the sensations of your clit it's... well... touch me and you'll find out."

I slide my tongue down her slit, lapping up her juices and moaning into her pussy as her tongue swipes down my heat. I circle her clit, licking and teasing until she's bucking under me. Her tongue draws long lavish strokes down my core. I can't focus. I don't know what's more delicious, the fact I'm ravishing her cunt or the fact she's doing the same to mine. And then, just as she promised, the sensations intensify. Instead of just the exquisite tingles of my own pussy, the pleasure ramps up.

It's everywhere. It takes over my entire body, rushing into my nipples, sliding down my spine like a river of electricity.

"Gods," I breathe.

"Don't stop," she pants, her fingers gripping my thighs tighter.

I lap harder, faster. I angle my body so I can slide a finger inside her. It makes her cry my name out, so I thrust quicker. And in response, both our pussies tighten and throb. Waves of electric pleasure pulsate out from my clit and rush around my body.

Everything slows. The garden vanishes and there is only her and me.

Our bodies, our pleasure.

It is blinding and all-consuming.

It's an infinite connection. I feel her, bonded deeper than flesh and bone.

The waves crashing over me are so intense I can barely see. It's as though she's punched a fist into the centre of my soul and clutches my beating heart in her fingertips. As if life has ceased and we exist outside of time and matter. Our souls are millennia wide and wrapped in a mesh of knots and tying us together forever.

We wind higher, tighter. Waves of pleasure clench both our cores. She rides me as hard as I ride her.

Bliss fogs my mind. It swirls around us, between us; her rising orgasm heightens mine which heightens hers. Until all I can see and feel and hear is her and us and our panting breaths and fevered bodies.

"Stirling," she gasps and together we ride over the precipice into something more than ecstasy, more than the orgasm. My whole body burns and glistens with the ferocity.

I can't breathe.

I can't see.

I can only feel the throbbing shivers wracking my body, stealing my voice and consuming my mind.

When it's over and we've stopped twitching, Morrigan reaches under the coffee table and brings a blanket out. She wraps it around both of us, and snuggles into me, resting her head on my shoulder and wrapping her fingers through mine. She points her other hand to the wood burner and the fire roars higher and hotter. The lights wrapped around the arbor flicker and twinkle like the stars popping to life in the dimming afternoon.

I squeeze Morrigan tight to me, our exhausted, satiated bodies press together, our legs and limbs tangled.

"This. This is what I've missed, these moments of peace. Just me and you. I should never have made that deal."

"It was a long time ago," she says and rubs her thumb along my jawline.

"I should've come back to you sooner, trusted that we

could find a way around Roman, found a way to protect you. I was just doing what I thought I had to." I twist to kiss the top of her head.

"I never stopped loving you, Stirling. Not once."

"I don't want to lose you, once this is over."

I grip her tighter. My fingers stroking her warm skin.

"I don't want to lose you either," she says peppering my skin with kisses.

"Then keep me."

She climbs on top of me and plunges her lips over mine. Her erect nipples skim my torso as she slides her hand between my legs. Her fingers find my swollen clit. She reaches down, dips her finger in my hole and brings it back to rub my clit.

And suddenly the future doesn't seem to matter anymore.

As I lose myself to her touch, somewhere inside, a part of me realises that instead of agreeing, instead of saying okay, and promising to find a way to be together, she chose to stay silent. For the second time today, she chose to say nothing at all.

CHAPTER 26

MORRIGAN

I should have told her.
I should have told her.
Things are a little more delicate now that Penelope is engaged to him. But thankfully, it's not public knowledge that she's the princess yet. So hopefully, by the time the investiture is over, it will be a scandal mother can sweep under some delicately negotiated carpets.

It does complicate things though, given our history. I almost told her. I almost told them both.

Penelope, for all her lack of brains has figured out something is off.

Stirling though, gods, she knows. And I wanted to tell her so badly this afternoon. But the way she looked at me, so full of hope, I couldn't. I didn't want to hurt her. I swear the words almost came tumbling out. But things are so complicated, so fragile. What's a couple more days? Maybe there's a way to just get through this whole thing and for her not to find out. But I know even as I think it that I'm deluding myself. And it will be so much worse if she finds out from someone else.

I decide I have to tell her today. I'll just pull her aside at some point during the auction, or maybe after and just blurt it out.

I have to.

The problem is the growing sickness in my gut. It's awful, the more time we spend together, the closer we're growing. There are these incredible moments when everything is just like before, us against the world. When I'm with her, nothing else matters. But then the second we're apart everything else rushes back into my reality and it hurts.

It hurts so much.

The annual auction is held in an enormous stately home in the heart of the city. It belongs to the Langfords. A tiresome family with egos the size of three cities. One of those typical legacies that feel blighted by the crown.

I can't blame them, though, they are a family of architects and one of the three original architect families who worked together to unearth and harness the magic running through properties. That's why they feel they're owed. It's entitled bullshit. Yes, they're powerful, but royal blood does not run through their veins. They've only lived in this home for five hundred years. So while they can trace their family line back thousands of years—almost as many as mother and I— they don't have the power or the history. And therein lies the reason we are sovereigns and they are not. The fact they lost power and regained it and lost it again is something they blame my family for, and they can't quite forgive us.

Quinn had to rush back to the Borderlands to help Malachi with something, so the team is down to Remy, Stir-

ling, Scarlett, and I. We approach their home in a carriage.
It rocks gently side to side, horses tethered to the front,
hooves clip clopping. Mother is using the plush carriages
for the dignitaries so we got lumbered with the old ones. Of
course, we can't be seen to be favoured otherwise it would
arouse suspicion, and with only a few days of freedom left, I
want to keep these precious days to myself.

The carriage draws to a stop in the circular courtyard in
front of the Langford home porch. A gaudy monstrosity
with six pillars and a red carpet stretching halfway down
the driveway.

We're greeted by several Langfords, all of them family
architects, all wearing matching navy slacks and shirts
emblazoned with their family crest. It's the identical sneers
they wear I can't stand.

Thankfully, they have no idea who I am. They will after
the investiture, though, and I'll take great pleasure in
reminding them of their behaviour towards me too.

The Langford home is an H-shaped building. Turrets
pierce the clouds on each corner. The stone is a washed-out
grey that despite its faded appearance is no less regal. The
house is proud, arrogant almost. It, like its occupants,
stands tall and illustrious.

"Good afternoon…" I'm greeted with an open palm from
one of the Langfords. His hair is a mop of midnight black,
his skin tanned, eyes the kind of sky blue you can lose yourself in—if you like that sort of thing.

"Morrigan," I say, putting my hand in his to shake. His
grip is just firm enough to whisper the threat of strength. It
makes me want to smile, naive fool.

Instead, I let my shawl fall from my shoulders and
display my collection tattoos. He flinches, releasing my
grip.

"Ah yes, Morrigan Lee, I've heard of you. A most learned guest. The pleasure is all mine. Do come in. The auction will be held in the main banquet hall. There are refreshments at the back should you require them."

"Lovely..." I wait, indicating he didn't give his name.

"Elias. Elias Langford."

"Pleasure, Elias." It was anything but pleasurable. I glance at the rest of the team, who seem to have faced the same greeting and look like they're trying not to roll their eyes.

I enter the stately house and a rush of pure power hums over my skin. It's clean and the pure scent of lilac and mint is so strong I can taste it. Under the lilac is a woody earthen smell, like raw minerals and forest bark. What I'd do to learn the magic of this house, be collected by it. As if Stirling can read my mind, she raises her eyebrows at me as she steps into the corridor and mouths "Wow."

I nod, and mouth "I know," back at her.

There are butlers and staff members lining the corridor to make sure we stick to the assigned path through the mansion, lest we wander into a secret room or try to steal their house's power. The walls of the corridor are adorned with rich fabrics and paper. An array of burnt ochres, muted mustards and terracotta colours. Sculptures of buildings and mansions sit at uniform distances lining the corridor—all the families work no doubt.

Oil paintings hang on the upper part of the walls, some ancient, others newer. I recognise the chap who greeted me in one.

We're shown into a room of cavernous proportions. Three enormous crystal chandeliers hang from the ceiling. Gems and diamonds sparkling from the fittings. At one end of the room is a stage, the other the buffet of refreshments.

And dotted around the room are dozens of boards hosting property information.

"Shall we check the property boards out? See if any look like they're going cheaply and therefore might be a target for Roman?" Scarlett says.

I nod, and she vanishes with Remy.

"Let's start here," Stirling says indicating the nearest board to us. We make our way past, examining the mansions, but most are huge estates going for millions of coin.

We go past two more rows of boards when Stirling sucks in a sharp breath at the fourth.

"What's wrong?" I say.

"Nothing," she says. But her fingers skim the board, tracing the outline of the property.

I glance at it. It feels familiar. It's much smaller than the others we've looked at. The front of it has ocean coloured shiplap covering the front. That's when I realise. It's the house behind her boat shed. The same house we slept together in the conservatory. The same one that two years ago, we...

I don't finish the thought. Today is not the day to reminisce. "Buy it," I say bouncing on my toes.

"I can't. Much as I'd love to. I have to look after Castle Grey. I can't just leave."

"I didn't say leave. I said buy it. Why not have another property in your portfolio?"

She looks at the floor. "What am I going to do with another property? It's not like I can live there. You definitely can't. It's just one of those nice dreams that can never actually come true despite the fact we hold memories there."

I glare at her. "Stir—"

Roman and Penelope walk into the room, and the

atmosphere visibly tenses. His reputation really does proceed him. I can't believe I was ever... Well, anyway, it won't matter in a few days, because if we can't pin him with crimes, I'll kill him myself.

As if he can read my mind, his eyes find mine. A hard stare, his dark eyes filled with hate.

Well, Roman, the feeling is mutual. He holds my gaze a moment longer than necessary and then he breaks it off, laughing at something Penelope said.

Bile claws at my throat. *Keep going Roman*, every dig you make is another dose of resentment, another injection of motivation to cut you off at the knees.

I'm vaguely aware of my name being called.

"Morrigan. Morrigan. *Morrigan*. What the fuck?" Stirling yanks my hand bringing me back to her.

"What?" I say, irritated.

"You nearly set fire to the tablecloth."

I look down at the table. It's singed and still smoking. I bend my fingers and draw a little water out of the atmosphere and place my hand over the steaming fabric. It hisses and cools. Alas, the black stain doesn't disappear.

"What the hell happened?"

My eyes flick to Roman. But instead of understanding, Stirling narrows her eyes at me, folding her arms.

"I'm fine. Okay? Completely fine."

"You're aware that I'm a negotiator? I try extremely hard not to use my ability to read your emotions, but I don't need to use my magic to know that's a baldfaced lie. I thought we resolved everything the other night. Or are you still keeping things from me?"

"Stirling, please, we don't have time for this today."

Remy appears, her usually pale face ghost-green. "We have a major problem."

CHAPTER 27

STIRLING

Three Years Ago

E ven dressed in oversized beige rags, Morrigan is still the most exquisite woman I've ever laid eyes on.

Her silky black hair, far too shiny and clean for the quality of clothes we're wearing, is the only tell that we shouldn't be here, that the clothes we stole from a washing line don't really belong to us. I've thrown my locks under a cap, but Morrigan's hair is so thick it wouldn't fit.

This is the furthest south we've travelled together. Most of our trips have been to the cities next door to New Imperium. But Morrigan was insistent she wanted to find some rare grimoire from a mansion made from obsidian and quartz. She coveted the ability to bend light and shadows to her will. And I found myself unable to resist following her. We've only been together five months, but I swear I'd give this woman my soul if she commanded it.

We enter the market. This far south, the midday heat is

scorching. It makes the rags stick to my arms and sweat roll down my legs. I'll be glad when we can leave this godsforsaken city. The creatures here are odd. Cold, and calculating, with pointed ears so sharp they could cut. I can't quite get a read on them. Their magic doesn't work like magicians. But that only makes them more interesting.

On the way here, Morrigan gave me a potted history from one of her books. There's another city containing their cousins. So the stories say, these two groups used to be united. But civil war forced half the population to migrate to the northern reaches of the realm.

But we're not here for people, we're here for the book.

The market is busy, creatures of all kinds meander from stall to stall. The air is full of the smells of roasting meats, warmed wine, and burning herbs. There are stalls and vendors as far as I can see in every direction.

Morrigan is marching so fast through the throngs of people that I lose sight of her for a moment. My chest clenches. I break into a jog dodging people and ducking in and out until I spot her and slide my hand into hers.

"Slow down, you gave me a scare," I say.

She halts, her eyes bright as they take me in. Her hand cups my cheek, "I'll never leave you," she smiles, and pulls me in placing a soft kiss on my lips. My hand skirts around her waist.

She swats me away. "But you keep touching me like that, and we'll never make it out of the market. Come on, I sped up because I spotted a grimoire selling up ahead."

She slides her hand into mine and tugs for me to hurry up. Together, we dart in and out, passing herb sellers, candle makers, stalls with coins and gems, a cauldron seller, card readers, another with elements inside orbs.

Finally, Morrigan stops in front of a stall covered in

books. Her eyes scan the array, her fingers dancing over the spines.

The seller, a particularly tall and sinewy creature, with ears so long and pointed they look like blades nods at me.

"Good afternoon," I say.

"Lookin' fer summat in par'cular?"

I let my magic seep out. Since their systems work differently to ours, I'm hoping he won't know I'm using it. There's a coldness to his aura, something off, sour almost.

"Nothing much, she loves to read," I say tipping my head to Morrigan.

"Gosh you have such pretty books," she says, sounding nothing like her at all. Morrigan knows exactly how 'pretty' the insides of these tomes are. But I realise she's going to try and charm the book out of him.

"Busy day?" I say, distracting the seller.

He shrugs. "Aye, ne'er as good as yer wan it though."

"Ooh, this one, this one." Morrigan bounces on her toes, pointing at a particularly stunning book. Its cover is so dark it seems to absorb the light around it. It makes my eyes hurt staring at it. Parts of the leather are marbled, wisps of quartz-white streaking the front.

"Tha's an spensive one tha'."

I'll bet it is. I'll bet they all are when you think you're able to rip someone off.

"How much?" I say, as Morrigan pulls it out and opens the cover. She glances at me, inclining her head in the faintest of nods. It's the one she came for.

Right. I push my sleeves up. This fucker isn't tripping me off.

He narrows his eyes at me, "Yer can't 'ford it yer can't."

"Go on, try me."

"'Undred coin."

I laugh. He's a right joker this one. "Why's it so much?" I ask.

He hesitates, his eyes flicking between the two of us. And I realise he was bluffing. He hasn't got a clue about the real value of this book, or what lies inside its pages, he was just trying to pull a fast one.

"Er. Well, 'cause umm."

"Mmm. That's what I thought. I'll give you thirty coin, and let's call it quits. The cover's worn thin. Look at those streaks, and what about the spine? The leather's hanging off."

I waft the book in his face and pull it back, not wanting him to check too close.

"Thirty-five and you got a deal."

I hold my hand, "Thirty-two."

"Ugh. Fine, yer drive a tuff bargain, yer do."

He shakes on it, and I toss him the coin. Morrigan slides the book under her arm. And we leave. It takes us a day to travel to the next city. One so far south, the weather is tropical. Three minutes after arriving, I decide I never want to visit again.

We enter an ivy covered building, and the air dries instantly. The walls, even inside, are green and covered in plants, as if the very building itself is made of ivy.

"Amazing, isn't it?" Morrigan says.

"Is the building alive? Like is the structure actually made of plants?"

She nods, and my mouth drops open. She pushes the sleeve of her off her shoulder and reveals a tiny green ivy-leaf tattoo.

"You studied here?"

She grins at me. "I've studied most places. Come on,

there's an herbalist in the back I need to see, and then we'll rest in the heart of the building."

She guides me through the winding rows of book-shelves. I follow, while her eyes skim the spines of the grimoires frantically. Even through we're just passing through, it's an obsession for her, like she can't help herself.

I smile to myself. This woman, who has more knowl-edge than anyone I know, still hungers for more. I wonder if she'll ever sate her appetite. I hope she doesn't; even in proximity to knowledge she glows radiant like the sun.

"Wait here," she says as we break into an open space. The leafy roof breaks open. Light pours down into the grassy area beneath.

"What the?" I say.

"It's a picnic field mostly, for people to eat and read the library books."

I frown, "What if it rains?"

"Roof seals itself shut. Anyway. Sit, hold this, I won't be long." She dumps her bag and a pile of books on me and vanishes.

A few minutes later she returns, holding three conical vials and slips them into her bag. She sits and picks up the book we collected from the previous city, its dark cover sucking the light from the air.

She lays her head on my lap, the sun beating down on us both, opens to a random page, and begins reading.

"In this ancient grimoire lies the sacred lore of Light and Dark, governed by quartz and obsidian. Quartz is the conduit of ethereal radiance, it's opposite the enigmatic obsidian, stone ruler of shadows. Together, they maintain a delicate balance within existence, binding day and night in divine harmony."

I yawn.

"Oi," Morrigan says, reaching up to dig me in the ribs.

I chuckle at her, "Sorry. But why do they have to make it all so stuffy?"

She rolls her eyes at me. "I'm pretty sure you were the one who told me the verbiage was everything."

I open my mouth to respond, and promptly shut it. She has a point.

We spend the afternoon there on the field inside the ivy building, the sun beating down, bronzing our skin and warming our hearts.

She reads from half a dozen books. With each one, she lights up more, until she's practically vibrating with excitement.

The words slide out of my mouth before I can stop them. "I just realised something."

"You did?" she beams, the dying sun radiates through her shadow-kissed locks, her fringe blunt, her eyes big.

I glance around the field. There's no one else here. The sun dips low beneath the holey ceiling, the sky smeared with dusky pinks and burnt orange. The air is plump with the scent of old books and leafy plants.

My stomach flips, as the words dance on my tongue. I want to tell her. I want to pull her in and curl my arms around her neck and confess what I've known since that night at the poker club.

I tilt us down until we're laying on our sides on the grass, I push a lock behind her ear.

"I realised, Morrigan Lee... That I'm utterly, unequivocally, and most definitely dangerously in love with you."

The smile she gives me is better than any the books created. It is blinding and all consuming. It makes my heart swell.

She leans in, her breath trickling over my ear and down my neck. I can tell she's smiling by the way the words curl.

"Took you long enough, Lady Grey."

And then she kisses me until our lips are sore and the sky is black.

CHAPTER 28

STIRLING

"Define problem," I say pulling Morrigan, Remy, and Scarlett into the corner.

"Don't look now, but you see the woman approaching Roman? She's wearing gloves, tanned skin, walks like she owns everyone in the room."

"Yeah?" I say turning to ogle the woman. Remy grabs my shoulders and yanks me around.

"I said *don't* look. Gods."

I shrug Remy off.

"What about her?" Morrigan says.

"Her name is Bella Blythe," Remy answers.

And then I realise why Remy is so pale. Surprisingly, I don't know Bella. But I know a girl who does and Bella is not one to mess with.

Scarlett slides closer, "Sounds like I need to cut her throat." She shoves three hors d'oeuvres in her mouth and chews like a hamster.

My nose crinkles. I'm not sure what I'm more grossed

out by, her free ability to kill anything with a pulse or the fact she just dropped several crumbs out her mouth. "Remind me how you landed Quinn again?"

"Go fugg yurseff, sisfta," she says around the mouthful of food.

"Look, can someone please explain who the hell this Bella woman is?" Morrigan whines.

I glance around again, recognising the curve of Bella's plump lips and the stare in her eye that promises death to anyone that crosses her from the photo hanging in Remy's house.

Remy, if it's at all possible, grows paler. "She was Roman's apprentice for a while. Around the same time I was apprenticed to Marcel Corbin. I had a number of run-ins with her. She's incredible, frankly."

I'm not sure if it's fury or awe in her tone. I think both.

"You have a lady-boner for her," Scarlett says smirking.

"Scarlett," I say.

"What?" she shrugs.

"Must you be so crass?" I go to give her a sisterly wallop, but she lunges for me. Morrigan balls her hand into a fist, and Scarlett freezes mid-lunge.

"Not the time," Morrigan says.

"A girl I know has spent time with Bella. Apparently she's a force to be reckoned with. A super tactical magician."

Morrigan releases Scarlett who shimmies her shoulders and gives her the middle finger.

Remy ignores the pair of them and continues, "Bella might not have as many collection tattoos as you, Morrigan, but she chose the houses she studied from with extreme precision. That woman is a menace. I'd heard she'd gone to another city, but it looks like she's still working for Roman."

The four of us turn in unison as Bella strides across the room and pulls Roman aside without a care in the world, as if he isn't the second most powerful magician in here and like she has absolutely no fucks to give about his authority.

Remy sucks in a breath, and I have to rub my mouth to stop the grin.

Remy shakes herself. "If Bella is involved with Roman, we could be in trouble."

"What's she known for?" Morrigan asks.

"Security, like me. Hence the run-ins when I was an apprentice," Remy says.

"Security as in forcefields and lattices?" I say memories of the lattice symbol in the suburb properties flashing through my mind.

"Exactly like that, which is why we have a major problem," Remy says.

"What I want to know, is why is she wearing gloves? What's she hiding under there?" Morrigan asks.

"Magic. Collection tattoos I'd wager. I'm going to bump into her," Remy says. "Stirling, how nimble are your fingers?"

I grin, "Ask Morrigan."

Scarlett retches.

Morrigan gawps at me. And I snigger.

"Nimble. I can slide one off her, don't worry. If she's hiding lattice work tattoos, then we'll have our confirmation that she's in on the job."

Remy and I approach Bella. Remy from her front to grab her attention, me from the rear. Bella catches sight of Remy and her body shifts. She turns away from Roman mid-sentence and heads towards Remy. I have to adjust course not once, but twice, when I realise Remy is going to get to her before me.

I scurry across the floor, barging magicians out the way and extend my hand, whipping the glove down as I faux trip and collapse into her.

Remy, the fucking gentlelady that she is, open arm catches Bella, a sly grin spreading across her face as she dips her down and brings her slowly back up.

Smooth motherfucker, is the last thing I think before dropping ass first to the floor and taking out two other magicians with me. Honestly, the shit I do for the team.

Remy helps Bella to her feet as I scramble up, mumble an apology to the other two magicians, and get the hell out the way.

Remy grasps Bella's hand and brings it up to her mouth, kissing Bella's knuckles. I can't work it out. Remy has an odd expression, her jaw flexing like she's irritated, but her eyes tell a different story. Either way, she's flawlessly charming as she bends to pick up Bella's glove. She glances at Bella's arm, her eyes widen, then narrow.

"I believe you dropped this," Remy says handing the glove over.

Bella snatches it out of Remy's hand.

"Still picking up after me, I see," Bella snarls.

"You should be more careful with your belongings," Remy says.

"Remy Reid, come near me again, and it will be the last thing you do."

By the time Remy joins us, her eyes are glazed.

"Is that rage or lust in your eyes," I say. "I'm confused."

"Do you know she used to hack mansion security systems before I could and then change the algorithms just so I couldn't get in," Remy says.

"A bit of both then," I laugh. But Remy ignores me.

"What was she hiding under those gloves?" Morrigan asks.

"It was exactly as we thought. Lattice collection tattoos," Remy says and then wipes her face, the heavy-lidded fog lifting from her eyes.

"At least we know what we're dealing with. We knew it was lattice work from the marks on the walls. But now I know *whose* work it is," Remy says.

"Which is good news?" I give her a friendly pat on the back.

"It is because I can reverse engineer it based on what I know of her. But the bad news is that her lattice work is an extremely high-tech form of magic. Some of the casino clubs use lattice magic to protect their vaults. A couple of the banks too."

"That explains the rumours about Roman's men robbing banks," I say.

Remy nods, "And how he didn't get caught. It's an extremely technical and complicated system using a non-binary functional cog-lattice of—"

"Remy!" I cut her off.

"Sorry. The point is, she is as good as me. And we only have a couple of days. I don't know if I can hack her system in time."

Morrigan kneads her temples.

Scarlett leans forward, poking her head into the middle of the group, "So like I said, I'll cut her throat, and then the problem's eliminated, yes?" Scarlett says.

"No," Remy and Morrigan snap.

I frown at Scarlett. "No one is killing anyone. Gods, is this how worked up you get when Quinn is away for a couple of nights?"

She pouts at me, so I turn to Remy. "You're the best hacker I know, why are you so twitchy?" I ask.

Remy swallows audibly. "Because her lattice-security work is second to none and even though I know her, have seen her work before, I have no idea how to hack it. And unless I can, then we're not going to be able to get access to Roman's embezzled magic. And if we can't do that, then he's got all the power he needs to take the crown down at the investiture."

CHAPTER 29

STIRLING

The following night, I'm heading to the suburbs of the city with Scarlett.

I knew a girl that went to the same guild as Bella, and after a brief chat costing me both coin and an hour of my time hunting for a decoder, she told me that Bella came top of their cohort, and her final year project was on lattice magic.

Which is why Morrigan and Remy are holed up in Remy's gaff working on hacking the security guild's historical records.

While I drew the lattices on the walls from memory, Remy wanted specifics with angles, lengths and dimensions so we're headed back to the houses now. She thinks if they can get Bella's project off the guild system, even if it's a crude version of what she can do now, then combined with accurate renderings of the lattices in the houses, Remy might be able to hack Bella's work on the properties.

Scarlett and I are both carrying video orbs, and once we're inside, we'll call her so she can scan the buildings from the inside.

Or that's the plan.

"So, you and Morrigan..." Scarlett says as we round a corner into a residential area.

"Yeah, totally not up for discussion."

"Well we all know you screwed at DnD the other night, but like you're *screwing-screwing* again, aren't you?" It's less a question and more of an accusation. "Is that wise?"

"Do we have to do this now?"

"I mean yeah, Stir. You had lots of opinions about me and Quinn. Karma's a bitch."

I pout at her.

"Fine. What is it you want to know?"

"Are you happy?"

That is not what I expected her to say.

"I... when I'm with her, yeah. We're closer than ever."

Scarlett is silent for a moment, weighing up everything I've said.

"What happens after?"

"I have absolutely no idea. If we haven't taken Roman out, then I guess I end up in jail. Or the same way our parents went."

"You know I'll never let that happen." Her words are as hard as steel.

"I love you, but you don't get to go swinging your samurai swords ar—"

"Katanas."

"Katanas. Whatever. You don't get to go swinging your swords around just because I got myself into shit. This one is on me. I fucked up."

She grabs me and pulls me to a stop and into her arms.

"Stirling, you listen to me. I will gut every prick in that palace including Calandra herself before I let you go to the gallows. You did nothing wrong. *Nothing*. You hear me?"

I fling my arms around her neck and squeeze her, "I love you."

"Love you too. Now, come on, let's break into some buildings and cause a little chaos, shall we?"

I laugh, "You almost sound like me."

We leave the residential area and head through a grassy field onto a chalky path.

"There," I say pointing at a lone house in the middle of the next field.

We approach the house cautiously.

The only piece of the puzzle that makes any sense came from Morrigan. She found something in the Sangui Grimoire I acquired for her. Apparently in Sangui City, vampires can't get into properties owned by the living. She thinks he's taken their magic and used Bella to twist it for security purposes, stopping anyone but the property owner from entering. Since he'd put them in my name, that explainecd why I could get across the threshold and no one else could.

"Remy?" I say into the earpiece.

"You're all clear to approach. I don't see any additional fields."

"You sure you can check that shit through this orb? I'm going to be super pissed if I get electrocuted or something," I say.

"You're good, it's a clear run right through to the house."

Scarlett glances at me but gives me a nod and then we edge into the garden and up to the front door.

The house is a simple stone cottage. No magic, just like

all the others. There's no hum or vibration coming from the brickwork. The door doesn't swing open to greet us and the air isn't alive with static or cinnamon.

Despite that, the cottage is a sweet thing. While everything is unkempt and worn, under the mess is the potential of what was. Bushy flowers with velvet petals sit in overgrown pots. Trellises covered in hanging plants separate the garden from the house.

Pots lay scattered and smashed, soil leaking from their wounds.

Scarlett opens the door, pushing it wide, a waft of stale air rushes out, and beneath the musty scent is the faintest trace of mint and cinnamon. She glances at me, her eyes hard.

I step over the threshold into a hall, "Come in sister."

Scarlett flinches as she steps inside and then breaks into a wide grin. "It worked." "I have got to study how he did that," Morrigan says through the earpieces.

"Move west through the living room, out to the back room and then upstairs. The house floor plans indicate it's a reverse layout of most of the cottages we've investigated," Remy's voice echoes through my head as we follow her instructions and move to the back of the house.

"Orbs on," she says.

The pair of us do as we're told and climb up the last few steps into the large central bedroom.

"There," I say, pointing to the lattice mark on the wall.

"Just like I thought," Remy breathes. "Gods, it's a work of lattice art."

"Here's the lattice snake." I hold the orb up to the wall and the symbol by the door.

"I hate that I have to cover my tracks so that she won't know I broke her security," Remy grumbles in our ear.

"Didn't know you were so viciously competitive, Rem," Scarlett says.

"Only with her."

Scarlett looks at me, raises an eyebrow and covers her orb to mouth the words. "She wants her so bad."

I have to crush my lips down hard to suppress the cackle that wants to burst out. I nod my head violently and wipe a pressure tear out from my eye.

"So bad," I whisper.

"What's happening?" Remy says in our ears.

"Nothing. Right, what do you need boss?" I say.

"Place the rune-orbs in the corners of the room. And then open the canister. It's going to take me a while."

'While' was an understatement. Scarlett and I were sat in that property for five very long hours. Long enough the first whisper of dawn cracked the sky, streaking it with purples.

"How much longer?" Scarlett yawns.

But even as she's saying it, I'm shifting off the floor as the air grows thick, choking, wisps of smoke burst to life at random spots in the room. The orbs brighten, balloon and vibrate.

"Rem...?" I say grabbing Scarlett and shuffling out of the bedroom.

"Just hold on... *Get down now*," she shouts.

There's a flash, searing white. I throw the pair of us out of the bedroom. There's a rushing explosion of noise, the light blooms, windows shatter, and then, silence.

"Shiiiiit, Remy. What the hell did you do?"

My ears ring from the explosion, Scarlett rubs her eyes.

"You okay?" I ask.

She nods and then her eyes widen. "Jackpot."

I scramble around and my jaw hits the floor.

"Fuck," I say.

"Now what?" Scarlett asks.

CHAPTER 30

STIRLING

The night before the investiture, the team is tense. We know Roman has power and that he is planning to use it at the investiture, he confirmed as much to me yesterday. Plus his guard numbers had quadrupled at the club.

His last words to me were, "Meet me before the investiture and I'll tell you everything."

Which means we're left working on best guesses. Remy is sat crossed legged in Morrigan's cottage living room, her usual whiteboard hovering open in front of her, her face furrowed, her shock of white hair tousled and messy where she's yanking her hand through it in frustration.

Morrigan and Scarlett bring mugs of coffee through.

Morrigan and Scarlett take a seat on the big sofa. Both of them with dark bags under their eyes. I daren't look in the mirror.

Several property files appear on Remy's board; she swipes through them faster and faster.

"We know all this shit. There's pages and pages of data. So what are we missing? We must be looking at this wrong. I just can't work out what we're missing," she barks, wiping her hand over the board and making all the files vanish.

I stare into my coffee cup, the bubbles from the foamy milk bursting and frothing. She's right we are missing something.

"We know he chose those properties because he's hiding his magic in plain sight," I say.

There's a mumbled agreement.

"And we know he's got my name on the properties to try and frame me for whatever he's going to do."

I narrow my eyes at the mug of coffee, the swirling contents, the perfect circle of each milk bubble until it bursts. And that's when it occurs to me.

"Remy?"

"Yeah," she sighs.

"Did you ever plot the houses on a map?"

She yanks her hand through her hair again. "Not all together. Each one is individually plotted in its file." She pulls a file up and scrolls down zooming in and showing the map with a single house.

"Plot them all. Overlay each of those maps onto each other and see where they all are in relation to each other."

Her hands move as fast as Scarlett's bikes, so quickly a sheen of sweat beads on her forehead. A map forms, and slowly, the houses dot on the map. One after another after another.

"Fuck," Morrigan says as a shape appears on the screen.

"I'm not done yet," Remy says.

"No but, look," Scarlett says pointing to the map.

Remy's eyes are ocean wide, but her hands don't stop

moving; she continues to layer and layer until the last house slots into place.

Roman's houses form a perfect set of concentric circles around the city with the palace at the centre. The four of us stare at the whiteboard, the cottage the kind of silent that's reserved only for death.

"He's going to use Bella's lattice magic to harness the power he's embezzled, and trap the palace and all its power in a lattice only he controls." Morrigan says her voice barely a whisper. "And if he harnesses that amount of magic, I won't be able to stop him." She paces across the living room back and forth.

But an idea starts to form.

"Remy how much do you trust your crew?" I ask.

"With my life."

"Then I have a plan."

The cottage door swings open, startling us. Quinn appears in the living room, her curls tight on top of her head and misted from a spatter of rain. But what concerns me is how sheet-white she is, her normally bronze skin ghost-like.

Scarlett is standing and reaching for Quinn but she holds her hand out to stop her. I thought something was wrong. But now I see the paleness isn't fear but rage. The trembling isn't a shiver but a fury.

She holds up a piece of paper. It's old and crumpled and stained like it's lived a long life. I frown.

"You're back. Wh—" I start but she cuts me off. All her fury and rage is angled at Morrigan.

Quinn snaps to me, thrusting the paper out. "This is for you. The records were wiped clean, so it got me thinking ..."

I glance at Scarlett, but she shakes her head. I stand and

take the paper off Quinn. It's dated eight years ago. The more I read, the more blood drains from my face.

> ### THE DAILY IMPERIUM
> *The Daily Imperium has an exclusive, unprece-dented reveal for you today. It appears Imperium DnD club owner and hottest off-the-market Bachelor is, in fact, back on the market. A source close to the couple revealed that they had an explosive argument yesterday morning, which resulted in Morrigan Lee leaving the apartment, and she has yet to return. Our source also revealed that a ring was returned to the family vault just hours after she left. We wouldn't want to speculate, ladies of Imperium, but it might be time for a night out.*

The piece of paper drifts from my hand to the floor, floating like a feather, this way and that until it lands face down.

Morrigan knows. I can tell because her eyes well up and her lips tremble.

"You. Lied." My words are more breathy than whole. I can't bring myself to look at her. The air evaporates from my lungs. My throat dries.

"Stirling," she says.

"Don't say my name."

Scarlett glances from Remy to Quinn and then reaches down to pick up the piece of paper, her eyes widen.

"Oh," Scarlett breathes. Remy snatches the paper out of Scarlett's hand.

Morrigan holds her hands up, a plea of innocence.

"You didn't think this was worth mentioning two years ago?"

I can feel Scarlett's frown on me as she pieces together everything that's being said.

"How was I going to explain that my parents had arranged my marriage to him? We had minutes. Minutes, Stirling. I chose to tell you the most important thing. He was on our tail. We had to make snap decisions."

Water splashes on my sock. I glance down and then touch my face. It's me. I'm crying. I shake my head, my ribs crushing my chest so it's hard to breathe. I want to leave. But then where will that leave us? We have to see this through. We have to see what we started through to the end.

Morrigan takes a step forward, but I inch back.

"Would it have changed anything? Back then? If you'd known who he was to me? That I was meant to marry him? Would you have left and not agreed to the plan? Would you have made that deal?"

And I don't know how to answer that.

Would knowing he was meant to marry her have changed anything?

That bastard.

"All these years. No wonder he hated me. No wonder he's trying to frame me. Gods, Morrigan."

Morrigan hangs her head.

"Gods, how long were you fucking him?" I'm snarling. I don't really want to know; my stomach is already curling.

"Stirling... please..."

"*How long?*" My insides are iron and coal and a writhing mess of toxicity. My mouth tastes like ash and death.

Morrigan's eyes drop to the floor. "Three years. But... It was clear from the start we would never work."

I'm going to be sick. I want to claw my heart out, stop the aching spasms in my chest. All the words I want to say are caught in my throat. My mind is thick and clogged, and the irony is that for once it's me that needs to go and think and not Morrigan.

"Baby please, remember that night. Remember the promise we made. No matter how long it took, we'd find each other again. Find each other where blue meets blue. That's now. We've found each other. We have to see this through."

Quinn shifts beside me. "What do you mean see it through? See what through?"

"Can someone explain what's going on?" Scarlett asks.

Morrigan glances from me to them.

"Stirling please?"

I stare into her eyes, and for the first time in almost a decade I see the shiver of fear flicker through her expression. And I know no matter how angry I am, no matter how stupid her mistake was, she regrets it.

"I made a deal, and I will see it through. But when this is over, we're done. Do you understand?"

A tear falls from her lids, her lips tremble so much she can't speak, so she presses her lips together and nods solemn and quiet.

I turn to the team. "We have something to tell you..."

CHAPTER 31

MORRIGAN

Two Years Ago

Two days before Stirling makes 'The Deal'

Tonight is our three-year anniversary, so I'm taking Stirling to a stunning fish restaurant on the beach near the harbour. It's fast becoming her favourite location in the city, so I've arranged a candle lit dinner for two.

My flip flops slap against the cobbled path leading to the beach front. Stirling is already there. She opens her arms, her hair fresh cut, long at the front short at the back, the tips razor sharp.

"You look gorgeous tonight," I say as I take in her sun-kissed skin in her shorts and t-shirt.

"As do you," she says taking my hand and twirling me around so my yellow beach dress twirls.

"Shall we?" I hold my hand out and she takes it and I

lead us into the restaurant. The waiter seats us on the ocean front, in a private wooden arbor with curtains on three sides. The open front has a stunning view of the sun dripping into the horizon.

The waiter snaps his thumb and the candles on the table and the lights hanging from the wooden construction flick to life.

"Can I get you something to drink?" the waiter says.

"Wine?" I ask.

Stirling nods.

"Rosé please."

He bows, hands us menus and leaves.

"I was thinking we'd share a platter," I say.

"Sure."

I frown at her, "You're quiet this evening."

She takes my hand across the table, bends my palm to kiss my knuckles. "Just basking in your beauty," she grins at me.

"Sleaze." But I'm laughing as I say it. "Seriously, what's wrong."

"How was your mum this afternoon?"

I look out to sea, avoiding her gaze because she knows damn well I hate it when she asks about my family. It's not that I want to keep it a secret, it's that I have to.

But Stirling has been pushing harder and harder. She's so close to Scarlett, their sister bond unbreakable especially after what mother did to her parents.

And there's another secret I keep from her.

The waiter brings us two glasses and a bottle. He pours an inch into the glass and waits. I sniff and then take a drink.

"Delicious, that's great, thanks. We'll have the sharing platter too please."

"Perfect, I'll bring it along shortly," he says and disappears.

The sun has all but melted into the ocean horizon, the sky daubed in rouge and umbers.

"Morrigan?" Stirling says.

"Huh?" I snap out of the reverie.

"Your mother?"

"Right, yes," I pull a hand through my hair. "She's good, yeah. Great. Busy with work. Anyway, how's Scarlett? Still having trouble with that poisoner?"

Stirling nods, but her face has hardened. Her eyes are vacant, void of emotion and I know she's pissed at me.

"Don't. Please? Not tonight. We're meant to be celebrating," I whine.

She shakes her head at me but can't bring her gaze to mine. "I have to go to Sangui city on business next week." Her words are clipped.

I don't want our night to be like this, but I don't know how to fix it without breaking my vow of secrecy.

"Stirling, please."

"What? You didn't want to talk about your family. So I'm making conversation."

I sigh, rub my forehead. "We're doing this now are we?"

"We're going to have to at some point. We've been together three years and I've never met your family. What normal couple does that? What are you keeping from me?"

The waiter returns with the sharing platter and two plates, some bread and olives. "Enjoy your meal."

"Thanks," Stirling says a little too sharply.

A breeze whips around the arbor, ruffling the curtains, I take a sip of wine before picking an oyster and several prawns off the platter. "I'm not keeping anything from you."

She huffs at me and then downs her glass of wine.

"How can I make this better?"

She glares at me. "You're going to introduce me?"

"I will."

"Eventually?"

I press my lips together and nod. "But not now."

Her shoulders sag, her eyes glisten like she's going to cry. But she wipes her face and says. "Fine. Then tell me something true."

I chew on a prawn. Its dressing is a little spicy and gives a kick as it slides down my throat. The breeze is tight, and I swear it's the waves of irritation peeling off Stirling. I decide to get as close to the truth as I can. Give her as much truth as possible without revealing who my family are.

"My sister is beautiful on the outside, but ugly as sin on the inside."

That makes Stirling crack a small smile. "Surely not."

"Oh gods yeah, she's an awful, awful magician. She hates that she's the second born. Got a real sense of entitlement that one."

"What does she do?"

"Swan around, attending parties and discussing fashion trends mostly."

"She sounds hideous."

"You see?" I say and grin.

Stirling's whole body relaxes, she picks up an oyster and swallows it down. "Tell me about your father."

"I have his heart, inherited my mother's mind for strategy though. She's as ruthless as they get. A brilliant businesswoman. Father has always been softer, he spends a lot of time working with people."

"What do you mean working with people?"

I pick out a crab leg and take a bite, trying to find a way

to explain that my father hears Magician complaints, deals with policy changes for the land and works to help the magicians in most need.

"I guess, he's a humanitarian. He works with a lot of campaigners and tries to advocate for change for the benefit of those that can't."

"Wow. He sounds amazing."

"He is," but I can't quite make myself smile because he's grown sick of late, and the whispers from the medics have me concerned.

"You know, if we're ever going to get married, you're going to have to introduce me to him so I can ask for your hand in marriage."

I drop my fork. "You... want to... marry me?"

A crease furrows into her forehead. "Well, not today, but obviously, I've been in love with you since you walked into that poker room. Why... don't you want t—"

"It's not that."

"Then what is it?" she says her frown growing deeper.

"It's... I..."

"Oh, let me guess. It's complicated. You can't explain. I wouldn't understand." She throws her hands up. "Just when I thought we were getting somewhere."

She pushes her chair out, is up on her feet before I can attempt to explain myself.

"Wait. Please. Just let me explain..." I say.

There's a pause, she hovers by the table, her hand on her hip. I try and form the words, a dozen different sentences run through my mind but none of them work. How do you explain that you're a princess and you're contracted to marry someone. How do you explain that your parents had your girlfriend's family executed? Gods.

There's too much that needs to be unravelled. I have no idea where to start.

So instead, I slowly close my mouth, and look up at her.

"Typical," she tuts. "More lies, more secrets. Gods, Morrigan. I adore you. I really do. But I don't want to be with you tonight. I can't keep doing this. *We* can't keep on like this. I mean is a secret really any different than a lie?"

I find my words then. "Of course it is. I haven't ever lied to you. There are just certain things I can't tell you. That's completely different."

"Is it? Well, it feels the same to me. Happy anniversary, Morrigan."

She steps onto the beach and disappears around the back of the arbor and off into the distance leaving me alone with nothing but the darkening sky and my heart breaking.

CHAPTER 32

STIRLING

Two Years Ago

Two days *after* 'The Deal'

I won't lie, the lady-balls I had on me last night to barrel up to Roman's party was... well, quite something even for me. If Scarlett hadn't been with me, I may have pussied out. But I was such a mess after Morrigan and I broke up that I think Scarlett felt bad letting me go anywhere on my own. And thank the gods because last night was everything. However bad Scarlett felt, it couldn't have bothered her that much, because she skulked at the edge of the garden party for most of the afternoon and evening and then disappeared with some woman into one of the sex rooms. Gods knows who it was. I'm sure I can pick her brains this evening though.

I waltz up to DnD, Roman's nightclub headquarters—and cover for all the illegal shit he's no doubt doing—and I thrust open the club doors. They smash against the hall walls, flooding the dim corridor with beams of morning light.

He has no idea I'm coming, of course, though if he doesn't at least suspect I'll be hungry for some kind of revenge, then he's more of a fool than I took him for.

No matter, he'll never expect the deal I'm about to offer him.

A young man with long blue hair and stick like limbs hurries from around the counter and flaps at me, a chain of keys jangling on his trouser pocket. Excellent. I'll have those.

I take a step forward, a faux stumble, knocking into him. A sleight of hand and the keys are in my pocket.

"Who are you? You can't barge in here like this," he says when we're both upright again.

"I'm Roman's new employee. Who the hell are you?"

He opens his glossy-lipped mouth and wafts his painted nails in my face. "You're not in the books, and there's no record of any meeting this morning, so try again missy."

"Look. I'm short on time, and trust me when I tell you Roman will be expecting me. Are you going to disappoint him or are you going to trot behind that there little counter and ring up to your boss's office?"

He presses his shiny lips together and folds his arms, glaring at me. Then he slouches, "Fine. Name?"

"Lady Grey. He'll know who I am."

He marches back around the counter and snatches an orb and dials up to Roman's office.

"There's a woman here to see you."

There's a pause.

"Lady Grey. But there's nothing in the diar—" he stops mid-sentence. "B—"

He fires me a shitty glare and huffs.

"Fine, I'll send her up."

He slams the orb back into the receiver and points at the end of the corridor. "Push the wall, door will open. Good day."

He turns his back on me and disappears into the darkened corners of the reception.

I move to the end of the corridor, push the door open and hesitate; the stairs are glass-clear. I can see all the way down to the ground outside. Weird.

I climb, my stomach bottoming out the higher I get, which is unusual as heights aren't an issue for me normally.

I push open Roman's door and find him sat at a huge desk, behind him a floor-to-ceiling bookcase with racks and racks of books. There's even a ladder to slide across the case to reach the highest tomes. In one corner is a bar and scattered around the room are a few sculptures.

Behind the desk, Roman puffs on a newly lit cigar. He holds it out to me, indicating I should take it. I do.

"Well, I must say, this is unexpected. I ruin your life and what... you come back for more?" he says snipping and lighting another cigar. "To what do I owe this unexpected pleasure?"

If I'm going to play this right, I need to be bold. I suck on the cigar and blow out the smoke. It's acrid. I've always preferred cigarettes. I stroll across his office and right behind his bar.

I run my fingers along the line of bottles, there's some seriously expensive drink here. He might be a complete life-ruining cunt, but the man has taste. I waggle a bottle of... I glance at the label. Shite. It's whiskey.

He raises an eyebrow at me, "Sure, help yourself,"

I pour two tumblers of whiskey and bring the bottle back to the table.

"So?" He takes his tumbler and drinks a huge gulp down.

I tip half the shot straight into my mouth and suppress the urge to hiss. Fuck I hate whiskey.

I swill the rest of the contents of my cup and then lock eyes with Roman. "You're going to give me a job," I say and puff cigar smoke rings out.

He laughs, full bellied, head rolling back.

I stay stone-still. Pour every ounce of concentration I have into staring this son of a bitch down. He stops laughing, the faintest hint of a crease between his brows.

"You're serious?"

"Deadly."

He shifts in his chair.

"I know what you're going to say," I start. "And no, I haven't forgotten what you did to me two nights ago."

"Then... why?" he says.

I take a deep breath, smile sweetly at him, but there's no mistaking the lethal blades in my eyes. "Let me be clear, I think you're the worst magician in New Imperium. I hate every fucking cell in your body."

He huffs out an indignant laugh. "Good start, my friend. Really selling yourself to me."

I let my magic ease out, the smooth warmth tingling beneath my skin. No doubt Roman has anti-magic protections so he can't be coerced, so I'm not even going to try. I can, however, loosen him up, make the atmosphere conducive to negotiations. I push out a little magic, let it seep into the cigar smoke and float through the room.

"I don't need to sell myself. By the end of this conversation, you'll want me to work for you."

He raises a single eyebrow. "What a difference two nights makes, so bolshy, so aggressive," he says, his upper lip curling.

He glances at his watch, son of a bitch pretending he's got other shit to do, when the throb in the air tells me he's engrossed in this dance. I decide to up the ante.

"I think it's obvious neither of us like each other. But that doesn't mean we can't work together. The way I see it, there are two reasons we should at least consider a negotiation."

He raises his whiskey glass to me and sips, "Go on..."

"One, given the deal you made me agree to, my hands are tied. As long as you pose a threat to Morrigan, I can't make a move against you. And two, the enemy of my enemy is my friend. Everyone knows you hate the crown. And Calandra took everything from me. My home, my titles, my land and my legacy status."

His eyes narrow at me, but he leans forward.

"Besides, there is no negotiator better than me in the whole of New Imperium."

"Prove it," he sneers.

"Can't reveal clients or sources, you know that."

He leans back. "Then I'm not interested."

I grit my teeth, the bastard playing hard ball. "Fine. Remember Giant Jake?"

"That wasn't you..."

I grin, "Of course it was me. Who else could get that beast of a man to give up his infamous blade?"

"And how did you get him to give it to you."

I shrug, "Gave him something he wanted more..."

"Which was...?"

"Privileged information that. If you need more proof, do you remember that job on the weapons quarter in the palace a couple of months ago?"

Roman nods.

I dust my shoulder.

"Intriguing."

"Oh, and one last thing." I whip out the keys I swiped from the receptionist and drop them onto Roman's desk.

He glances down at them and slowly looks back up at me.

"Thing is, Roman. You don't just want me, you *need* me to work for you. Because if you don't hire me, I will go out of my way to make your life very, very difficult." I get up and pace around his office, sucking the cigar smoke down, and threading more magic through the puffs.

"Is that a threat?"

"Not unless you want it to be." I sit down again.

"There's just one little thing you're forgetting."

"Oh?"

"I stole the love of your life, why would I ever trust you?"

"Because I want Morrigan safe."

His jaw flexes, one hand slides under the desk, the other reaches out to me. "Alright, Little Stir. Let's shake on it."

Something's off. There's a twitch in the air like a worm burrowing through the earth, there's a wrongness.

I slide my hand into his. His grip tightens. He slams my hand onto the desk, pulls out a knife from under the table and places it on my forearm, the tip just scraping the skin, a bead of blood forming at the point.

I hiss.

"So prove it. Mark yourself as mine, and I'll agree to the

deal. I'll leave Morrigan alone for as long as you work for me."

He releases the blade and hands the hilt to me.

"You're a psycho," I spit.

"And you're desperate. You stink of it."

He grabs the scruff of my collar and yanks me forward. "You listen to me, you legacy shit, I don't need you. I don't need anyone. One day, this city will be mine, the palace will crumble under my feet and I will ruin Calandra. You threaten me again and it won't just be your arm that's scarred. You understand?"

Roman's unhinged, his eyes feral and wild.

However hard I thought it was going to be to play this son of a bitch, I'm going to have my work cut out. But I will find dirt on him. I will ferret my way into his business, I'll earn his trust, and then I'll cut this motherfucker down from the inside out.

I breathe deep, never taking my eyes off him and sink the blade into my arm. My teeth grit down. The slice of flesh and muscle sends pulses of agonising heat coursing through my limbs. But I keep staring at him, holding his gaze, never bending. Goosebumps fleck down my back, static plagues my vision as bile claws at my throat. But I keep pushing. I will not let him win.

When the blade hits the table, I let go of it and release the faintest of whimpers. It makes Roman jolt, breaking our gaze.

He hesitates, glancing at my arm, seeing the blade already through my skin. His head tilts, his bottom lip dropping. He's impressed.

"Fine. 8am Monday." He yanks the blade out of my arm. I hiss at the sudden rush of blood spilling out of my forearm. "Now get out."

My arm is excruciating but I refuse to let him think he has the upper hand. So I throw the rest of the whiskey down, stub my cigar out, and then I leave.

It's not until his office door is shut and blood drips down his glass staircase that I let the tears roll down my cheeks. I bite my lip hard enough to draw even more blood. I leave red breadcrumbs all the way down his stairs and through the hallway.

"Deary me," the receptionist says when he sees me. "Here."

He passes me a cloth and I wrap it around my arm. "Thanks. See you Monday."

He opens his mouth to say something and decides better of it, shutting it and opening the door for me.

"I hope you know what you're doing," he says as the door closes behind me.

And for the first time since I walked into his club, I have to wonder if I do.

CHAPTER 33

STIRLING

The Night Before The Investiture

I turn to the team.

"We have something to tell you..." I say.

"I don't think I can handle anymore revelations tonight without a glass of something strong," Quinn says and retreats to the kitchen to find a bottle of wine. She comes back with five glasses and two bottles, opening and pouring each of us an exceptionally large glass.

"I've ordered pizza," she says and then nestles onto the sofa next to Scarlett. Morrigan gets up, giving them space. She makes to sit with me, but hesitates when she catches the storm in my expression and stands instead.

The night I lost Morrigan was the worst of my life. I knew who Roman was, of course. But I didn't know who he was to *her*.

Not then. I still can't believe she lied. My chest spasms against the truth of it. We're so close to ending this I can't process the pain right now. So instead, I lock the screaming in my mind behind a mental door and tell the team everything.

I wipe my face, clear the tears and focus. "Roman must have been following me for a while. He found me at the docks, crept out from the darkness like a poisoned shadow," I say.

Funny thing is, I knew I was in trouble. The rumours of his penchant for violence and death went far beyond reputation and myth. Most of my underground colleagues already bore scars carved by Roman or one of his henchmen.

Perhaps then, our meeting was always inevitable. Like calls to like, after all. And while I might not murder so freely as he, my soul isn't any whiter. Not now, not after two years with him. And sure, it was in the name of love, in the name of finding my way back to her. But it doesn't make my conscience any cleaner and it doesn't remove all the crimes that stain my hands.

I still remember the way he moved. A dark mountainous hulk, all shoulders and fists. But it wasn't his bulk that had me sliding my fingers into my waistband to grab my knife. It was the look in his eye.

He was hungry for blood. And something about the sharp flex of his jaw, told me it was my blood specifically.

Morrigan's voice is quiet, the shiver of shame drawing through her trembling tone. "It was the same thing for me. Only, he knew where I lived, had already been in my house many times. Despite my protestations. Despite the fact I'd warned him, told him I'd never marry him. He hid in the corner of my bedroom. Waited until I crept into bed and held the knife to my throat."

Scarlett's jaw flexes, her fists balled. She wants retribution as much as I do.

Morrigan slips her hand over mine, but I pull away. She flinches at the action.

"He threatened us both. Told me things about Stirling he shouldn't know. Things about our relationship. The places we went, the way she would touch me."

"He must have been spying for weeks. Because the things he knew about us, about her—? It was enough to convince me he could end her if I didn't comply."

"Didn't you ask why he was doing it? What he wanted?" Remy says.

"Of course, but he said the same thing to us both," Morrigan says.

I deepen my voice, do my best impression of Roman. "Why doesn't matter. What matters is that I'll do it. Will knowing *why* change your answer? Will you suddenly say no and let her die?"

Quinn presses her lips together and nods. "Bastard."

I grit my teeth, pull the stinging memory forward. "He had me surrounded on the dock, and then he dragged Morrigan out from the darkness. She was bound, gagged, her lip split. I swore right then that I'd do anything to take him down. But it wasn't just her."

"What do you mean?" Quinn asks leaning forward.

"He threatened Scarlett, too. He knew about several jobs you'd done. I think he'd set them up, so he had evidence to frame you if I didn't comply. I was cornered. So I did the one thing Morrigan constantly cusses me out for."

Scarlett huffs, "Shoot first, ask questions later?"

"I didn't have time to think. All I cared about was protecting Morrigan."

"I was screaming behind the gag, begging her not to do it. But it was pointless. She'd already made her mind up."

"So I agreed to a blood bond."

"Gods, Stirling. What the hell did you agree to?" Remy asks.

I adjust my voice, deepen it like Roman's. "Leave her, Stirling, and I'll let her live. That's the deal. Take it or leave it."

"So she took it," Morrigan says.

"Yes, Morrigan. But the devil is in the detail, and the art of every deal is the wording. Even in the height of panic, I knew that. I drew first blood, so I made the terms."

Quinn and Scarlett's eyes both darken. Like hunters, they can sense the turning of the fight, they can smell Roman's blood.

"What did you agree to?" Remy asks.

"I said 'I'll leave Morrigan tonight, in exchange for her life. Of this I promise in blood and bonds.'"

The room is silent, each of the team rolling the words back over and over until Scarlett barks out a laugh. "Oh, well done, sister."

I shrug. "I did what I said. I knew I'd have to leave her. I knew we'd have to break up *for the night.*"

"Yes, but you didn't bank on my resistance," Morrigan says. "As it happens, I was rather more insistent on a longer break up. I didn't want any repercussions from the deal. If Stirling came running back to me and Roman knew he'd been duped, he'd have killed us both."

"Ruin the story why not," I glare at her.

Morrigan pouts, "Thankfully, he didn't need me to make a bond, he stupidly thought Stirling's was sufficient. Didn't matter he had enough shit against me."

Scarlett turns to me, "Well you clearly didn't leave."

"Oh no, I did. I had to. Otherwise, Morrigan's life would be forfeit."

"So what happened?" Quinn says.

"I found her, later that night, roaming the harbour," Morrigan says.

"There's a watery-blue mansion on the harbour," I say.

"The one near your shed?" Scarlett asks.

"That's it."

Morrigan sips her wine, "It took me a couple of hours, but I managed to escape. I used locator magic and found Stirling there. We snuck into the garden of the mansion."

Quinn claps her hands over her mouth and gawps at me. "Didn't Roman follow you?"

"He didn't need to. I'd made a blood oath. If I broke it, Morrigan's life would be over," I say.

Morrigan pushes a loose lock of hair behind her ear and takes a sip of wine. Her eyes are so distant, as lost in the memories as I am. I tear my gaze away.

I can't bear to look at her.

Eventually, she continues. "It's all about the wording. Stirling said she'd leave 'tonight'. And thank the high magician, I found her before midnight, so we had a chance to say goodbye. Roman is an arrogant bastard—he didn't bother following me or sending any men after me. He knew I had no choice but to adhere to the deal. Stirling had laid blood on it."

Remy's face contorts into a sneer, "Piece of shit."

"His ego has always blinded him to his weaknesses," I say. "But by the time Morrigan got to me, we were both furious. Instead of sorting out a plan, we spent the night arguing,"

"We did try to strategise. We ran through scenario after scenario. But we were both so furious, we couldn't agree on what we should do. We didn't have enough time."

"As usual, you were livid with me for acting without thinking and agreeing to a deal in the first place, like I had any other choice."

Even from the corner of my eye I can tell Morrigan's face is pinching. She folds her arms and continues.

"Stirling wanted to break up that night and get back together the next day. But I wouldn't have it. It was too dangerous, not least because it could cost me my life, but because for all of Roman's arrogance, he isn't a fool. I knew he'd watch us, at least for a while. He wanted the crown and a marriage to me. It's what he was promised, and Stirling was in the way of that."

"So we agreed to end things for real," I say and my voice cracks and wobbles, the memories still sharp and wretched and so entangled in the heat of what I feel today. "We didn't set a time, only a promise that we would end him."

"I told her, I'd always find my way back there. To that mansion. It became our symbol. We said that one day, when it was safe, and we knew he couldn't threaten us anymore, we'd find each other where blue meets blue. Where the ocean meets that house."

I huff out a laugh. It all seems so pointless now. "I told Morrigan that one day I'd be able to say I'd come home. To her. To us."

Tears well in Quinn's eyes. "You gave up two years together hoping you'd be able to find your way back?" her words are breathy.

Then she pokes Scarlett in the arm. "Gods, why aren't you that romantic?"

Scarlett glares at her, "I'm going to sp—"

"And that's enough of that conversation," I say cutting her off and punting her in the shin with my toe.

Remy has been quiet this whole time, taking in the story, she leans forward now. "So much makes sense. You two bang way too often to hate each other."

Morrigan stifles a laugh, quickly squashing it as Scarlett turns a pale shade of green.

"But that doesn't explain how you ended up working for him," Quinn says.

I laugh, for real this time. "That was the easy bit. The enemy of my enemy is my friend," I say.

"The crown," Remy says nodding.

"Roman hated the palace as much as I did back then. So I used it as an in. He ruined my life, and the dock lads owed me, so I blocked his imports and fucked his business up enough to get his attention. Then I went and had a little chat. We both knew that if I went near Morrigan he'd kill her. So I used that, told him she was his leverage over me. I didn't know she was the princess, of course. And he waited, bided his time before he told me that little truth. But in his eyes, that only gave me more reason to act against the crown."

"But that's not what you want, right?" Quinn asks, her gaze flicking between Morrigan and I.

"It wasn't. I was using it as a way to get closer to him. Figured I'd gather dirt in a couple of months and take him out and find Morrigan again. But a couple of months turned into a year and a year into two."

I glance at Morrigan, who gives me a limp smile. "When the team came together a few months ago, it was a shock seeing Stirling. I was furious with her for coming anywhere near me when we didn't have a solution. But it was more fear for her life than anything."

I nod. "Morrigan tried to stay as far away from me as possible. She didn't want Roman or his spies to discover we were back together. It wasn't until her mother announced the investiture that we really started working together to bring him down. And here we are nearly two and a half years later."

Morrigan stands. "So... I know you hate me right now, but are you still willing to see the deal through? Make one last plan."

She holds her hand out to me. I hesitate. My body coursing hot and feverish with betrayal. And while Morrigan's hurt me, I want vengeance more.

I shake her hand and stand. "Tomorrow, we take Roman down once and for all. He thinks he's got access to three dozen houses packed full of stolen power, and I need to lure him into a deal. I think it's time for a little payback, don't you?"

"About damn time," Morrigan says.

CHAPTER 34

MORRIGAN

The Investiture Part 1

Convincing mother to allow me to be invested before I took Roman out was the hard part. We spent several hours hashing out the variables and options last night. Stirling didn't look at me once, just agreed to whatever request I made.

I've fucked up.

Despite the fact she's refusing to talk to me, she came with me to speak to mother. When we laid out the plans, and I assured mother that if I failed, I'd step aside, she agreed. Of course my word wasn't quite satisfactory and I had to swear to her in a blood-bonded oath I'd step down if we failed.

It meant the real investiture would be done in the middle of the night and recorded for the public. The High Magician—although rattled at being spontaneously dragged out of bed in the middle of the night—agreed to do the ceremony.

Which is how I came to stand in the ceremonial room in the palace. For all the pomp and flare and importance of tomorrow, the real thing is a modest affair. A private moment between the three of us: the High Magician, mother and I.

In a way, I rather like it this way. More intimate, less pressure. I just wish Stirling was here with me. I fucked up, bad. I should have told her who he was to me, but how could I?

The way she looked at me, the way her soul fell apart, her heart breaking in front of me. I don't know how to fix it, how to repair the damage I've done. But when this is over, I have to try. I can't let her go, not again.

The High Magician recites the official texts and incantations. I lay my hand on the skull of the original High Magician and swear my oath. Herbs mixed with Sanatio are burnt, smeared on my forehead and across my wrists. The High Magician then tattoos the royal Collection Sanatio sigil over my heart.

The whole process is recorded ready to be aired on the screens in the city centre for the magicians of New Imperium to watch later. They'll never know it wasn't live. In order for our plan to work, it was too risky to allow Roman anywhere near the palace before I was already invested. At least now I can fight with the palace's magic in my control.

When it's over, my skin itches where the new tattoo is bonding to my existing magic. But aside from that, I don't feel too different.

The same impending loss of freedom that's always hung around my neck still looms heavy. The same knowledge that I'll spend my life in service is true, as is the aching awareness that Stirling is lost to me.

What sours my day further is Penelope. Given her connection to Roman, she too had to be part of the plan.

She saunters in at the end of the ceremony. Doesn't matter, she's here and that's what I need.

"Pen," I say, my voice thick with ice, as I walk out of the ceremony room and down the hall. I don't wait for her to follow me. I know she will be desperate to dig her nails into me.

She follows, like I predicted. I draw her away from the ceremony room and down the hall where I need her.

"Delightful little ritual," she says a snarl dripping through her tone.

"Ah yes, jealousy. Your favourite emotion," I spit.

"And ungrateful, entitled pretentiousness seems to be yours."

I stop dead. "Oh look, Penelope used a four-syllable word. Careful sis, you might give yourself a headache."

She bares her teeth at me, a nasty little smile, all teeth and gums and sharp eyes.

"Just here to say congratulations, *heir,*" she drags out the last word.

She's pathetic. When you look at Stirling and Scarlett's relationship, their closeness, the tender love and sibling banter, it makes me sad knowing we'll never have that. I'd kill for a relationship like that.

But Penelope was spiteful from birth. Born resentful that I came first. Even before she could speak she hated me. Would scratch and kick me, steal my toys and bite me when the nanny wasn't looking.

Could I have tried harder? Been a better sister?

Possibly.

Probably.

Too late now. Pen can go fuck herself. She just needs to stay out of the way today.

"Yes. Thank you *spare*. Now, if you'll excuse me, your fiancé needs dealing with, which means you... need to be otherwise occupied."

I glance at the end of the corridor. Scarlett and one of Remy's crew appear. Penelope's expression crumples.

"What are you doing?" she says as she glances from me to them.

"Can't have you in the way. But don't worry, you won't feel a thing."

She turns around ready to bark some petty shit at me when Quinn appears and places a chemical-rich cloth over her mouth. Pen's eyes widen then narrow into furious slits. But before she can snarl anything else at me, her knees buckle.

Scarlett's there to catch her. "Got her," she says.

"Good, get out of sight quick," I say and turn to Quinn, "How long have we got?"

"I made the concoction a little stronger than necessary. I'd say a good few hours."

"Excellent. On to phase two."

"Everything is on track. Stirling's already with him," Scarlett says and starts to leave. I hold her back.

"I fucked up," I say.

Scarlett's eyes soften. "I know. But she does love you deep down."

"You really think I can fix this? What if she's mad enough to betray me...?"

Remy's crew member carries Pen down the hall and off toward her bedroom.

Scarlett hugs me, then holds me by the shoulders, "This

is one of those times you're going to have to keep faith. I've never known Stirling not to keep her end of a deal."

She sprints down the hall to catch up to Quinn and Remy's crew. My gut is in knots. Stirling may not have ever broken a deal, but there's always a first for everything.

CHAPTER 35

STIRLING

The Investiture Part 2

I meet Roman at the front of the palace, my heart shattered in two. All this time, she lied. Over and over.

And Roman has been laughing in my face this entire time, humiliating me. No wonder he wanted to frame me.

"Roman..." I say. "At your service, as promised." I bow deeply to him, more to keep the snarling rage from my face than in deference, but the bow serves both purposes.

"I wasn't sure you'd come."

"I told you, the crown can fuck itself. Morrigan's a liar."

He nods, a sneer creeping over his lips. "Then let us begin."

"Begin?"

"There's no point going in through the side door. The staff need to meet their new king. Might as well walk in like I mean to."

A man built more like an ocean liner than a magician walks up to Roman. "Men are in position, Sir."

"Excellent. And the alarm system?"

"Bella disabled it."

"Then it's time."

Roman walks up to the front of the palace, the marble pillars glisten cream in the sunlight.

"Good morning, Sir, do you have your identification and ticket?" the guard says.

Roman draws a line through the air and the guard's uniform slices in half.

There's a moment where his eyes widen in recognition of both his injury and of who I am. My heart is in my mouth. I wonder whether he'll cry out and ruin everything. His mouth curves around my name.

So I do the unthinkable.

"Move," I bellow at Roman as the guard draws a sword. Even as the soldier stumbles forward, blood spilling down his uniform, his guts in one hand a trembling blade in the other, I bring the man's head down low and cut his throat so deep the only thing he can do is gargle.

It's a savage death. He doesn't deserve it. He's never been anything other than civil. But I cannot allow one man to undo everything I've sacrificed.

A chill spreads through my heart, a vile sickness claws at my throat. His blood spills onto my hands and spreads like hives. I scream internally and plead to the High Magician to wipe his blood from my soul. I pray I can make his sacrifice worthy.

Another guard appears at the end of the corridor. His eyes widen. There's a single second of frozen time. It stretches long, almost like a kiss, only this time it's not love but death that hangs between us.

"Go," I scream at Roman.

And then we're charging into the palace. Guards swarm the corridor. Roman, drunk on power, forces his way through man after man.

There are fists and limbs everywhere. I'm forced to stay behind him. Scarlett's taught me well over the years, but my skill is with words not knives.

Still, the guards are outmatched. No one expects an assault on the palace. Their weapons, while sharp are only ever used ceremonially. The palace's protective guards and soldiers are located in the assassin's guild. Scarlett has already taken out the traitor guards working for Roman, but as planned, she's also deactivated the security alarms. Remy sent word of warning to Bella in the form of a lap dancer with a penchant for handcuffs and ropes. Bella is safe and secure and not culpable for today. But it also means for now, at least, no one is coming.

These guards are going to be slaughtered and no one is coming to rescue them, all for the sake of appearances. We have to lure Roman into the courtyard. We have to allow him to commit treason before we take him out.

Nausea lines my throat as I slice and stab at flesh.

Fists fly towards my face, but I block and feint, kick out and drive swords into flesh. Roman uses nothing but magic and might; his knuckles break cheeks and knees.

I'm panting hard by the time we reach the end of the corridor. I'm slicked in blood and ache in places I didn't know existed and my hands tremble. I didn't want to do this. I didn't want it to get this far.

A hand grabs my throat the cold pressed steel nicking my skin. I still, the icy trickle of fear flowing down my spine.

"*Hurry up*," Roman barks, but I can't move, a guard has me and if I budge an inch I die.

"*Stirling*?" He bellows, and finally he turns around.

The guard increases the pressure of the knife to my throat. I swallow; the sharp edge digs in hard enough a dribble of blood oozes out and tickles my neck as it falls beneath my shirt.

"Give it up, Roman," the guard says.

Roman laughs, "You think I care about her? Do it. Kill her. I'm still going to gut your queen from end to end, and there's nothing you can do about it."

There's a moment of sinking, my stomach and my heart falling, as I realise I'll never get to see Morrigan.

Isn't it odd, that in these moments of life and death, when the veil between breathing and not thins like air, that we realise what matters?

A hardness lines my gut, a resilience made of pure steel.

I can't quit now.

I slam my foot down on the guard's toe, and he yelps, releasing my throat.

Roman swipes his arms through the air and the guard freezes. I'm splattered with blood. It covers my face, my arms. Droplets fleck my lips and skin. My nose wrinkles as the guard's eyes go vacant and then he splits in half and slides to the floor in pieces.

I gag, wipe my arm over my face but it does nothing to clean the blood away and I wonder whether I'll ever be free of it.

"Thank you," I say to Roman.

"I hated you once. But you have proven time and time again the depths of your loyalty. Today, I'm proud to have you by my side. We're going to finish this together." He gives me his hand, and I take it.

Lies.

It's all lies. He needs me here so he can lay the blame on me. The paper trail already leads to me, he just needs the world to witness it.

The pair of us are panting by the time we've battled our way through the palace corridors. Gods knows how many guards are dead. Guilt wraps cold fingers around my belly. If I think about it too hard I won't be able to follow through, won't be able to get my head on straight to make this happen. And I have to. I have one chance at finishing this.

My muscles scream from the abuse. I'm not the fighter in this family. That was always Scarlett. She's trained to maim and kill. She's trained to fight for more hours than I can count. Inside, I'm sickened. I've never seen so much blood. My skin crawls with it, dried flakes peel like leaves off my arms, dark crusts form under my nails. I have to keep going so I grit my teeth and forge on.

We're close now.

We pull into the Sanatio courtyard. The architects have made the courtyard ten times the size it normally is. Five hundred magician's fill rows and rows of seats and there at the head of the courtyard stood upon a stage backed by the oldest Sanatio tree in the city is Calandra.

This is it. The moment Morrigan's life changes the moment she loses a life and gains a crown.

"Ladies, gentlemen, magicians, dignitaries, and friends! Welcome." Calandra's smile is wide. The music flares to life, a drum beat that matches the thudding in my own heart.

"Ready?" Roman's dark eyes have a nasty glimmer, and gods, am I ready.

Just not in the way he thinks.

I'm ready for his world to come crumbling down.

Every truth he thought he knew. All the holds he

thought he had over me. This is where it all comes to fruition. I hated him before, now I want to destroy him and all it will take is one last deal.

He steels himself, steps behind a pillar. "Remember. When I break up the central aisle, you're going to go left, charge up the side of the stage. My men should be filing into the palace as we speak.

He's ready to step out of the shadows and down the main aisle.

Morrigan sweeps on stage to a crescendo of applause. Roman practically vibrates with desire. It crawls over him, mixed with magic. I can smell the stench of his jealousy. It's bitter like stale sweat. I hate this man as much as he hates me.

He takes a step, a single toe onto the purple carpet, ready to fire magic down the aisle and take the whole palace down. He opens his arms, draws them into the circle he needs to access his stored magic.

Nothing happens.

He frowns.

Draws his arms into a circle again.

"The f—"

"Ohhh, Roman," I trill, with as much potency as I can.

I know what comes next, and it takes a colossal feat of willpower not to let a smile creep into my voice.

I reach out, grab his arm, my fingers gripping tight. I never do this. I don't take liberties with him, I'm his marionette, his *Little Stir*.

Patronising cunt. He thinks I'm just a puppet ready to do deals on his behalf. And I was happy to let him think it. I've never acted like I'm the one with power.

But I am.

I always have been.

Confusion ripples across his brow. I pull him back into the shadows.

"What's going on?" he says. "We haven't got time."

"Is there a problem?" I say, light, sweet. "Trouble accessing the power?"

"N—" his closes his eyes, reaches for the power he should be able to access. Silvery lattice marks flare bright over his arms, burning through the spilled blood. And then the light drops out. The magic fades.

His expression stills into the coldest steel I've ever seen. If I were anyone else, I'd leave a puddle of piss right here in the courtyard. But this is my time. And it is my day.

"What. Have. You. Done?" he snarls.

I lean back against the marble pillar, pick at the crusty blood beneath my fingernails. "It's not what I've done, Roman. It's what you did. Did you really think I wouldn't discover that you tried to frame me? That you put my name on those property records so that if anything went south, you'd be able to pin this on me."

His mouth parts ever so slightly and then the darkness is back and his face hard like rock and death. It takes everything I have not to look at Morrigan. Not to hesitate. This is it, this is the moment we've all be working towards.

Will he take the bait?

"But you see, that's put you in a bit of a predicament. Because now the properties and everything in them are mine."

He sniffs, glances at the proceedings on stage. Calandra knows she must drag the speeches out, give me time to convince him to my way of thinking.

"What do you want?" he growls.

Ahh, there he is. No hesitation, no flicker of fear. Sheer arrogance, and that's how I know I've got him.

I curl his words around my tongue, the sugar-sweet treat of knowing they're bait. This is just the final mouthful, every step he's taken has led him here. He's already in this deal, he just doesn't know it.

"I want, *Roman*, what I'm owed."

He recoils, the words so familiar, so alien.

"I'll give you the properties back if you give me Calandra and Morrigan."

His eyes narrow. He glances at the stage.

"You showed me who they really are. Who she really is. A liar, a whore. Her family took everything from me. My parents. My titles. And then Morrigan tried to take my heart."

I spit on the floor. I draw all the hurt, the aching, the agony of the last two years and funnel it into my expression.

He steps back, raises an eyebrow. This was unexpected. Good. He's on the back foot, exactly where I need him. I focus on his expression, let my magic curl through my system and read his body language. I sink hook after hook into him. React just as he expects me too.

"Fuck the crown. Fuck Morrigan. I won't be fooled by them again. So yes, I want what's owed to me. When you take the palace, you give me back my standing in the legacies. Fuck your job, and you for lying to me. But, as a courtesy for being good to me these last two years, I'll give you back your properties in exchange for doling out their punishment."

I kick off the pillar, spin the blade on my finger the way Scarlett always does. "I like to think of it as justice. It's only fair."

His eyes are feverish; he doesn't want to be stood here debating, he wants to take the crown.

"Tick tock, Roman. What's it to be?" I let the blade fall into my hands, clench it hard until the metal bites into my skin. Blood drips to the marble floor.

I land the final blow. "She took my heart, Roman. Let me give you hers."

He glares at me, fury etching feather lines into his expression. Beat after beat crawl by but finally, he says. "You play a good game Stirling."

He claps as he closes the distance between us.

I hand the blade to Roman, hilt first.

He takes it. "There's something delicious about the full circle of revenge: a heart for a heart. So fitting. So poetic."

I shrug. "What can I say? I have a way with words."

He slices the blade down his palm, the wet squelch and slice of skin my new favourite sound; the sound of him looping a noose around his own neck.

I hold my hand out, "I vow to give you the properties in exchange for Morrigan and Calandra. Of this I promise in blood and bonds."

He slaps his hand to mine, our blood mixing. "I vow to give you Morrigan and Calandra in exchange for the properties. Of this I promise in blood and bonds."

Our palms lock, sucked tight like a vacuum. A hissing emanates from between our hands, it's the sound of fate and fury. Of two long years of sacrifice and loss. Of aching hearts and precious hopes.

But more than anything, it's the sultry sound of vengeance ringing true.

CHAPTER 36

MORRIGAN

The Investiture Part 3

Roman steps out from the shadows, an ugly sneer twisting his lips. I could never be wedded to this man.

And now I won't have to be.

As Roman charges the stage, his arms out wide, his henchmen flood the courtyard. He draws his fists in a full circle, accessing his power.

Stirling, from the corner of the courtyard, contorts her fingers. She's using the illusion magic I taught the team months ago after the heist to thread just enough power into Roman that he thinks he's won.

Stupid, arrogant man.

He thrusts his hands in every direction, firing magic into the crowd. Stirling lazily flicks her fingers left and right, following his movements so explosions rip through the court.

She makes him a puppet.

I know she hates me right now, but I'm so proud of her, it's a glorious irony turning him into the very thing he made her. For all the plans we had, even I didn't come up with this. Stirling is on fire, the way she's acting. No. She's reacting, in the moment. Tweaking and adapting to control him, own him. She was right: there is so much worth in being spontaneous and not planning everything out.

The chairs and pillars erupt, marble and wood splinters fly through the air.

Roman makes it halfway up the central aisle before he skids to a halt. His men circle the courtyard all wearing the same crumpled expression.

Confusion.

Chairs lay scattered, pillars broken, and yet, the crowd of magicians are still seated, albeit now without the aid of chairs.

Remy steps out from behind the stage and draws four fingers down the knuckles of her other hand. The mass of magicians flickers and then simply evaporate.

It's only then, once the noose is firmly around his throat, the evidence of his treason live-streamed on orbs throughout the city that Roman realises he's been duped.

He spins on Stirling, who is marching up the aisle. I bolt off the stage to protect her. Even without access to his magic, he's more powerful than her.

The thud of boots against stone booms around the court. Finally, Scarlett and an entourage of Assassin Guild members pour into the courtyard followed by Remy's exhausted crew.

"Kill them!" Roman screams to his men.

Quinn darts between the marble pillars throwing

poison dust at Roman's men. Remy fires runic cogs at legs and limbs.

The clash of steel and slicing of wet flesh fills the air as assassins crash against Roman's men. My nose fills with the thick stench of cinnamon and iron. Magic flies through the air bursting marble and slate cobbles.

"Protect the tree," I scream, and two assassins break off with Remy, whose eyes darken and hands vibrate as she erects a field around the tree. Bodies fall to the floor crumpled and limp.

But I only have eyes for Roman.

I fling ribbons of magic. Draw upon the palace, beg it and plead with it to help me. To my horror, I'm met with silence.

As I sever the limbs of Roman's men, I whisper prayers of servitude. As blood sprays through the air like rain, I breathe promises to the palace. Promises of loyalty and fealty to my role as queen. Vows of servitude and allegiance.

Someone smacks into me. I lurch forward rolling on my ankle as a body topples into me. The full force of his dead weight ploughs me into the ground. I howl as my ankle pops and searing pain shoots through my calf.

Quinn is already on it, her eyes following me from the edge of the court. Her hands slap together, her fingers dancing over her palm.

Even as I hit the courtyard's slate slabs, the pain is easing and the ligaments meshing back together.

I scramble to my feet and go still. Roman has his hand around Stirling's neck. His fist is squeezed tight.

Please, please hear me palace. Don't let me lose her. Not again. I give you my life, my soul, I swear I will serve this palace, just don't take her from me.

Stirling's turning a vicious shade of red, her lips swollen and blue. Her eyes are bulging. A river of red drips from her nose.

In the corner of my eye, I see Scarlett running full pelt towards us. But I'm already there. I already have him. His rage blinds him, his ego failing to reveal his enemies.

Something loosens inside me.

I stumble forward and my power cracks wide open.

A gasp rips from my chest. A surge of thrumming magic pours into me. Every single collection tattoo on my body flares to life. Light courses through them.

Thank you, thank you.

The courtyard ruptures, but this time, under my control. Ribbons of pearlescent palace power tear through the marble slabs. What chairs remain fissure and explode, fragments of slate and stone fracturing as I pull more and more magic from the palace.

I weave rope after rope of pearlescent thread around Roman. I don't want him dead. I want him off Stirling and alive long enough to know he lost to me.

He fights and wriggles against my tightening grip, but my hands are faster than his and Stirling is stronger than he realises. She wrenches herself back and slams her foot in his groin. He drops her and she collapses to the floor spluttering and gasping. She steadies herself and then staggers to her feet, yanks her fist back and slams it into his nose. It erupts; blood pisses down his mouth and chin.

But I can't stop. Not yet. I have to make sure he's secure. I weave and bind and knot him into place, keeping him hovering a foot above the floor. I lock my index fingers together ensuring he won't be released.

And then finally, the courtyard is silent.

Stirling staggers forward. She's covered in blood. I can't

work out if it's hers or his or the dead guards. I hobble towards her, my ankle still sore. She holds her own weight, though she's obviously carrying an injury too. She stumbles forward and wobbles, but I catch her.

"Quinn," I bellow and she sprints from the other side of the courtyard to Stirling's side, she slides herself under Stirling's arm, steadying her.

Roman's eyes are wide and round. I step up to him and pull off the ribbon of magic sealing his mouth shut.

He spits in my face.

I grit my teeth and wipe it clean, suppressing the urge not to level another punch to his nose.

He leers down at me. "Do you have any idea what she's done? The crimes she's committed against the crown?" Roman wriggles against the bindings but he can't escape.

I laugh. It bubbles up and out; I'm exhausted and hysterical and free. I slide my hand into Stirling's.

"Every. Single. One," I say.

I want her to grip me tight, hold me like I know I'm safe, that we will pull through this. But she doesn't. Her hand is limp, but she holds it long enough to see the deal through.

His brow wrinkles. His eyes flash between us, realisation dawning on him.

"How long?"

"Two years, four months and seventeen days," Stirling says, her voice is hoarse. She sticks a finger in his chest.

"You think threats and blackmail is enough to keep me away from the love of my life?" she snorts. "Unlike you, I'm willing to do anything, sacrifice anything for her."

"But you hate her, you hate the crown. She killed your parents." Desperation leaks into his voice in broken trembles.

Stirling laughs. "No, Roman. The Border Lord killed my

parents. And I've long ago forgiven Calandra. You, however, I do not forgive."

"Where the fuck is my magic?" He snarls.

Stirling straightens. "Gone, as it happens. Last night, we took a team out and hacked the lattice security. Emptied the properties of everything."

"You piece of traitorous shit," Roman spits.

"Your Majesty?" Stirling says.

Mother appears from the back of the stage. She waves her hand, and more guards pour into the courtyard.

"Roman Oleg, I sentence you to life imprisonment."

I lay my hand on mother's arm. "I have the perfect prison on the edge of the city. A cute little cottage, not a drop of magic."

Roman's eyes flash. "You wouldn't dare."

Stirling smirks. "Tut tut Roman. Didn't you learn anything from working with me? Always check the wording. You didn't ask for the magic. You asked for the *properties*. So enjoy your deal, because it's the last one you'll ever make."

Stirling lets go of me and limps away. Quinn slides under her arm supporting her across the court. Every inch of her is covered in blood, but her ocean blue eyes are warm until I catch up to them.

"You're finally free," she says as we exit the courtyard to the sound of Roman's screaming. "I hope you're happy."

And then she's gone, limping out of the palace and out of my life.

EPILOGUE

STIRLING

Two days after the investiture, I'm sat on the dock. My feet are bare and dangling into the cool water. It's late afternoon, my favourite time to watch the ocean. My body still aches and I have a black eye from where I caught a couple of punches. I'm also carrying a number of bruises. But none of it matters, I'll heal. I need to take the herbs Quinn gave me to speed up the recovery. But there's something comforting about the physical ache matching the way my insides feel, the constant throbbing like I had a tooth pulled, only the pain isn't in my mouth, it's in my chest.

A pod of dolphins swim half a click off the shore. A salty breeze strokes my cheeks. I close my eyes, remember that night. The night I lost her. The deal I struck.

I wonder now if Morrigan was right and I shouldn't have acted first and agreed to a deal.

Perhaps.

But maybe that deal is the very reason I'm here. The

reason we're both still alive and Roman is now trapped without access to magic in a cottage for the rest of his hopefully short life. It's certainly the reason I could convince him to make another deal with me.

There's something beautiful about that. It really was the perfect deal. I stand up, pad down the docks towards my boat and the beach mansion Morrigan and I thought of as home despite never living there.

It was our symbol. It became my ray of hope. I think that's why I chose to rent the shed right in front of it. It made me feel like I was nearer to her. Nearer to a solution.

Claude plods along the sand until he finds me staring up at the house.

"You like house, hmm?" he says.

I nod. "It sold recently," I say. "At the annual auction."

"I know."

"You do?" I ask.

"It was my house. I lived there with my wife, our entire marriage. But when she passed, I couldn't stay anymore. I held on to it for a while, but I knew if I was going to heal, I needed to move on from the house too."

It's the most words I've ever heard him say. And I'm a little slack-jawed at the confession. There's a pang deep in my chest for the loss of a thing I never had.

I should've bid on it.

I wish I'd bid on it.

"Has it gone through contract?" I could maybe slide in, undercut the buyer and offer him more money, or a crate of Sanguis Cūpa.

"Fraid so."

My heart sinks. "Right. Right, fair enough." I pause, staring at the house, the shiplap blue slats adorning the front of the mansion. It's the same colour paint I've bought for the boat.

"When do the new owners take possession?"

Claude doesn't say anything, he just smiles at me. I don't think I've ever seen him smile.

"You still don't know," he says.

I frown. "Know what?"

He shakes his head at me, but it's not malicious. He's smiling and chuckling to himself as he takes my hand and deposits something cold and hard into it.

I glance down at my palm. My vision glazes over. My eyes sting with wet pin pricks.

"She didn't?"

"Yes, actually, I did," Morrigan says appearing from behind the shed.

She's grinning like an idiot, and suddenly I'm bawling.

I am joy and grief, two years of loss, and a single moment of unison. I pull her into my arms, pick her up and swing her around and around until we collapse in the sand and are a mess of tongues and teeth and lips.

"I promised you I'd find you where blue meets blue," she says.

I kiss her again and again until my lips are sore and swollen. I pull away and haul her off the sand. We make our way across the dune, up onto the road and over to the front of the house.

"I don't know that we can live here," Morrigan says. "Not now I'm the heir apparent. But I thought, maybe it could be... Our home, our safe space. Even if we don't live here. We can spend weekends or vacations... That is... if you'll forgive me."

I stiffen, untangle myself from her arms, the last week rushing back to me.

"Morrigan... I—"

"Look, the mansion is yours. No matter what. If you don't want to be with me anymore, I understand. At least let me show you around..."

She pulls me toward the door, we walk up the path in silence, she slides the key in and opens the mansion.

She turns to me, touches my cheek. "I swear to you, Stirling Grey, I will never, ever keep anything from you again. I am so, so sorry."

Her eyes are bright and wet and her face so open, so innocent I know she means it. We've both fucked up along the way, but forgiveness is the only way relationships work. And I do love her. I wouldn't have spent two years working for that bastard if I didn't.

"Stirling, please. We went to the ends of the realm for each other. After everything we had to do, after everything we've sacrificed, stolen, broken, killed and lied about. Please tell me you still want me...?" Her words quiet, a single tear rolls down her cheek. I brush my thumb over her skin, wiping the tear.

"For the record, I am so, so deeply pissed at you for lying about Roman. But I suppose I owe you an apology for working for him."

She tuts at me and pulls me into an embrace, "Of course I forgive you... Does this mean..." She looks up at me, her gaze expectant.

"Well, I did just make the deal of my life for you. So I suppose I should enjoy the spoils..."

Her whole body sags, a huge grin peels across her lips, and then she plunges her mouth against mine and it's the deepest most hungry kiss she's ever given me.

We stand there, on the hearth of the mansion, where

blue meets blue, the sun showering us in warmth and for the first time in a decade, I feel like I found home.

She peels herself off me and smiles, "No more secrets."

"None. Not ever. Where do we go from here? What happens now you're the heir apparent?"

"It can all wait," she says, her fingers skimming the waistband of my trousers.

"Can it? I just..."

She places a finger over my lips. "Mother isn't going to attempt to marry me off again. She's pissed that I'm thwarting tradition. Like *really* pissed. I doubt I'll hear the end of it for a while. But she's also stopped mentioning arranging a marriage, and that is the only concession I'll get. She's still a queen. She won't admit I'm right. But you know what? After she saw you battered and broken running to my defence, you earned some brownie points. We're going to be okay."

"So I don't have to worry about some strapping wannabe prince from the underworld coming to steal your heart?"

"Not unless he has a death wish," she grins.

"Well, that's a relief."

"So I guess we should go I—" she makes to walk inside, but I grab her hand.

"Wait," I say pulling her back. I lift her into my arms, and carry her. She squeals but I'm not letting go. "Now we go in."

We pass the threshold, and the house greets us with a hug. It is the warmest of welcomes, my whole body pressed into an embrace the way mother would hold me when I fell over. The air smells of Sunday roasts, warm chicken and herby vegetables. The house, while a shell, has so much love to give.

When I rather ungracefully drop Morrigan on her feet, her eyes are full of unspent tears. "It's even more perfect than I imagined."

The ground floor of the mansion is decorated in pale blues and seafoam white. It has an open plan living room and kitchen with a grand marble staircase splitting and spiralling up to each side of the top floor. Despite the fact it's almost sunset, there's so much glass in the living room that the whole house is bright.

In the middle of the room is a wooden crate, two deck chairs, two glasses and a bottle of champagne facing the ocean.

"Is this really ours?" I whisper.

"It's really ours."

Morrigan opens the bottle of champagne and pours two glasses and holds one out so we can clink.

There's a rabble of people on the beach, whooping and hollering. I grin, realising it's the rest of the team. They stroll in, brandishing plastic cups and demanding fizz.

"We won't stay long," Quinn says.

"We just wanted to toast your new home," Jacob says pulling me in for a hug. I want to ask him how things went in the Borderlands, whether he and Malachi are a thing yet, but it doesn't seem like the right time.

"We're having a barbecue on the beach. This lot bent my arm," he says.

Quinn bounces on her toes, "We figured he owed us one, for fucking off for a month."

Jacob tips his head.

"But perhaps you're both too busy?" Quinn winks.

I roll my eyes at her and open my arms. One by one each of the team congratulates Morrigan and I. We descend into chatter and catching up.

Remy peels off from the group and pulls me aside. "How are you feeling?"

"Okay. A little sore. But I have the herbs Quinn gave me. But enough about me. A little birdie tells me you had an invitation yesterday."

Remy runs her hand through her updo. "Rumour has it Bella is pissed at me for breaking her lattice. And even more pissed that I saved her arse from prison."

"Pissed at you?" I raise an eyebrow. "So, nothing to do with the way you look at each other then?"

"Don't be ridiculous. The woman was a constant thorn in my side while I was mentored to Marcel. But she's also so talented it would be a crying shame for her to waste away in jail."

"Some of us like thorns."

She glares at me, but it's the kind of glare that makes me smirk.

"So this invite..."

Her eyes light up at this. "It's the Runic Games. All the top hackers, technicians and security magicians across New Imperium and several other cities compete to be the best there is."

"Ooh, and the prize?"

"Other than glory and pride you mean?"

I laugh, "Other than that."

"Well, there's money, but we both know I don't need it."

"Go on... what's the real reason you're going?"

"One, I didn't say I was going but two, let's say I am—"

"Which you are."

She ignores me and continues. "Let's just say there's something rather delicious about the prospect of finally proving I'm better than Bella."

"Well, cheers to that, Remy Reid, future Runic champion of the world!"

We clink glasses and I have a funny feeling she's letting herself in for a whole lot more than she's bargained for.

The team drift off back to the beach slowly. It's a painful amount of time before Morrigan and I are alone. But finally, she twists the key on the sliding doors, shutting the sand and ocean and team out, and us in.

In silence, she slips her fingers into mine and pulls me away and up the marble stairs.

"I didn't get a chance to show you up here. I've only done one room. I figured we would decorate the rest together."

"When did you have time to—" I stop talking.

There's a string of twinkling lights, and a bed in the middle of the first room. There are candles littered around the floor. She waves her hand through the air and they all spark to life.

"I wanted t—"

I silence her with a kiss. This is where I take control. I slide my hand up her neck and into the back of her hair. When I run my hands through her locks, the scent of rose petals and cinnamon and the faintest hint of old books fills my nose. She smells like home. She smells like mine. I push her lips open, slide my tongue inside her mouth until she moans into me.

I break off the kiss.

"Take your top off," I demand. And then decide to add, "Your highness."

Her eyes glimmer at me, the candlelight flickering and casting shadows on the ceiling. She does as she's told. Her nipples hardening as the lace of her bra falls away. I stroke my thumb over her nipple bar, trace the new Collection tattoo marking the space between her breasts, right over her heart. She pulls my top off, unbuckles my trousers and helps me out of them.

"And now your underwear," I say.

She goes to pout but unclips her bra and take her knickers off.

"Get on the bed, Morrigan."

"What if I don't want to?"

"Don't be a brat. It's been a long month, and an even longer week. I'm going to ravish you. Like, right the fuck now. So do as you're told, and get on the bed."

She grins at me, her eyes darkening. She wants to behave like a brat, but the warning look I give her tells her not to misbehave.

"No sex magic," I say.

"But," she opens her mouth, sticks out her tongue and contorts her ring finger. Her tongue flicks up and down vibrating so fast it blurs.

I open my mouth, close it. "Okay, maybe a little sex magic. But I'm having my way with you first..." I nudge her onto the bed.

She squeals as she bounces onto the soft mattress. I climb on top of her, shower her tattooed skin in kisses. Running my tongue over her body. Kissing every collection tattoo, every ounce of her power. I know in my heart I will worship this woman until my last breath.

"Stirling..." she says.

"Yes?" I inch down her body. "I've waited for this. For you, for us to be free for so long. I don't want to wait any more."

She tilts her head up. "Fuck me like you'll never leave again."

"I will never leave you, Morrigan. Not tonight. Not ever."

"Show me," she breathes.

I push her legs apart and slide between her thighs, drawing my tongue over her warm centre. Gods I missed this, missed her. I part her pussy, my tongue slipping between her folds and down her core.

She's wet, as wet as I am. I know by the slick between my thighs. I'm desperate for her.

I draw neat circles around her clit, lapping soft then hard. The taste of her glistens in my mouth, like sweet magic and raw power. I want to drink her in. Her clit hardens under my tongue. The sensation sets my body on fire. I want to touch myself.

But I don't. I hold back, so I can give everything to her. I run my hands along her thighs, lapping at her centre until her back arches and her legs twitch.

She pants and moans, her hands find their way to my hair. She's ready. I know she wants me to tip her over. But I want to tease her. To draw this night out.

But then I also know how much she needs me, how much I need her. So I slide my fingers inside her pussy and curl them to the perfect spot. I thrust in and out, my fingers riding her g-spot, flooding her with pleasure and coaxing her orgasm to come and play. Her hands claw at the bedding, find my shoulders, run through my hair.

"I'm close," she pants. "Don't stop."

I lap at her faster, harder, I pulse my fingers until she tightens around me, her moans send shivers down my back.

"Stirling. Fuck I'm going to come."

She bucks against my mouth, pulls my hair until my

face is crushed against her pussy. She rides my mouth, calling my name, making my body melt as hers comes apart. She releases me, lies still, her breath panting as fast as mine.

And then she pulls herself up and grins at me. She doesn't luxuriate in her orgasm, instead she takes my hand and tugs me close. And then she's pushing her fingers to my cunt. I'm so wet she gasps.

"All for me?" she bites her bottom lip.

"I'm always wet for you."

Her eyes burn with desire as she brings her fingers to her mouth and sucks them dry, and I swear my soul cracks wide.

She bends, clasping one of my breasts to suck my nipple between her teeth, grazing it with her tongue. It earns a moan, my head tips back. One of her hands caresses down my belly, leaving a trail of tingling flesh in her wake. Her fingers find my pussy and circle my wet hole. She dips inside me.

Teasing.

Testing.

"How much do you want me?"

I grab her wrist. She gasps at the sudden grip. Her eyes glint at me. She knows exactly what she's doing.

"I swear to gods, I'm either going to spank you or fuck you until you're a quivering mess."

She giggles as I lean into her neck and draw a line of hot kisses down her collarbone. My teeth kiss the meaty bit of flesh just hard enough it elicits a hiss.

She pushes me until I'm lying flat on the bed and wiggles her way down between my thighs. She is magnificent. And she's all mine.

Her tongue skitters out over her lips as if she can

already taste me and is hungry for more. She nudges my legs wider, stares at me fully parted for her.

And then she dips her mouth to my wet pussy and laps up every last drop of my excitement.

She moans before I do. Like the very taste of me is ecstasy. It makes my skin flush hot, my cunt wet all over again.

She slips a single finger inside me, stroking my g-spot tantalisingly slow. My body aches for her, I tighten and relax, the first shivers of orgasm consuming my body. My nipples harden, my clit swells. And still, her tongue and fingers ravish my pussy. She thrusts inside me until I beg for release.

When I don't think I can take anymore, when she's pulled me to the edge and my whole body is shutting down, she stops suddenly.

"Stirling?" she says.

"Yes?" I say trying not to sound exasperated. I was so close to coming. I can't believe she's edging me like this.

"I'm going to do the thing with my tongue now. And you're going to come for me. Do you understand?"

"Yes my queen."

She plunges down onto my clit, her fingers sliding in and out of me. Her tongue flickers once, twice, and then my world blows apart and all I am is sensation. I am vibrations and stars, golden electricity and tingled pleasure. Thread by thread, my world ebbs into bliss.

I come undone for her.

For us.

I come undone because I know we're safe and no one can ever tear us apart.

I come undone because she is my safe space and we finally found each other where blue meets blue.

When my body calms, I pull her up to my head, run my hand through her hair pushing the locks away from her face. I place a single, slow kiss on her lips.

"How about we make a deal," I say.

"I'm listening," she says.

"If you give me your heart, I'll give you mine."

"Be careful now Lady Grey, the verbiage is important."

I nod, solemn and serious. "What are your terms?"

She pouts, pretends to think. "Lifetime agreement. No returns, no exchanges, and absolutely no more negotiations."

"One last deal to rule them all. You drive a hard bargain, Princess."

"I learned from the best," she winks at me. "So...?"

I lean close, brush my lips over hers. "You got yourself a deal."

The story is not over! Discover what happens with Remy and Bella in book 3: *A Game of Deceit and Desire* read on here: rubyroe.co.uk/AGDD

Thank you so much for reading *A Game of Romance and Ruin*. If you'd like to read an extra steamy prequel novella involving Scarlett and Quinn's enemies to lovers romance, you can do that by signing up here: rubyroe.co.uk/signup.

Last, reviews are super important for authors, they help provide needed social proof that helps to sell more books. If you have a moment and you're able to leave a review on the store you bought the book from, I'd be really grateful.

ABOUT THE AUTHOR

Ruby Roe is the pen name of Sacha Black. Ruby is the author of lesbian fantasy romance. She loves a bit of magic with her smut, but she'll read anything as long as the characters get down and dirty. When Ruby isn't writing romance, she can usually be found beasting herself in the gym, snuggling with her two pussy... cats, or spanking all her money on her next travel adventure. She lives in England with her wife, son and two devious rag doll cats.

instagram.com/sachablackauthor

tiktok.com/@rubyroeauthor